MW00398261

"It *is a*

Even as he snapped out the words, threats of white light lanced downward from the ship. The three people heard the characteristic *crack-sizzle* of a plasma fusillade and then the boom of an explosion.

The Deathbird dropped violently on its belly within a few yards of an outcropping. The landing gear collapsed and its nose tipped up.

As Brigid, Grant and Kane watched in wide-eyed silence, the portside cockpit hatch flew open and a small body plunged out through the billows of smoke, falling to all fours only a few feet away.

The body appeared to have been dyed jet-black from the neck down, but after a half second of staring, the three outlanders realized the figure wore the same kind of formfitting bodysuit as they did.

Brigid Baptiste, still gazing through the ruby-coated lenses of the binoculars, managed to break the spell of shock that paralyzed all of their vocal chords. She blurted, *"Sindri!"*

Other titles in this series:

James Axler
Outlanders®

SKULL
THRONE

A GOLD EAGLE BOOK FROM
WORLDWIDE®

TORONTO • NEW YORK • LONDON
AMSTERDAM • PARIS • SYDNEY • HAMBURG
STOCKHOLM • ATHENS • TOKYO • MILAN
MADRID • WARSAW • BUDAPEST • AUCKLAND

If you purchased this book without a cover you should be aware
that this book is stolen property. It was reported as "unsold and
destroyed" to the publisher, and neither the author nor the
publisher has received any payment for this "stripped book."

First edition May 2007

ISBN-13: 978-0-373-63854-3
ISBN-10:   0-373-63854-X

SKULL THRONE

Copyright © 2007 by Worldwide Library.

Special thanks to Mark Ellis for his contribution to
the Outlanders concept, developed for Gold Eagle.

All rights reserved. Except for use in any review, the
reproduction or utilization of this work in whole or in part
in any form by any electronic, mechanical or other means,
now known or hereafter invented, including xerography,
photocopying and recording, or in any information storage
or retrieval system, is forbidden without the written permission
of the publisher, Worldwide Library, 225 Duncan Mill Road,
Don Mills, Ontario, Canada M3B 3K9.

This is a work of fiction. Names, characters, places and incidents are
either the product of the author's imagination or are used fictitiously,
and any resemblance to actual persons, living or dead, business
establishments, events or locales is entirely coincidental.

® and TM are trademarks of the publisher. Trademarks indicated
with ® are registered in the United States Patent and Trademark
Office, the Canadian Trade Marks Office and in other countries.

Printed in U.S.A.

Evil, much evil passes here
on earth. Perhaps
I will never stop crying.
Without family,
alone, very lonely I walk,
crying day and night
only cries consume my eyes and soul.
Under evil so hard.
Ay ay, my Lord!
Take pity on me, put an end
to this suffering.
Give me death, my Beautiful Lord,
or give my soul transcendence!

—*Mayan Mourning Song*

The Road to Outlands—
From Secret Government Files to the Future

Almost two hundred years after the global holocaust, Kane, a former Magistrate of Cobaltville, often thought the world had been lucky to survive at all after a nuclear device detonated in the Russian embassy in Washington, D.C. The aftermath—forever known as skydark—reshaped continents and turned civilization into ashes.

Nearly depopulated, America became the Deathlands—poisoned by radiation, home to chaos and mutated life forms. Feudal rule reappeared in the form of baronies, while remote outposts clung to a brutish existence.

What eventually helped shape this wasteland were the redoubts, the secret preholocaust military installations with stores of weapons, and the home of gateways, the locational matter-transfer facilities. Some of the redoubts hid clues that had once fed wild theories of government cover-ups and alien visitations.

Rearmed from redoubt stockpiles, the barons consolidated their power and reclaimed technology for the villes. Their power, supported by some invisible authority, extended beyond their fortified walls to what was now called the Outlands. It was here that the rootstock of humanity survived, living with hellzones and chemical storms, hounded by Magistrates.

In the villes, rigid laws were enforced—to atone for the sins of the past and prepare the way for a better future. That was the barons' public credo and their right-to-rule.

Kane, along with friend and fellow Magistrate Grant, had upheld that claim until a fateful Outlands expedition. A displaced piece of technology…a question to a keeper of the archives…a vague clue about alien masters—and their world shifted radically. Suddenly, Brigid Baptiste, the archivist, faced summary execution, and Grant a quick termination. For

Kane there was forgiveness if he pledged his unquestioning allegiance to Baron Cobalt and his unknown masters and abandoned his friends.

But that allegiance would make him support a mysterious and alien power and deny loyalty and friends. Then what else was there?

Kane had been brought up solely to serve the ville. Brigid's only link with her family was her mother's red-gold hair, green eyes and supple form. Grant's clues to his lineage were his ebony skin and powerful physique. But Domi, she of the white hair, was an Outlander pressed into sexual servitude in Cobaltville. She at least knew her roots and was a reminder to the exiles that the outcasts belonged in the human family.

Parents, friends, community—the very rootedness of humanity was denied. With no continuity, there was no forward momentum to the future. And that was the crux— when Kane began to wonder if there *was* a future.

For Kane, it wouldn't do. So the only way was out— way, way out.

After their escape, they found shelter at the forgotten Cerberus redoubt headed by Lakesh, a scientist, Cobaltville's head archivist, and secret opponent of the barons.

With their past turned into a lie, their future threatened, only one thing was left to give meaning to the outcasts. The hunger for freedom, the will to resist the hostile influences. And perhaps, by opposing, end them.

Chapter 1

Pakistan, the Indus River valley

The Moon sank beneath the curve of the Sind Desert, leaving a heavy cloak of darkness over the eastern bend of the Indus. The black waters flickered with flares of red, reflecting the discharge of weapons from the skirmish line along the banks.

Standing on the parapet of the ancient wall, Kane heard the distant reports as a series of muffled thumps and staccato finger snaps. He glimpsed long ribbons of orange and yellow streaking across the river's sluggish current a split second before the sound of the detonations reached his ears.

As the echoes of an explosion faded, the voice of De-card, husky, hoarse and tight with tension, filtered over the Commtact. "They've breached the outer perimeter, sir! Blown away our cover!"

"I figured that out for myself," Kane replied dryly. "And don't call me sir. Casualties?"

"None. We were lucky."

"Good. Start pulling your people back."

Decard's voice rose in a strident protest. "But sir—I mean—"

"That's an order," Kane broke in, an iron edge in his tone. "Do it now. Acknowledge."

After a few seconds, Decard responded with a weary resignation, "Acknowledged. Will comply."

Kane understood Decard's reluctance to retreat in the face of the enemy, but he had learned long ago that survival was the touchstone of success in any line of work, particularly his. No one accomplished anything by dying and even less by capture and interrogation.

He heard another jackhammering fusillade of autofire, punctuated by the heavier *crumps* of the detonating grenades launched by the H&K XM-29 assault rifles carried by Cerberus Away Team Alpha.

"The Nephilim are crossing the river," Decard said breathlessly. "We're falling back."

"Roger that," Kane said, striving to sound calm to the point of nonchalance. "Keep your heads down."

Reaching up behind his right ear, Kane made an adjustment on the Commtact's volume control. The little comm unit fit tightly against the mastoid bone, attached to implanted steel pintels. The unit slid through the flesh and made contact with tiny input ports. Its sensor circuitry incorporated a subcutaneously embedded analog-to-digital voice encoder.

Once the device made full cranial contact, the auditory canal picked up the transmissions. The dermal sensors transmitted the electronic signals directly through the skull casing. Even if someone went deaf, as long as a Commtact was worn, he or she would still have a form of hearing, but if the volume was not properly adjusted, the radio signals caused vibrations in the skull bones that resulted in vicious headaches.

Lifting a compact set of night-vision binoculars to his face, Kane switched on the IR illuminator and squinted through the eyepieces. Viewed through the specially coated lenses, which optimized the low light values, the riverbank seemed to be illuminated by a lambent, ghostly haze. Where only black had been before, his vision was lit by various shifting shades of gray and green.

The Indus was less than a quarter of a mile away, and in daylight details along the opposite shore were easily visible. Now all Kane glimpsed was the amorphous, armored shapes of the Nephilim and the renegade Magistrates as they flitted back and forth. He was careful not to focus the binoculars on the discharge of weapons, particularly those of the Nephilim's ASP emitters, because the IR optics enhanced the energy bursts to nova blasts of intolerable brightness.

He knew the river flowing past Hardpan was little more than fifty yards wide and very shallow, a ford used by traders and nomads. All along the banks were marshes and islets overgrown with reeds. Hardpan had itself had once been the site of a fair-sized metropolis. The ruins of old outbuildings were scattered up and down both sides of the Indus. The warm, humid breeze smelled of swamp, raw sewage and the smoke from the fishermen's huts that had been caught in the exchange of fire and burned to the ground.

Juballah, the Devi of Harappa, stepped up beside him and murmured bleakly, "Soon it will be dawn and we will be overrun."

The brown-skinned woman's voice reverberated within Kane's head, first as a conglomeration of liquid syllables, before the translation program from the PDA in the pocket of his field jacket fed him the English translation.

In conjunction with a sophisticated lingual translation program within the PDA, the Commtacts analyzed the pattern of a language and then provided a real-time audio translation. Some foreign phrases and words would not be exact translations, but the program recognized enough words to supply an English equivalent. Conversely, the program supplied him with the appropriate responses in the language it heard.

Glancing over at the woman, Kane once again wondered why she chose to stand with him at the walls, clad only in the clinging fabric of a red-and-gold silk sari. Her heavy black hair was cut square at her shoulders and artfully streaked with gray. Juballah was not old, but her dark face was that of a matronly aristocrat, locked tight with the stamp of harsh determination. She might have been beautiful, if not for the austerity of her features.

With an assurance he did not feel, Kane said, "Overlord Nergal isn't interested in taking your city." Although tempted, he didn't add, "Only because he thinks he owns it already."

Juballah nodded. "He wants what lies beneath it…and he will not hesitate to destroy Harappa if we stand in his way. There are many legends about the ruthlessness of Nergal and his armies of darkness."

"If Nergal wanted to destroy your city, he would have done it as soon as he arrived yesterday, not waited until now."

"Our refusal to allow him entrance may have made him angry enough to do it," Juballah said quietly.

"We'll take every countermeasure possible to stop him." Kane knew how lame his words of encouragement sounded. To cover his discomfort, he raised the binoculars again, gazing at the armored figures wading through hip-deep water. at the shallowest point of the ford. His stomach muscles fluttered in adrenaline-fueled spasms.

Kane estimated the Nephilim at fifty, with a handful of former Sharpeville Magistrates swelling the ranks. Leaning over the edge of the mud-brick wall, he watched the members of CAT Alpha running across the open ground between the hastily constructed fortifications. With crackling hisses, balls of plasma streaked through the darkness after them, exploding against heaps of broken masonry, raining shards of rock in all directions.

Like himself, the dozen members of Team Alpha wore tricolor desert camouflage BDUs, helmets and thick-soled jump boots. Unlike Kane, Personnel Armor System Ground Troop vests encased the team's torsos. Weighing seventeen pounds, the PASGT vests provided protection from even .30-caliber rounds, but their ability to withstand the accelerated streams of protons fired by the Nephilim's wrist pods was unknown.

The nine men and three women swiftly took up positions behind the cover of stacked rocks and brick, returning the ASP fire with short bursts from their H&K assault rifles. Stuttering roars overlapped as the barrels of the autorifles lipped short tongues of flame. An RPG-7 grenade fired from Decard's weapon lit up the darkness with an eye-searing blaze of orange and red.

"We've slowed their advance," Decard said over the comm. "At least for a few minutes."

"Don't let them outflank you and pin you down," Kane replied. "Keep working your way back in."

"Roger that."

Globes of incandescent plasma darted from the direction of the riverbank and splashed against the bulwarks of stone amid showers of multicolored sparks. Kane resisted the urge to order the team to retreat into the city of Harappa proper. He had faith that Decard, despite his youth, would know when a full withdrawal was necessary.

Kane adjusted the chin strap of his own tan-and-brown helmet, wishing not for the first time since arriving in Pakistan that he wore a black shadow suit. He would have been cooler, if nothing else. Standing an inch over six feet, Kane was built with a lean, long-limbed economy. Most of his muscle mass was contained in his upper body, much like that of a wolf. A wolf's cold stare glittered in his blue-gray eyes, the color of dawn light on a sharp steel blade. A faint hairline scar showed like a white thread against the sun-bronzed skin of his clean-shaved left cheek.

The BDU was a departure from the skintight shadow suit he preferred to wear on dark territory missions, but Lakesh had suggested that the more conventional clothing would make him and his team appear less sinister to the people of Harappa.

Diplomacy, turning potential enemies into allies against the spreading reign of the overlords, had become the preferred tactic of Cerberus over the past couple of years. As the canvas of their operations broadened, the personnel situation at Cerberus redoubt also changed.

No longer could Kane, Grant, Brigid Baptiste and Domi undertake the majority of the ops and therefore shoulder the lion's share of the risks. Over the past six months, Kane and Grant had seen to the formation of three Cerberus Away Teams—Alpha, Beta and Delta. At the moment Alpha Team was undergoing its baptism of fire. Led by young Decard, a former Magistrate from Samariumville, none of the troopers had received so much as a scratch during the hour-long firefight down at the riverbank.

Through the binoculars, Kane studied the approaching Nephilim. Broadly built men who had a look of impassivity about them, they strode forward with the single-minded purposefulness of the march of automatons. That assessment wasn't too far wrong, he reflected sourly.

Set deep beneath jutting brow ridges, the white eyes of the Nephilim did not blink, nor did their craggy, scaly faces register emotion. Kane knew why. Ovoid shells of alloy rose from the rear of their dark red body armor, sweeping up to enclose the back and upper portion of their hairless skulls. From the undersides of the shells, hair-thin filaments extended down to pierce both sides of the Nephilim's heads, a bioelectronic interface that for all intents and purposes turned them into mind-controlled drones.

Conduits stretched down from inch-thick reinforcing epaulets on their shoulders, connecting to the alloyed gauntlets that sheathed their hands and forearms. From raised pods on the gauntlets rose three small flanges that flared out like cobras' hoods. Red energy pulsed in the gaping mouths of the stylized serpent heads of the ASP emitters.

Kane tightened the focus of the binoculars, noting that the Magistrates marching among the Nephilim displayed neither their discipline nor fearlessness. Although the Nephilim employed the wrist-mounted ASPs almost exclusively, the Magistrates were armed with the standard-issue standbys of Copperheads and Sin Eaters, neither of which had the range, stopping power or versatility of the XM-29s. Their black polycarbonate armor was far less resistant to damage than the smart-metal alloy worn by the Nephilim.

Grant's lionlike voice suddenly came over Kane's Commtact, so brusque and loud he was glad he had turned down the volume. "What the hell's going on up there? We hear a hell of a lot of fire."

"That's because there *is* a hell of a lot of fire," Kane responded. "As in a hell of a firefight right outside the walls. How's it going down there?"

Grant's reply was so long in coming, Kane almost repeated the question. "I just asked Brigid for an update," Grant said. "She thinks she has the combination decoded but she needs a little more time to make sure. How close is Nergal?"

"That depends on how much more time Baptiste wants," Kane said. "If she waits another ten minutes, she can probably ask him for the combination in person."

"Why doesn't he just use his damn ships?" Grant demanded. "He could level the city with them."

"I don't know," Kane answered. "Maybe he has a sentimental attachment to this place."

The Commtact accurately conveyed Grant's snort of derision. "I can't imagine why."

"Me either." Turning on the narrow parapet, Kane swept his gaze over the city. What Harappa lacked in beauty was more than made up for by its mathematical symmetry. The buildings were mainly houses, constructed of mud bricks dug out of the banks of the Indus.

No lights showed in the windows of the squat and low buildings. A broad patchwork of lanes ran between the dwellings. There were places for pens and livestock and small gardens. No animals or people stirred on the streets. Most of the inhabitants had fled when Nergal's three sky disks arrived the afternoon before.

The main thoroughfare ran straight through the city and ended at a time-eroded pile of stone that might have been a palace or temple—three thousand years ago. A colonnade of square, squat pillars ran across its front, and a pair of heavier ones stood at its entrance on either end of a half-built stone wall. Wooden scaffolds rose at various points around the temple as it underwent restoration. Although Kane couldn't see the entrance from his vantage point, he knew Grant and Brigid Baptiste were within a vault beneath the structure.

Kane started to turn, saying to Grant, "I'll have the CAT pull back inside the walls, and we'll start working our way to you."

"Copy that."

Out of the corner of his eye, he glimpsed a globule of plasma jetting toward him from the darkness, like a fireball launched from a catapult. Grabbing Juballah around the waist, he wrestled the woman down just as a kaleidoscopic bolt of colors and energy bit a deep notch out of the top of the wall. Fist-sized chunks exploded from the wall, and Kane felt a wave of heat slapping against the back of his neck. Gravel rattled on his helmet. The Devi cried out something the PDA couldn't translate and Kane was just as glad.

"The ship!" Decard yelled angrily.

Quickly, Kane pushed himself away from Juballah and climbed to one knee, fanning away the smoke as he peered toward the Indus. A featureless disk of molten silver rose vertically into the sky, its configuration and smooth hull reminiscent of a throwing discus used by athletes—if the discus was twenty feet in diameter and coated with mercury. Perfectly centered on the disk's underside bulged a half dome, like the boss of a shield. Three of the ships had landed the afternoon before, sinking out of sight behind the crest of a low ridge on the far side of the Indus.

As the craft took to the air, Kane realized with a sinking sensation in the pit of his stomach that the fourteen-hour-long siege was about to come to a decisive end. Whatever had prevented Overlord Nergal from taking an active hand in the engagement was no longer an issue. Kane had survived so long by taking nothing for granted, so the sight of the airborne silver disk didn't surprise him. He had known that the overlord would eventually tire of exchanging ineffectual shots across the Indus.

"Break off the engagement and withdraw the team," Kane ordered Decard tersely. "Pull all the way back and make for the vault. We're out of here."

"Yes, sir," Decard responded. "I mean—"

"Just do it," Kane broke in impatiently, eyes fixed on the disk.

He hefted his own Copperhead, knowing the abbreviated subgun would be less than effective against the ship, composed as it was of smart metal. The Copperhead was under two feet long, with a 700-round-per-minute rate of fire, the extended magazine holding thirty-five 4.85 mm steel-jacketed rounds. The grip and trigger units were placed in front of the breech in the bullpup design, allowing for one-handed use.

Optical image intensifier scopes and laser autotargeters were mounted on the top of the frames. Low recoil allowed the Copperheads to be fired in long, devastating, full-auto bursts, but Kane knew from experience a long or short burst wouldn't do much more than ding the hull of the disk ship.

Hauling Juballah to her feet by her wrists, he said, "We're about to be seriously overexposed. Let's get to cover."

As the pair ran along the narrow walkway to the stairs leading down to the street, Team Alpha sprinted through the open gate in an orderly deployment of personnel and firepower. The raised portcullis was made of black iron bars and set between two flanking towers, but lowering it would make no difference to either the oncoming Nephilim or the sky ship of Overlord Nergal.

At the foot the stairs, Kane paused to call Grant. "We're on our way back to you. Nergal is finally using his air support."

"Acknowledged," came his longtime partner's response. "I think we're about done."

"Yeah," Kane replied dourly. "Us too."

He waved the team and Juballah onward into the city, but Decard and Halloran dropped back to stand beside him. A fair-skinned man of medium height and build, Decard breathed heavily as perspiration glistened on his flushed face.

"We couldn't hold them," he snapped bitterly.

"You weren't supposed to," Kane retorted, casting an anxious glance through the open gate. "You knew that."

"With all due respect, sir," Halloran challenged, "then what was the point of this?"

Halloran was not very tall, but her full-cheeked face beneath the overhang of her helmet showed the intense expression of a veteran warrior. She was actually a cartographer and a raw recruit on her first away mission, forgetting the chain of command in the excitement of battle.

Coldly, Kane answered, "Your team bought us time and that's all I expected. Let's move out."

The three people stepped away from the wall. There was no warning. The shaft of light flashed down from above like the sudden thrust of a lance, bright and dazzling. The concussion felt like a battering ram of hot, almost solid air that knocked Kane off his feet. He slammed down on the hard-packed ground with a nerve-numbing jolt. All the air went out of his lungs in a pained grunt.

Kane lay where he had fallen, the stink of scorched human hair and flesh thick in his nostrils. His stunned eardrums registered little more than a surflike throb. He was dimly aware of a fine rain of pulverized pebbles and sand drizzling onto him, clinking dully against his helmet.

He saw nothing but a white haze, like the searing brilliance of burning magnesium, but Halloran's shriek of agony filled his head.

Chapter 2

Dust sifted down from the ceiling, coating Grant's helmet. Far in the distance came a low rumbling, and above the walls of Harappa the predawn darkness lit up intermittently with the distant flare of explosions.

"I don't know," Kane's voice said over the Commtact. "Maybe he has a sentimental attachment to this place."

Grant snorted derisively. "I can't imagine why."

"Me either," Kane answered, his tone of voice distracted. "I'll have the CAT pull back inside the walls, and we'll start working our way to you."

"Copy that," Grant replied. A few seconds later, he heard a whip-crack detonation and glimpsed a brief blaze from the direction of the gate.

"Anything happening?" Brigid Baptiste's voice floated up from the foot of the stairs.

Still peering out from beneath the archway toward Kane's position on the wall, Grant answered, "Maybe nothing, maybe everything."

"More of the same, sounds like." Brigid's response was studiedly indifferent. "Come down here and give me a hand, will you?"

After a moment's hesitation, Grant turned and strode down the stairwell. The steps were steep and wide, almost like separate levels, three feet across and four feet deep. They disappeared into a yawning black abyss. The variety of grenades and the Copperhead clipped to his combat webbing clinked faintly with every move.

Grant walked very lightly for a man of his size. He towered six feet five inches tall in his thick-soled jump boots, and his shoulders spread out on either side of a thickly tendoned neck like massive planks, straining at the seams of his desert camouflage field jacket.

Although he looked too huge to have many abilities beyond sheer strength, Grant was an exceptionally intelligent and talented man.

Behind the fierce, deep-set eyes, down-sweeping mustache, black against the dark brown of his skin, granite jaw and broken nose lay a mind rich with tactics, strategies and painful experience. Like Kane, he had lived a great deal of his life by and in violence. He had been shot, stabbed, battered, beaten, burned, buried and once very nearly suffocated on the surface of the Moon.

In the shadows of the stairwell, red jewels winked. On the walls glittered little squares of colored tile, part of an elaborate mosaic that had long ago been chipped out of recognition by the hand of time.

At the foot of the stairs a gallery opened up into a natural, bowl-shaped cavern. Firelight flickered from a half-dozen copper braziers placed in a circle around the curving granite walls. Three PVC equipment cases were stacked at the bottom of the stairwell, holding firearms, magazines of ammo, MREs and even a rocket launcher with a dozen rounds.

Deeply engraved into the rock floor was a large geometric design, a complex series of interlocking cuneiforms that formed a spiral of concentric rings twelve feet in diameter.

The pattern of symmetrical hieroglyphs bent, twisted, swirled and intersected to meet in the raised center ring upon which rested the gleaming pyramid-shaped interphaser.

Grant knew the design cut into the floor was an ancient geodetic marker, chiseled into the naked stone as a two-dimensional representation of the multidimensional geomantic vortex points that comprised the natural electromagnetic grid of Earth energies. He and his friends had seen similar markers in the past, in places such as Iraq, China and even on Mars.

Grant skirted the outer ring of the marker, careful not to tread on the intricate labyrinth of lines. He didn't understand the scientific principles of geomantic vortex points, but he respected their power, as had the ancient peoples who engraved the rock floor with the symbols. He had no idea of how old it was, but the chamber itself felt more than ancient and exuded an aura of the primeval.

On the opposite side of the chamber, light glinted dully from a verdigris-streaked bronze portal. Rust flecked the iron cross braces. The door was ten feet tall and very nearly that in width. The flickering firelight glinted from the symbols embossed on the surface of the door, smaller versions of the hieroglyphs carved into the floor. Little squares of paper bearing handwritten numbers were taped to the bottom edge of the symbols.

Brigid Baptiste stood before a sheared-off pedestal that she had turned into a makeshift workstation. Her long fingers flew over the keyboard of a laptop, a clattering accompaniment to the thumping barrage outside and above them. A tall woman with a fair complexion, Brigid's high forehead gave the impression of a probing intellect, whereas her full underlip hinted at an appreciation of the sensual.

A mane of red-gold hair fell down her back in a long, sunset-colored braid to the base of her spine. Her emerald eyes were narrowed behind the rectangular lenses of her wire-rimmed spectacles. Like Grant she wore desert camouflage, but her helmet lay in a corner. An autopistol was snugged in a cross-draw rig strapped around her waist.

Grant walked around the pedestal, asking, "Which hand do you need?"

Brigid nodded to the laptop. "That depends on the final result of the decrypt. The program is just about done—I hope."

The monitor screen glowed with digital representations of the symbols on the door, flipping and shifting through a CGI grid network.

"When that's finished," Brigid continued in her characteristically crisp and precise tone of voice, "we'll both need to press the appropriate symbols in the right sequence, probably at the same time."

Dubiously, Grant eyed the door, the images flashing on the screen and then Brigid. "You sure that's safe?"

Absently, her gaze still fixed on the computer, she inquired, "Why wouldn't it be?"

"Just off the top of my head," Grant replied, not bothering to disguise the sarcasm in his voice, "we could activate an Annunaki death ray or an Annunaki nerve-gas dispenser or an Annunaki doomsday bomb." He paused, then added, "And that's just off the top of my head."

Brigid's lips quirked in a half smile. "The Annunaki didn't usually booby-trap their own property. Besides, I'm certain this vault was built by the original inhabitants of Harappa, using left-over Annunaki tech. As it is, the symbols I've deciphered don't warn against opening the door."

Grant nodded, hoping he hadn't provided Brigid with an excuse to launch into a historical dissertation. Although he didn't possess her eidetic memory, he clearly remembered the details of the briefing in Cerberus two days before.

According to both Brigid and Lakesh, the vast subcontinent of India-Pakistan contained a number of lost cities, some of them dating back over three thousand years before the beginning of the Christian era. A highly civilized people occupied the Indus River valley for at least two millennia and were responsible for building two great cities—Mohenjo-Daro, near Punjab, and Harappa, on the border between India and Pakistan.

Although excavations began in Harappa in the 1920s, archaelogoists were never certain who actually built the city or when, although some scholars argued that Harappan civilization arose around 2500 B.C. or even earlier.

From information gleaned from the Cerberus database, Brigid postulated that Harappa served as the foundation for the legends of the so-called Nameless City that figured in the esoteric traditions of the region. Muslim and even Hindu texts hinted that the site of Harappa at one time lay beneath the ground but came to the surface after a cataclysmic earthquake.

A species of humanoid reptile, possibly a branch of the Annunaki royal family, occupied the city. When humankind rose to dominance in the Middle East, the reptilians withdrew, leaving their city uninhabited until wandering tribesmen took it over and built additions over the long track of centuries.

Like the civilizations in Mesopotamia and Egypt, Harappa grew on the floodplains of a rich and life-giving river, the Indus. Eventually, ancillary settlements spread along the banks of the Indus and its tributaries, and just as eventually, the Harappan people finally disappeared, their civilization vanishing without a trace.

Some historians believed that Harappa was overrun by the warlike Aryans who rushed in from Euro-Asia and conquered Persia and northern India. All anyone knew was that somewhere between 1800 and 1700 B.C., the Harappan cities and towns were abandoned and finally reclaimed by the rich soil from which they had sprung.

But as so often had happened in the two centuries following the global nuclear holocaust of 2001, old cultures were revived, often as bizarre re-creations of societies that had vanished long, long before. Over the past four-plus years, Grant, Brigid and Kane had come across many examples of ancient cultural resurrection.

This latest incarnation of Harappa was not as strange as many they had seen, but it was strange enough. However, the people were not as murderously xenophobic as some they had encountered in their journeys.

Juballah, the high Devi, was a surprisingly learned, open-minded woman and allowed the Cerberus team to study the vault. Of course, the decision had not been totally hers since the interphaser had opened a parallax point there, atop the geodetic marker. However, the Devi had been convinced the strangers meant her and her people no harm.

Due in part to her eidetic memory, Brigid Baptiste spoke a dozen languages and could get along in a score of dialects, but knowing the native tongues of many different cultures and lands was only a small part of her work. Aside from her command of languages, Brigid had made history and geopolitics abiding interests in a world that was changing rapidly.

She and all the personnel of Cerberus redoubt, over half a world away atop a mountain peak in Montana, had devoted themselves to changing the nuke-scarred planet into something better. At least that was her earnest hope. To turn hope into reality meant respecting the often alien beliefs of a vast number of ancient religions and their accompanying legends, myths and taboos.

"If you deciphered the symbols, then you must have an idea of what's behind the door," Grant said.

"Not really," Brigid admitted. With a forefinger she pointed to a column of symbols pulsating on the screen. "It's a type of Sumerian cuneiform, but it also has borrowed from the Akkadian system."

"There's a difference?"

Brigid shrugged. "Sumerians preferred the pictographic form that wasn't dissimilar to Egyptian hieroglyphics. Individual words were represented by over six hundred symbols that resembled the object in some way. Later they merged with the Akkadian system, which developed into more abstract symbols, the ideogram. What we've got here is a blending of ideographic and hieroglyphic."

"And you're able to read it?" Grant asked skeptically.

"After a fashion...I get the general gist. Very loosely translated, the glyphs and graphics on the door say, 'Behind this portal sleeps the knowledge that leads to the mother of all knowledge, slumbering above the blanket of the stars.'"

Grant's brow furrowed, casting his eyes into little pools of shadow. "Even loosely translated, that doesn't make a whole hell of a lot of sense."

Brigid nodded. "Not to us. But apparently it does to Overlord Nergal, or he wouldn't be here in force." She tapped the monitor screen. "Here are two ideograms that correspond to his name, so he had something to do with this place."

Not even Grant could argue with that, even if he had been so inclined. Four days ago, the Cerberus satellite-system began transmitting ELINT signals that indicated overlord activity in the vicinity of Harappa.

Although most satellites had been little more than free-floating scrap metal for well over a century, Cerberus had always possessed the proper electronic ears and eyes to receive the transmissions from at least two of them. One was of the Vela reconnaissance class, which carried narrow-band multispectral scanners. It could detect the electromagnetic radiation reflected by every object on Earth, including subsurface geomagnetic waves. The scanner was tied into an extremely high resolution photographic relay system.

A year's worth of hard work on the part of Lakesh's apprentice, Donald Bry, at long last allowed Cerberus to gain control of the Vela and the Keyhole comsat. Knowing that the Annunaki empire had been centralized in Mesopotamia, Bry programmed the Vela to transmit any imagery from the subcontinent that fit a preselected parameter.

Only three days before, Cerberus downloaded a telemetric sequence that showed an object resembling a silver disk skimming over the Indus River valley, hovering over the only city in the region, then shooting out of sight so rapidly it almost seemed to vanish. Computer enhancement of the image proved what Lakesh and Bry had suspected anyway—the disk was one of the small fleet of scout vessels carried by *Tiamat,* the inestimably ancient, mind-staggeringly enormous Annunaki starship in Earth orbit.

A quick check in the database brought up the connection between Harappa, the Nameless City and the Annunaki. By questioning Devi Juballah, they learned about the vault buried beneath the temple, and Brigid guessed that was the object of the overlord's interest. It wasn't until the ships landed the day before that they learned the overlord involved was none other than Nergal, whom they had contended against in the past in his guise as Baron Sharpe.

As Nergal, he was worshiped by the ancient Sumero-Babylonians as the god of the netherworld, an evil deity who brought war, pestilence, fever and devastation. His symbols were the club and the sickle, and Brigid had found corresponding cuneiforms on the door leading to the vault.

The laptop emitted an electronic beep and Brigid leaned forward eagerly, the lenses of her glasses holding eerie reflections of the glowing CGI glyphs. Triumphantly, she announced, "Got it."

"Got what?" Grant asked.

"The numeric sequence, the combination." She stared at the images on the screen, committing to memory the order in which they were arranged. "Six numbers, but like I said they're probably designed to be activated simultaneously to get the door open."

Straightening, she studied the portal, then switched around several of the paper squares beneath the symbols. As she worked, she said, "The combination is binary, divided into two sequences of three. The glyph pairings are separated by a couple of yards so two people are required to unlock the door. A single thief or heretic couldn't manage it. More than likely it was designed to be opened by a high priest and an acolyte."

She removed her glasses, folded them and placed them in a jacket pocket. Turning her bright jade gaze on Grant, she asked, "Ready?"

Although his impassive face didn't register it, he felt a surge of apprehension. "Now? Shouldn't we wait until Kane and the rest of the team are back?"

"There's no better time than the present," she countered impatiently. "Besides, once we get it open, we can see what's in there and jump back to Cerberus."

Brigid gestured toward the pyramidion positioned in the center of the geodetic marker. "I've already recalibrated the interphaser for Destination Zero, so getting the vault open is the last item on our to-do list."

Grant knuckled his heavy jaw for a thoughtful moment, then gusted out a resigned sigh. "All right, let's get it done."

Following Brigid's instructions, Grant stepped to the left side of the ponderous bronze slab. The marked symbols were almost at eye level, and with the wide span of his hand, he rested his fingertips lightly atop all three of them.

Brigid was not so equipped and she spread both of her hands over the embossed hieroglyphs. Glancing over at him, she asked, "Are you set?"

Grant opened his mouth to answer, then Kane's voice came over the Commtact. "We're on our way back to you. Nergal is finally using his air support."

He sounded so casual, Grant knew he was very worried. "Acknowledged," Grant said. "I think we're about done."

"Yeah," Kane replied dourly. "Us too."

"Kane?" Brigid asked.

Grant nodded. "He and the squad ought to be here in a couple of minutes."

"Then let's do it. On three. One…two…*three*."

The two people pressed the symbols, pushing them down hard with all the strength in their hands. After an initial second of resistance, the glyphs sank beneath the surface of the door. Tiny hidden locks caught them fast. For a long, tense moment, nothing happened.

Grant favored Brigid with a bleak gaze. "That's exciting."

She smiled ruefully. "Wait for it."

Mystified and annoyed, Grant bit back a profanity. The portal suddenly quivered. A grinding rumble slowly built, punctuated then overlaid by a series of squeaks, creaks and rattles as a long disused system of gears and pulleys laboriously began to move. As he and Brigid stepped back slowly and smoothly, the bronze door slid to the right. A puff of clammy, stale air assaulted their faces.

In the deep shadows within the vault, a ghostly, spectral light glowed. Grant felt the fine hairs at his nape stir as he stared at it. Dimly visible in the murk floated a human skull, hanging in the darkness like an opalescent, disembodied head. He was aware of Brigid standing at his side, as wide-eyed and entranced as him. Once their eyes adjusted to the murk, they realized the skull did not float, but rested atop an oblong black stone pedestal.

The skull was crafted of gleaming, translucent crystal, every detail and facet so perfectly fashioned, it was as if it had not been sculpted but was the remains of a beautiful celestial being.

The underground chamber suddenly shuddered, the ceiling showering them with grit and rock chips. The sound of the explosion broke the spell woven by the grinning, bodiless skull. Brigid and Grant involuntarily turned toward the stairwell, peering up it.

Brigid began to speak—then the scream of agony filled their heads.

Chapter 3

Kane elbowed himself onto his back, blinking to clear his vision of the molten afterimage of the blaze of light. His sight returned in hazy, piecemeal fashion.

The first thing he saw was a smoking crater several feet deep. Next he saw Halloran, sprawled on her back. She no longer screamed because she had lapsed into unconsciousness. Decard lay beside her, stirring feebly.

Forcing himself to his knees, Kane tilted his head up. A funnel of incandescence flowed down, casting a halo as bright as the noonday sun around him and his two companions. He didn't need to see the ship hovering fifty feet overhead to know it was there.

Shielding his eyes, he crawled toward Halloran, and the sharp reek of seared flesh and scorched cloth cut into Kane's nostrils. Blood puddled the dirt beneath Halloran's hips, her uniform torn and burned, little wisps of smoke rising from it. The pulse-plasma bolt had caught the woman in midbody, and the PASGT vest turned to slag and disintegrated even as it distributed the heat and kinetic force. Beneath it, her burned flesh was red with congealed blood and black with charred patches of Kevlar.

Despite the wound, Halloran still breathed, but her respiration was labored and fitful. Kane wasn't surprised she was alive—the very nature of the weapon prevented excessive blood loss by cauterizing the ruptured blood vessels, but she had passed out from the shock.

"Decard!" Kane half shouted. "Get it together! Decard!"

The man slowly raised his head, teeth bared, eyes glassy beneath the rim of his helmet. They reflected only pain and confusion. Kane rose to his feet, swaying back and forth, grimacing at the sharp needles of pain in his right rib cage. "Take care of Halloran, get ready to move out with her."

He didn't wait to find out if Decard followed his order. Moving swiftly, he unbuckled the chin strap of his helmet, casting it off and staring upward so his face was fully revealed in the spotlight. His hair, a shade between chestnut and black, glistened with sweat.

"What are you doing?" Decard croaked in dismay.

Not shifting his gaze from the underside of the disk, Kane replied quietly, "Your team bought us some time—now I'm returning the favor."

The funnel of light shifted away and a giant figure suddenly shimmered into existence within it, standing between Kane and the city gate. Decard murmured wordlessly, fearfully. The holographic image of Overlord Nergal loomed nearly fifteen feet tall. He looked much the same as when Kane had last seen him nearly two years before, on the bridge of *Tiamat* in the company of the nine other members of the Supreme Council.

Elaborate body armor tinted a dark, rich burgandy encased his gaunt frame. The armor was inscribed with leering demon faces and serpentine writhing dragons. A swirling cuneiform symbol, the insignia of Nergal, rose in relief on the left pectoral.

The skin of his face, stretched drum-tight over strong, high-arching cheekbones and brow ridges, was of a ruddy hue. Beneath overhanging brow arches, sunken very deep in his head as if hiding from the light, his fierce eyes shone like drops of burnished brass. Black, vertical-slitted pupils bisected them.

The quality of the hologram was such that Kane could easily see the delicate pattern of scales glistening along the line of his jutting jaw. A back-slanting crest of red spines sprouted from his hairless skull. Nergal's lips peeled back over his teeth in either an angry grimace or a grin of savage satisfaction.

"Kane," he said, his amplified voice reverberating with a metallic, whispering echo.

Affecting an exaggerated tone of ebullience, Kane said loudly, "Nergal—buddy! Long time no shoot at. How's your mom getting along up there in orbit?"

Nergal did not respond to Kane's oblique and disrespectful reference to *Tiamat*. "What are you doing here? How dare you oppose me…this is a blatant breach of the accord you struck with Enlil."

"Maybe," Kane conceded, noting out of the corner of his eye that Decard cradled Halloran's head in his hands. "But you weren't there, so the treaty doesn't really extend to you, does it?"

"Don't try to distract me with your dissembling!" Nergal's voice hit a strident note of outrage.

Kane kept the surge of relief that his gamble had worked from showing on his face. He and Overlord Nergal shared a history of sorts—several years ago, while in the persona of Baron Sharpe, he had been the recipient of a bullet fired from Kane's pistol. They had met a couple of times afterward, and as Sharpe, he had not borne Kane a grudge. But since his metamorphosis into Nergal, his vengeful nature could not have been more out in the open.

As Kane made a motion to brush hair from his face, he activated the all-channels frequency on the Commtact. He guessed that Halloran's comm had malfunctioned when the plasma bolt struck her, and so her scream was transmitted to all Commtacts within range.

"All right," Kane said, "I won't. I'm here to keep you from doing whatever you're trying to do."

"You don't even know what that is!" Nergal shot back angrily, with a hint of Baron Sharpe's characteristic petulance.

Kane shrugged. "Does it really matter?"

"Don't act like a bigger fool than I already believe you to be," Nergal spit, contempt dripping from every syllable. "It matters a great deal to me. If you continue to stand in my way, I'll have this city razed to the ground and every living thing in it put to death—man, woman, child, cat, dog and chicken. Then I'll go about my business at my leisure."

Nergal paused for a second, looking to one side as if something within the ship distracted him. "I had hoped you would withdraw when you realized how outmatched you were and therefore spare Harappa further damage. Clearly my hope was in vain."

"Clearly," Kane agreed. Through the open gate, he glimpsed the first of Nergal's forces entering the city. A four-man contingent of black-armored Magistrates walked point for the Nephilim, casting about nervously for an ambush.

"You may still depart the same way you arrived here," Nergal continued, "or you may remain and die. Those are the only choices open to you, but you must choose now."

Kane gazed at the overlord's holographic image without expression. "You don't believe in wasting time, do you?"

"Time is something you have no more to spare."

"How much do you happen to have?" Kane asked, half-glancing toward Decard as he rolled the unconscious Halloran over his shoulders in a fireman's carry.

"Far more than you or your friends," Nergal retorted, voice sibilant with menace.

"Speaking of friends," Kane said, striving for a friendly, conversational tone, "what happened to that little doomseer you used to hang with? Crawler was his name, right? And then there's my old pal, Sindri. Wasn't he your guest until your makeover?"

Nergal's eyes flashed in fury, and Kane's belly lurched with the realization that his time had run out. He, Decard and Halloran had the survivablility quotient of fish in a barrel.

"I've had enough of you," Nergal growled between gritted teeth, his voice dropping to a whisper of hatred. "I've had *more* than enough. I am going to do something that several of my brethren tried but failed to accomplish— I am going to watch you die in screaming, mad agony."

Kane tensed, clenching his fists, preparing to defend himself. He heard a ripping sound as of a stiff piece of canvas tearing in two. Then the rocket arced over his head, a short, slender projectile with a wavery ribbon of spark-shot smoke. It struck the disk ship broadside, the warhead detonating amid a billowing mushroom of black smoke and a gush of flame that rolled over the hull. Instantly, the image of Nergal winked out. The craft wobbled, tilting up on one edge.

The first explosion was followed by a staggered pattern of grenades bursting open against the surface of the disk and flying beneath it to detonate the mud-brick archway over the gate. Debris blew skyward and rained down, forcing the Magistrates to leap awkwardly for cover.

Thudding footfalls reached Kane's ears, and he heeled around as CAT Alpha pounded down the narrow street, their assault rifles hammering on full-auto and spouting grenades. The bullets sparked on the rim of the disk ship's hull, looking like miniature novas in the dim light.

Kane knew directing fire against the ship would accomplish very little, but he kept his opinions to himself. The semifluid composition of the hull was such it absorbed projectiles and the kinetic energy produced by their impacts.

A second rocket streaked overhead, missing the disk entirely but striking the wall. The archway collapsed completely, burying two of the Magistrates beneath a cascade of splintered timbers and pulverized stone. Their cries of shock and pain were brief.

Grant jogged up, a short-barreled, big-bored LAW-80 rocket launcher angled over his right shoulder. Shouting to be heard over the slamming, banging cacophony, he yelled, "I think we've overstayed!"

Bracing an overbalanced Decard with one arm, Kane shouted back, "You think?"

From the underside of the disk streaked short pencils of light. Craters opened up in the ground, and Kane felt the concussions of the impacts. Chunks of stone flew in all directions. CAT Alpha returned the fire with streams of steel-jacketed rounds and a flurry of grenades. For a long moment, the world became a thundering inferno. The disk rose vertically and slid across the sky eastward, out of range of the concerted barrage.

"Pull back!" Kane bellowed. "Everybody pull back!"

The team began an orderly withdrawal down the stark and bare streets of Harappa just as the Nephilim emerged through the piles of rubble partially blocking the gate. They extended their arms, and little fireballs of ASP energy blazed through the air.

Garsden took a direct hit to his head, and his face blew away in a pink spray. Only his helmet kept his skull from flying apart.

Two of the team took up protective positions over his body and raised the H&K XM-29s to their shoulders. They raked the armored, marching figures with a steady fusillade of autofire. The bullets struck sparks and bell-like chimes from their gleaming exoskeletons, ricocheting away with angry, buzzing whines. One of the Nephilim staggered under the multiple impacts, falling against a comrade, and for a few seconds, the ASP blasts flared wildly, like off-course comets.

Taking advantage of the confusion, the two CAT troopers secured grips on Garsden's arms and dragged his body with them, the heels of his boots cutting grooves in the dirt. His limbs were completely slack.

A second silver disk hove into view over the walls. Lances of white light stabbed downward from round ports on its undercarriage. Concussions knocked the two men who dragged Garsden off their feet, but they rose quickly.

"Leave him!" Kane shouted over his shoulder. "You can't help him now!"

The pair of troopers hesitated for a couple of seconds, then turned and sprinted after the rest of the team.

As Kane ran, helping Decard along, the darkness strobed with repeated explosions, the sharp reports slapping painfully against his eardrums.

Grant cradled the LAW-80 in his arms as he ran, not

daring to take the time to load another warhead and prime it. "Getting too old for this shit," he panted.

Kane winced as a blast of dust and rubble billowed in from a side lane and one of the team cried out as he was struck by flying debris. "I can't imagine what would make you feel that way," Kane said grimly.

BRIGID BAPTISTE WATCHED the eruptions that sent flames and shadows dancing over the tops of the buildings. From beneath the shelter provided by the framework of scaffolds, she and Devi Juballah peered up and outward, glimpsing the silver disk-ships skimming back and forth. Beams of incandescence darted down from the disk's undersides.

"It is over," Juballah intoned flatly. "But war never has a tidy ending. My city and my people will suffer because of this day for a very long time to come."

Brigid glanced at her, noting how calm and collected the woman appeared to be, despite the grim set her mouth. "It's only a battle in a far larger war," she said. "Not even that, really. Barely a skirmish compared to some of the engagements we've been in. We explained everything to you about the overlords and their agenda yesterday."

Juballah closed her eyes, veiling them with her long sweeping lashes. "Oh, yes…you told me all about how the old gods of this land were in reality alien monsters who came from another world thousands of years ago to enslave humanity. You said they never really went away, that they were only sleeping within the womb of their mother *Tiamat,* high above the Earth. They slept there, waiting until humanity nearly destroyed itself and Earth—and then the old gods awoke."

Brigid smiled wanly. "That's a pretty simplistic version of what we told you."

Juballah opened her eyes and they glinted with sudden, angry resentment. "We are a simple people doing our best to survive and preserve the ways of our forefathers, our ancestors. We lived here in the ancient city, clearing away the dust of centuries. And then you and your friends materialized in one of our sacred sites—" she gestured behind her toward the stairwell "—and informed me that everything we believed in, all of our old legends, were only lies."

"No," Brigid retorted firmly. "Not lies. Just misinterpretations."

Juballah waved away Brigid's objection. "You told us that Nergal desires to claim what is within our vault and that we should help you recover it before he does. And now that you've opened the vault, you will take it and leave us to face a god's vengeance alone."

Brigid hesitated, thinking through her response, automatically resting a foot atop the yellow plastic containment case at her feet. She understood and sympathized with Juballah's fear and confusion.

"I can promise you that you won't be abandoned," Brigid stated, knowing she couldn't fulfill such a vow alone.

Juballah's gaze flicked toward the box under Brigid's foot. "What treasure did the vault protect?"

"It wasn't a treasure exactly. I'd call it more of an artifact."

"An artifact of the ancient Harappans?" Juballah's tone of voice made her question sound more like an accusation.

"That's very doubtful," Brigid declared confidently. "What we found wasn't the kind of object associated with the cultures of this part of the world."

"But it belongs to the god Nergal and he wants it, nevertheless."

"He's not a god," Brigid retorted, anger edging her words despite herself. "And I seriously doubt it's his. I have an idea of why he wants it but—"

"But you want it because he does?" the Devi broke in, eyes slitted with suspicion.

Brigid sighed. "It's not that simple. Anything the overlords want won't mean anything good for humanity."

"Why should I take your word for that?" Juballah argued.

The woman's challenge startled and irritated Brigid. "We can prove what we say, but at the moment you'll have to take it on faith."

A shadow suddenly shifted overhead, and Brigid shrank back against the temple wall as a disk floated soundlessly fifty feet overhead.

Juballah didn't move. Quietly she said, "I have no faith in you."

Moving with surprising speed, Juballah bent and snatched up the box from beneath Brigid's foot. Alarmed, Brigid reached for the Devi, but the woman drove an elbow into the pit of her stomach, driving her backward. Loose stones turned beneath her boots and she sat down awkwardly.

Juballah dashed out from beneath the canopy of the scaffold, shouting shrilly. The disk seemed to freeze in midair. A cone of light sprang out from the domed underside and cast a circle of brilliance around the Devi. Stumbling to a halt, she held the yellow box aloft, as if it were an offering.

"No!" Brigid shouted, scrambling to her feet. "They think you're defying them!"

Juballah ignored her.

Lunging forward, Brigid grasped Juballah around the waist and hauled her back. The woman struggled, using one arm to fend her off. Reaching around her, Brigid wrestled the box from her grip. Heart trip-hammering within her chest, she realized there was no time to think or act except in self-preservation.

Brigid bounded back beneath the scaffolds just as a flurry of energy bolts arrowed down from the disk. Planks and chunks of stone exploded in a burst of smoke, flame and thunder.

Chapter 4

Brigid lay her on her stomach, clasping the box tightly between both hands, feeling her shoulders, legs and back pelted by debris raining down around her. Nothing too heavy came down to strike her. She heard a faint, strangulated female scream amid the crash and clatter of falling wreckage, but there was no hope of going back for Juballah now.

Slowly she raised her head, squeezing her eyes half-shut against the swirling particles of grit. She didn't rise, praying the gunner of the disk wasn't interested in firing blind into the rubble. The rumble of tumbling, settling rock slowly faded, and she squinted into the thick pall of dust.

Brigid could see very little, so after a moment she carefully climbed to one knee, aware of a trickle of blood on her left cheek from a shallow, stinging cut. Swiftly she examined the box, seeing with relief that the lid was still locked. Down in the vault she hadn't had the time to examine the skull before Grant had grabbed the rocket launcher and bounded up the steps to meet the CAT squad. As she placed the object in the foam-rubber-lined containment box, she noted it appeared to be made out of crystal, as she had guessed upon first glimpsing it.

She repressed the reflex to cough. Fanning the smoke and dust away from her face, Brigid inched her way through the scattering of debris toward the entrance of the underground chamber. She didn't see the disk overhead, so she sacrificed stealth for speed. Within a moment, she stood just inside the doorway, breathing hard, peering at the bursts of light flaring through the haze, listening to the crack-sizzle of the Nephilim's ASP emitters and the staccato hammering of the CAT squad's autorifles.

Thinking about Devi Juballah, Brigid shivered involuntarily, knowing that half a second had separated her from sharing the woman's fate. She, Kane and Grant had been in tight situations many times before and in more than a few of them she hadn't expected to survive. But she and her friends always did, even if they lost some blood, flesh and peace of mind in the process.

Lakesh had once suggested that the trinity they formed when they worked in tandem seemed to exert an almost supernatural influence on the scales of chance. The notion had both amused and intrigued Brigid. She, like Kane, was too pragmatic to truly believe in such an esoteric concept, but she couldn't deny that she and her two friends seemed to lead exceptionally charmed lives.

Kane and Grant had made something of a minireligion about the matriculation of luck, as if it were a finite resource that had to be periodically replenished. It was difficult for Brigid to keep in mind that the two men had spent their entire adult lives as killers. Both men had been through the dehumanizing cruelty of Magistrate training, yet had somehow managed to retain their humanity. But vestiges of their Mag years still lurked close to the surface, particularly in threatening situations. In those instances, their destructive ruthlessness could be frightening.

She heard the steady thumping of many running feet and stiffened. Vague, blurred shapes loomed in the veils of smoke and dust, quickly resolving themselves into the figures of Kane, Grant and Cerberus Away Team Alpha. A score of yards behind them she glimpsed the dull glints of the Nephilim's body armor. Bolts of orange-cored energy peppered the facade of the temple, bursting in kaleidoscopic blazes of sparks and flying shards of stone.

At a sharp command from Kane, the team whirled, formed a line, aimed and fired as one in a long stuttering volley. The air filled with a jackhammering racket as of a gang of blacksmiths pounding anvils in a crazed tempo. The Nephilim staggered and careened away beneath the barrage, sparks flaring from their body armor at the points of impact.

ASP emitters flashed and seething globes of plasma burst on the ground around the CAT squad. One of the team cried out and fell, clutching at his right leg. Grant dropped the rocket launcher and dragged the man to his feet.

Chill fingers of dread seized Brigid's spine as she

glimpsed the shadowy Nephilim, marching forward in a steady, relentless rhythm. They stepped heedlessly over their fallen brethren, not so much spurning death as oblivious to it. The pearl-eyed zombies were mortal, but their expressionless faces reminded her that in legend, the Nephilim were reputed to be the illegitimate children of fallen angels, wandering lost souls.

"Fall back to the vault! Fall back!" Kane yelled.

Brigid stepped aside as Decard stumble past her, a limp body slung over his shoulders. She caught a whiff of seared flesh and the acrid odor of scorched fabric. The squad retreated through the entrance to the subterranean chamber, moving swiftly but not running. Although she had at first been skeptical about the formation of the away teams, since they were composed of volunteers from the Manitius Moon base and disenfranchised Magistrates, Brigid felt grudging admiration for the discipline they displayed.

Grant handed off the wounded trooper to another man and crouched beside Kane and Brigid at the door. Panting, his pale eyes startlingly bright in his dirt-smeared face, Kane said, "Baptiste, please tell me you found something of worth in that vault. Grant claimed you got it open."

Brigid patted the lid of the container. "We did, but I don't know if it's worth risking the lives of any of our people."

"We already lost one," Grant bit out, putting his Copperhead to his shoulder and squeezing off a long burst at the armored soldiers. Bright brass arced out of the smoking ejector port, tinkling down at his feet. "I don't think what we found was worth his life."

"Who?" Brigid asked, feeling a chill fist knot in her chest.

"Garsden," Grant replied, lowering the subgun. "The Mag from Thuliaville. He was looking for a new way of life. That's an example of what you call irony, right?"

"There could be more examples if we don't get out of here," Kane said darkly, gesturing in the direction of the hovering disks. "The only reason Nergal hasn't flash-blasted this place is because he doesn't want to have to dig out the vault."

His gaze flicked back and forth as if a notion suddenly occurred to him. "Where's the Devi? I sent her back to—"

"She was here," Brigid interrupted, nodding toward a heap of broken stone and splintered timbers. "She tried to cut a deal with Nergal."

"Idiot!" Grant snarled out the word. "Why would the stupid bitch do that?"

Brigid glared at him in angry reproach. "Because she didn't think we had Harappa's best interests at heart."

"But she thought Nergal does?" Kane demanded.

"She didn't know," Brigid replied. "We didn't do an exemplary job of proving to her we were any better than him. She just wanted to stop the destruction of her city.

We can't really blame her for that." She paused and added bleakly, "Not exactly our finest diplomatic moment."

Kane opened his mouth to voice a profane rebuttal, but a bolt of plasma lashed through the air a finger's-width above his head, bursting against a pillar behind him with a shower of sparks and rock shards. He hunched his shoulders, wincing at the impact of the fragments against his back.

Grant rose and stepped back toward the stairwell, pulling Brigid and Kane with him by the sleeves of their field jackets. "Like I said before, I think we've overstayed."

"Yeah," Kane agreed sourly, eyeing one of the silver disks as it skimmed closer. "I imagine Nergal feels much the same way."

Apprehensively, Brigid said, "I don't know if we'll have all the time we need to activate the vortex and do a phase-out."

"I'll buy us some time." Grant half rose, gazing toward the approaching Nephilim, as if gauging the speed of their gait. He plucked a grenade from his combat webbing, unpinned it and lobbed it toward the base of the half-built wall.

"Fire in the hole," he said calmly.

The high-explosive compounds detonated in a tremendous cracking blast, a blinding burst of dust and sand erupting from the ground. The sound of the explosion instantly bled into a grinding rumble of a stony mass shifting. The groaning grate overlapped with the ringing echoes of the detonation then overwhelmed them.

As Brigid, Kane and Grant watched, a long section of the wall toppled forward in a crushing cascade of bouncing blocks and spurting dust. The Nephilim were engulfed, buried by the tons of collapsing basalt and granite.

After the rolling echo of the crash faded, there came a stunned silence, stitched through with a clicking of pebbles and faint moans. Dust hung in the air like a dingy blanket over the fallen mass of rock.

"Plenty more where they came from," Kane commented. "But maybe the others will take some time to come up with a new strategy and by then we'll be gone."

A gleaming disk ship slid to a halt twenty feet above the rubble, a shaft of light shining down from the half-dome bulging from the craft's undercarriage, playing over the heap of stone.

Gazing up at it, Kane murmured, "Uh-oh."

Short rods of light streaked down from the ship. Fist-sized craters opened up in the ground with spurts of flame, and they felt the concussions of the explosive impacts. Hastily Brigid, Grant and Kane withdrew into the stairwell, running quickly down the steps. With each sharp report, dust and rock particles showered down from above.

"I don't think Nergal cares if he has to dig the vault out now," Brigid commented breathlessly.

"Me either," Grant replied. "The whole point is probably to bury us alive."

The three people felt a surge a relief when they saw

that CAT Alpha had arranged themselves around the geodetic marker, as per their instructions. Halloran was still unconscious, tended to by Decard. The man with the leg injury was being treated by one of his comrades.

"I hope everybody is packed," Kane announced, stepping onto the floor carvings. "We're leaving in kind of a hurry."

"Not in enough of a hurry for me," Decard commented dourly.

Brigid moved swiftly to the raised center of the floor carving and knelt beside the interphaser. From the base protruded the blocky power unit and a miniature control keypad. She touched the inset activation toggles on the pad, and a waxy, glowing funnel of light fanned up from the metal apex of the pyramid. It looked like a diffused veil of backlit fog, with tiny shimmering stars dancing within it.

The light expanded into a gushing borealis several feet wide, spreading over the surface of the geodetic marker. A thready pulse of vibration tickled everyone's skin, and a faint hint of a breeze brushed their faces and ruffled their hair.

From above reverberated the thuds of three explosions. Grit poured down from the roof, mixed with larger chunks of gravel that clattered against the floor and bounced from helmeted heads.

"Don't mind us, Baptiste," Kane said with a forced calm, fanning grit away from his face and casting a sideways glance toward the stairwell. Stones rolled down the steps amid puffs of dust. "Take all the time you need."

"Done," Brigid announced crisply, standing and stepping away from the pyramidion.

A glowing, phosphorescent lotus blossom sprouted from the base of the interphaser. Skeins of blue-white streaked along the grooves and convolutions of the carvings, the light pulsing like the lifeblood in a circulatory system. In an instant, the entire inscribed surface of the geodetic marker was laced with a webwork of dancing light.

Even after all the phase transits he had made, Kane still wasn't sure how the interphaser did what it did, but the fact it functioned at all never failed to amaze him.

When making transits to and from the Cerberus redoubt, they always used the mat-trans chamber as the origin point because it could be hermetically sealed. The interphaser's targeting computer had been programmed with the precise coordinates of the mat-trans unit as Destination Zero. A touch of a single key on the interphaser's control pad would automatically return the device to the jump chamber, but sometimes the phase harmonics needed to be fine-tuned. The adjustments were normally within Brigid's purview.

The veil of light expanded from the apex of the pyramidion, stretching outward, giving the illusion of a Chinese hand fan spreading wide, with the interphaser acting as the centerpiece.

A new series of consecutive hammering blasts thundered overhead, and Kane guessed Nergal had notched up the power of his ship's weapons. The walls of the chamber showed a network of cracks, and the ceiling split. Rocks and dirt showered down. The ground heaved and shuddered and several of the braziers tipped over, sending embers flowing over the floor like lava. A fissure opened up around the foot of the stairwell with a clash of rending rock.

Kane swung his head toward Brigid, squinting through the pulsating waves of cold fire dancing along the carved lines and curves of the geodetic marker underfoot. He said loudly, "Somebody better start the evac and fast!"

Brigid didn't answer. She helped Decard heave the unconscious Halloran to her feet and carry her to the center of the marker. Gently, they pushed her into the fan of wavering light surrounding the interphaser.

Halloran toppled headlong into it—and vanished.

Chapter 5

If not for the artifact, Mohandas Lakesh Singh would have been singularly unconvinced that the expenditure of time, effort and a human life was worth the field op to Pakistan.

The artifact rested on the center of the trestle table in the long chamber that served as the testing facility and workroom of the Cerberus redoubt. Rows of drafting tables with T-squares hanging from them lined one wall. Upright tool lockers, a band saw, a drill press, lathes and various chassis of electronic equipment, including a spectroscope, lined the other.

Arms folded over his chest, Lakesh slowly walked around the table, examining the artifact from all angles with an impatient expression creasing his dark olive face. He held an aluminum ruler in his right hand and absently tapped the end of it against his chin. After another circuit around the table, he uttered a profanity-seasoned sigh.

Brewster Philboyd, perched on a stool at a computer station, looked up from the monitor screen and cast a surprised glance over his shoulder. Lakesh resorting to curse words was unusual, which only hinted at the high degree of consternation he felt.

"I thought you'd be excited," Philboyd said. "Not irritated."

Lakesh waved the ruler at the translucent skull grinning up at him from the center of the table. "We have quite enough bonfires burning around the world at this moment," he said sourly, his cultured voice underscored by a lilting East Indian accent. "Our resources to douse them are stretched thin in terms of personnel. And so Alpha Team brings this…*thing* back, and I don't know what we're supposed to do with it."

Philboyd hooked a thumb over his shoulder toward the spectroscope. "I'd suggest sticking it in there, for starters."

An astrophysicist in his midforties, Brewster Philboyd was slightly over six feet tall but very thin and lanky. Pale blond hair was swept back from a receding hairline, which made his high forehead seem very high indeed. He wore black-rimmed eyeglasses, and his cheeks appeared to be pitted with the sort of scars associated with chronic teenage acne.

Philboyd was one of a number of space scientists who had arrived in the Cerberus redoubt from a forgotten Moon base over the past two and a half years. Like Lakesh, he was a freezie, postnuke slang for someone who had been placed in stasis, although conventional cryonics was not the method applied.

Lakesh shrugged. "I know as much about crystal skulls as I care to."

A well-built man of medium height, with thick, glossy black hair and a long, aquiline nose, Lakesh looked no older than fifty, despite strands of gray threading his temples. In reality, he had observed his 250th birthday a short time before. He and Philboyd wore one-piece white zippered bodysuits, the unisex duty uniform of the Cerberus redoubt.

"I can't say as I do," Philboyd replied. "Particularly if this one is of Annunaki manufacture, like Brigid claims."

"It is," a decisive female voice said from the door. "I'm sure of it."

They turned as Brigid Baptiste strode in, walking with her characteristic mannish stride. She vigorously towel-dried her mounds of damp red-gold hair. A strip of liquid bandage shone on her left cheek. She wore a black T-shirt and jeans that accentuated her full-breasted, willowy figure. Her bare arms rippled with hard, toned muscle.

"How are you feeling?" Lakesh asked as she reached the side of the table.

"I think I'll be washing mementos of Harappa out of my hair for the next few days," she answered wryly, "but other than that, I'm fine."

Lakesh frowned. "Which is more than can be said for Halloran, Garsden and Falco."

"Falco will be all right after a week on crutches," Brigid said a little defensively. "No final word on Halloran's condition yet."

"But the word on Garsden is pretty bloody final," Lakesh countered, his frown deepening.

"I don't want to sound coldhearted," Brigid replied tersely, "but Garsden was a former hard-contact Magistrate from Thuliaville. He knew all the risks when he joined us."

"Suzie Halloran was a cartographer from Muncie," Philboyd interjected. "I'm not sure she knew *all* the risks. She was motivated more by pulling her own weight, making a contribution to Cerberus, like most of the Manitius personnel."

The people to whom he referred were expatriates from the Manitius Moon base who had chosen to forge new lives for themselves with the Cerberus exiles. Although the majority of the former lunar colonists were academics, they had proved their inherent courage and resourcefulness and wanted to get out into the world and make a difference in the struggle to reclaim the planet of their birth.

Nearly twenty of them were permanently stationed on Thunder Isle in the Cific, working to refurbish the sprawling complex that had housed Operation Chronos two centuries before and make it a viable alternative to the Cerberus redoubt.

The others remained in the redoubt concealed within a Montana mountain peak as part of the Cerberus resistance movement. For three years, Kane, Brigid and Grant had struggled to dismantle the machine of baronial tyranny in America. They had devoted themselves to the work of Cerberus, and victory over the nine barons, if not precisely within their grasp, did not seem a completely unreachable goal until unexpectedly, nearly two years earlier, the entire dynamic of the struggle against the nine barons changed.

The Cerberus warriors learned that the fragile hybrid barons, despite being close to a century old, were only in a larval, or chrysalis, stage of their development. Overnight, the barons changed. When that happened, the war against the baronies themselves ended, but a new one, far greater in scope, began.

The baronies had not fallen in the conventional sense through attrition, war or organized revolts. The barons had simply walked away from their villes, their territories and their subjects. When they reached the final stage in their development, they saw no need for the trappings of semidivinity, nor were they content to rule such minor kingdoms. When they evolved into their true forms, incarnations of the ancient Annunaki overlords, their avaricious scope expanded to encompass the entire world and every thinking creature on it.

The Cerberus warriors had hoped the overweening ambition and ego of the reborn overlords would spark bloody internecine struggles, but in the nineteen months since their advent, no intel indicating such actions had reached them.

So far, the overlords had been engaged in reclaiming their ancient ancestral kingdoms in Mesopotamia. They had yet to cast their covetous gaze back to the North American continent, but it was only a matter of time.

Before that occurred, Cerberus was determined to build some sort of unified resistance against them, but the undertaking proved far more difficult and frustrating than even the cynical Kane or the impatient Grant had imagined. Even long months after the disappearance of the barons, the villes were still in states of anarchy, with various factions warring for control on a day-by-day basis.

A number of former Magistrates, weary of fighting for one transitory ruling faction or another that tried to fill the power vacuum in the villes, responded to the outreach efforts of Cerberus.

"Every member of the away teams is a volunteer, Brewster," Brigid declared, "whether they're ex-Mags or ex-Moonies."

Philboyd stiffened at her usage of Kane's disrespectful slang for the Manitius émigrés. He said grimly, "That may be so, but the selection process isn't very exacting, either."

"That's the main reason I opposed the formation of these away teams from the beginning," Lakesh declared. "The pool from which to draw participants isn't very deep."

"I know that," Brigid replied coldly. "And I also know you were outvoted by the senior command staff. I had my own reservations, remember. But even Domi voted for the squads."

Lakesh swallowed hard, struggling to tamp down his anger. Brigid refrained from pursuing the matter out of consideration for his pride. When she, Domi, Grant and Kane first arrived at the Cerberus redoubt nearly five years before, Lakesh held the position as the primary authority figure in the redoubt. Within a few months, the staging of a minicoup dramatically changed the situation.

Lakesh hadn't been totally unseated from his position of authority, but he became answerable to a more democratic process. At first, he bitterly resented what he construed as the usurping of his power by ingrates, but he grew to appreciate how the burden of responsibility had been lifted from his shoulders. With the removal of that burden, the risk that his recruitment methods would be exposed also diminished.

Before the arrival of the Manitius personnel, almost every exile in the redoubt had joined the resistance movement as a convicted criminal—after Lakesh had set them up, framing them for crimes against their respective villes. He admitted it was a cruel, heartless plan with a barely acceptable risk factor, but it was the only way to spirit them out of their villes, turn them against the barons and make them feel indebted to him.

Brigid Baptiste did not enjoy scoring a debate point by raising an issue that her former mentor found painful. The argument regarding the away teams had not been protracted, but it had been acrimonious with Lakesh and the redoubt's medic, Reba DeFore, leading the opposition.

Returning his attention to the crystal skull, Lakesh intoned, "In that case, perhaps you'll be good enough to explain why this exceptionally morbid paperweight was worth a man's life."

Brigid's jade eyes flashed with annoyance. "You know why as well as I do. The skull is obviously a memory buffer for an Annunaki computer system."

Philboyd snorted derisively. "Obviously?"

Forcing a note of patience into her voice, Brigid said, "I saw one on *Tiamat,* remember? I mentioned it in the mission report."

One corner of Philboyd's mouth quirked in a smile. "That was almost two years ago and I don't have your photographic memory. But I do remember reading about the crystal skulls found here on Earth. Seems like most of them were revealed to be of terrestrial origin."

"I have no doubt they were," Brigid said coolly. "Since the Annunaki colonized Earth, it stands to reason they'd use terrestrial materials."

Lakesh leaned forward, gazing into the hollow, translucent eye sockets of the sculpture. "As I recall, crystal skulls turned up at various archaeological sites during the nineteenth and twentieth centuries, which excited all the wealthy occultist societies of the time. They put forth the belief that the indigenous peoples of various undeveloped nations consulted the skulls as if they were oracles."

Brigid shrugged. "If their own legends maintained the skulls contained encoded information, that's not surprising, even if they had no way to access them."

"Maybe so, but that doesn't make them the same thing as Annunaki computer memory buffers," Philboyd remarked skeptically.

"True," Brigid admitted. "But several skulls, found near the ancient ruins of Mayan and Aztec cities, were believed to be between five and thirty-six thousand years old."

"That's a hell of a gap," Philboyd observed.

"Mayan artisans were known for working in minerals," Lakesh argued. "Finding the skulls near those sites isn't unusual."

Brigid nodded, eyes fixing on the skull. "Yes, but there's not even an oral tradition among the Mayans that such things were ever made. Everything that is known about lapidary work indicates that the skulls should have been shattered, fractured or simply fallen apart when carved."

"That doesn't make them the result of Annunaki manufacturing techniques," Philboyd said.

"No, but that's just one unusual characteristic among many," Brigid responded.

"What are the others?" Lakesh inquired, sounding interested despite the skeptical angle of his eyebrows.

Brigid said, "The most widely celebrated crystal skull is the Mitchell-Hedges skull, for at least two good reasons. First, it is very similar in form to an actual human skull, even featuring a fitted removable jawbone. Most known crystal skulls were of a more stylized structure, often with teeth that are simply etched onto a single piece like this one."

"What's the other reason?" Lakesh asked.

"From a strictly technical standpoint, it appeared to be an impossible object, which the twentieth century's most talented sculptors and engineers were unable to duplicate."

"Where was it found?" Philboyd wanted to know.

"British explorer F. A. Mitchell-Hedges claimed that his daughter unearthed it in 1923 within some ancient Mayan ruins in Belize," Brigid answered. "Researchers found that the skull had been carved against the natural axis of the crystal."

"Is that significant?" Lakesh asked.

Brigid smiled wanly. "Modern crystal sculptors always take into account the axis, or orientation, of the crystal's molecular symmetry, because if they carve against the grain the piece is bound to shatter—even with the use of lasers and other high-tech cutting methods."

Philboyd gestured to the spectroscope. "What would we find if we subjected it to full spectroscopic analysis?"

Brigid combed her fingers through her tousled mane of hair. "I couldn't say. The Mitchell-Hedges skull showed not even microscopic scratches to indicate it had been carved with metal instruments. The best hypothesis for the skull's construction is that it was hewn out by rubbing it with diamonds, and then the detail work was meticulously done with a gentle solution of silicon sand and water. The job—assuming it could possibly have been done in that way—would have required three hundred years to complete."

"We don't know if the skull you brought back has the same properties as that one," Philboyd declared.

"No, we don't." She paused, her smile widening. "But I imagine it does."

Lakesh straightened from the table, casting her a questioning glance. "Why do you imagine that?"

"Mainly because Overlord Nergal wanted it so badly he was willing to bury us all alive to keep it from us."

Lakesh nodded sagely. "I can't argue with that. But still—"

The trans-comm on the wall emitted a harsh, attention-diverting buzz, followed by Donald Bry's voice. "Lakesh, are you there?"

Turning toward the voice-activated comm unit, Lakesh called, "I'm here, Mr. Bry, as well as Brigid and Dr. Philboyd."

The sigh that filtered over the comm sounded genuinely relieved. "Good. Would the three of you mind coming to ops as soon as possible?"

"Why?"

"I've picked up something on the voyeur channel you might find interesting. I know I do."

Chapter 6

Under the thinnest of transparent polyethylene tenting, Suzie Halloran looked like a woman embalmed. Her face was a parchment color, her eyes closed, her hair bound up beneath a white cloth cap.

The intensive-care room in the infirmary was filled with the ominous sounds of medical monitors and the hiss of respirators pumping life-giving oxygen into the woman's damaged lungs. A network of feeder tubes ran into the tent. An IV bag dripped slowly into a shunt in her left arm.

Kane stood at the foot of her bed, absently probing his rib cage with careful fingers. Halloran had barely survived the interphaser transit, and it had taken DeFore two hours to stablize her condition. Still, it was guarded and the medic's prognosis was not optimistic.

Auerbach, DeFore's aide, pushed aside the curtain and checked the icons on the diagnostic monitor and jotted down notes on a pad of paper. A burly, freckled man with a red buzz cut, he said quietly, "Damn shame. Suzie was a nice girl."

"Was?" Kane echoed sarcastically. "What are you doing, getting a jump on writing her eulogy?"

Auerbach glanced at him with an expression close to pity on his face. "Even if she recovers, she'll never be the same. Thirty percent of her torso is covered in third- and second-degree burns, her intestines and stomach have been perforated, her digestive tract is all but cooked and only one lung is working at full capacity. She's not getting up and walking out of here any time soon. The guy who got killed—Garsden?—might have been the lucky one."

Kane felt a quiver of nausea and turned away without answering, tugging down his black T-shirt.

"How are you doing?" Auerbach asked. "I saw you favoring your ribs."

"I'm fine. Look after Halloran."

Although he had known Auerbach for years and even saved his life once, Kane had never cared much for the man, for several reasons. Crossing the infirmary, he stepped inside a curtained alcove and found DeFore attending to Carr's elevated and thickly bandaged leg. A shard of sharp-edged stone had been driven deep into the man's lower right thigh, piercing the muscle.

"How are you doing, Carr?" he asked the raw-boned man.

"You might ask *me* that," DeFore stated peevishly. "I'm the one who treated him. I treated all the injuries this time around, except yours."

"I hurt," Carr said flatly. "That's how I'm doing."

DeFore said, "You'll recover. Next time, you might want to think twice about volunteering for an away mission before you know all the specifics."

The last was directed toward Kane. Reba DeFore, the de facto physician of Cerberus, had never been shy about voicing complaints when she treated injuries she believed had come about due to foolishness or carelessness.

The medic had at one time felt a great deal of antipathy toward Kane—or rather, what he represented. In her eyes, as a former Magistrate, he was the embodiment of the totalitariansim of the villes, glorying in his baron-sanctioned powers to dispense justice and death. At one time, she had believed that due to his Mag conditioning, Kane was psychologically conflicted and therefore couldn't be trusted.

But the woman wrestled with her own inner conflicts. Once, in a private, unguarded moment, DeFore had been driven by frustration to admit that she did not believe she was really a doctor, not by the predark definition of the term. She described her training as superficial, down and dirty. At best, she felt fulfilled the functions of what was once known as a general practitioner.

Although her attitude toward Kane had softened over the past couple of years, the earlier resentment now flashed in the dark eyes she turned toward him. A stocky, buxom woman in her midthirties, DeFore usually wore her ash-blond hair pulled back from her face, intricately braided at the back of her head. Its color contrasted starkly with the deep bronze of her skin and her brown eyes. She always looked good in the one-piece white jumpsuit most Cerberus redoubt personnel wore as duty uniforms.

"So Garsden didn't make it." Carr didn't ask a question; he made a statement.

Kane shook his head. "No. Was he a friend of yours?"

Carr shrugged. "I only met him here. He was an ex-Mag like me, so that made us more than friends, I guess."

Kane didn't respond, understanding that the bond between Magistrates could sometimes be closer than that shared by family members. For most Mags, fellow enforcers were brothers and shield mates.

A century before, the Magistrate Divisions were formed as a complex police machine that demanded instant obedience to its edicts and to which there was no possible protest. Over the past ninety-plus years, both the oligarchy of barons and the Mags that served them had taken on a fearful, almost legendary aspect. Kane and Grant had been part of that legend, cogs in a merciless machine.

All Magistrates followed a patrilineal tradition, assuming the duties and positions of their fathers before them. They did not have given names, each taking the surname of the father, as though the first Magistrate to bear the name were the same man as the last. The originators of the Magistrate Divisions had believed that family names engendered a sense of obligation to the duties of their ancestors' office, insuring that subsequent generations never lost touch with their hereditary roles as enforcers. Last names became badges of social distinction, almost titles.

As Magistrates, the course of their lives had been charted before their births. They were destined to live, fight and die, usually violently, as they fulfilled their oaths to impose order upon chaos. By a strict definition, Grant and Kane had betrayed their oaths, but as Lakesh was wont to say, "There's no sin in betraying a betrayer."

The bromide was easy enough to utter, but to live with the knowledge was another struggle entirely. When the two men first broke their lifetimes of conditioning, the inner agony was almost impossible to endure. The peeling away of their Mag identities, their Mag purpose, had been a gradual process. Now, nearly five years later, Kane's memories of his time as a Magistrate brought only an ache, a sense of remorse over wasted years.

But old Magistrate habits died very hard, particularly because of the rigorous discipline to which they had submitted themselves. Casting aside their identities as Mags and accepting new roles as rebels and exiles hadn't been easy for either Kane or Grant, and it was doubly difficult for the former enforcers who had been driven from their respective villes after the infrastructure of baronial authority collapsed.

Now the Mags who had joined Cerberus were learning the same painful lesson as Kane and Grant—coming to grips with the fact they had spent most of their adult lives supporting a system that was nothing more than old-fashioned fascism, prettied up with lipstick and rouge. It was institutionalized and standardized despotism, a foundation by which a far more terrifying tyranny could grow and spread over the entire world, without regard for borders.

"Casualties are part of the risk," Kane declared. "Garsden, Halloran and you were all briefed about what you'd be going up against if you joined Cerberus. The opposition is a little stiffer than Tartarus Pit jolt-walkers and outland Dregs."

Ville society was strictly class and caste-based, so the higher a citizen's standing, the higher he or she might live in one of the residential towers. At the bottom level of the villes was the servant class, who lived in abject squalor in consciously designed ghettos known as the Tartarus Pits, named after the abyss below Hell where Zeus confined the Titans. They swarmed with a heterogeneous population of serfs, cheap labor and black marketeers.

An abashed smile lifted the corners of Carr's mouth. "I'm not complaining, Commander."

"Don't call me that," Kane retorted automatically, his tone harsher than he intended. "Nor sir or 'my lord Kane,' either. I'm just an ex-Mag like you. You don't have a division commander's ass to kiss anymore."

Carr's eyes widened, then narrowed. He laid his head back on the pillow. "Sorry. Whatever you say…Kane."

DeFore jerked her head meaningfully toward the exit.

"Get him back on his feet as quick as you can, Doctor," Kane said gruffly, then left the infirmary.

As he entered the twenty-foot-wide main corridor, he smiled slightly at the way DeFore's eyes widened in surprise when he addressed her by her honorific. The woman wasn't accustomed to it, even though Reba DeFore was one of the few exiles who acted as a specialist.

The threescore people who currently lived in the Cerberus redoubt, regardless of their skills, acted primarily in the capacity of support personnel. They worked rotating shifts, eight hours a day, seven days a week. For the most part, their work was the routine maintenance and monitoring of the installation's environmental systems, the satellite data feed, the security network. However, everyone had been given at least a superficial understanding of all the redoubt's systems, so they could pinch-hit in times of emergency.

Constructed primarily of vanadium alloy, all design and construction specs had been aimed at making the Cerberus redoubt a self-sufficient community of at least a hundred people, although Lakesh preferred to think of the trilevel, thirty-acre facility as a sanctuary. The installation contained a frightfully well-equipped armory and two dozen self-contained apartments, a cafeteria, a decontamination center, an infirmary, a swimming pool and even detention cells on the bottom level.

The Cerberus redoubt had weathered the nuclear holocaust of 2001 and all the changes that followed. Its radiation shielding was still intact, and its nuclear generators still provided an almost eternal source of power.

The facility also had a limestone filtration system that continually recycled the complex's water supply.

Kane turned right into the armory, intending to cut across it to the adjacent workroom where he knew Lakesh and other tech-heads would be pawing over the crystal skull. The overhead fluorescent fixtures blazed, flooding the armory with a white, sterile light, causing him to squint.

He heard a sound from the rear of the big square room and walked toward it, wending his way among the crates and boxes that were stacked nearly to the ceiling. Many of the crates were stenciled with the legend Property U.S. Army.

Glass-fronted gun cases lined the four walls, containing automatic assault rifles, many makes and models of subguns and dozens of semiautomatic blasters. Heavy-assault weaponry occupied the north wall—bazookas, tripod-mounted M-49 machine guns, mortars, tripod-mounted 20 mm cannons and rocket launchers.

On the day of his arrival at the redoubt, Lakesh informed him that all of the ordnance was of predark manufacture. Caches of matériel had been laid down in hermetically sealed Continuity of Government installations before the nukecaust. Protected from the ravages of the outraged environment, nearly every piece of munitions and hardware was as pristine as the day it rolled off the assembly line.

Lakesh himself assembled the arsenal over several decades, envisioning it as the major supply depot for a rebel army. The army never materialized—at least, not in the fashion Lakesh hoped it would. Therefore, Cerberus was blessed with a surplus of death-dealing equipment that would turn the most militaristic overlord green with envy.

. To his disquiet, Kane saw Decard standing before two suits of Magistrate body armor mounted on metal frameworks, gazing at them with something akin to reverence in his hazel eyes. The black exoskeletons stood there like silent, grim sentinels. The armor was close fitting, molded to conform to the biceps, triceps, pectorals and abdomen. The only spot of color anywhere on it was the small, diskshaped badge of office emblazoned on the left pectoral.

It depicted, in crimson, a stylized, balanced scales of justice, superimposed over a nine-spoked wheel. It symbolized the Magistrate's oath to keep the wheels of justice in the nine villes turning.

Like the armor, the helmets were made of black polycarbonate and fitted over the upper half and back of the head, leaving only portions of the mouth and chin exposed.

The slightly convex, red-tinted visor served several functions—it protected the eyes from foreign particles and the electrochemical polymer was connected to a passive night sight that intensified ambient light to permit one-color night vision.

Kane cleared his throat, and Decard turned quickly and a little guiltily. He had stripped out of his desert camo BDUs and was attired in the same clothes he had worn upon arriving at Cerberus ten days before—khaki pants, sandals and an olive drab T-shirt.

Kane and Grant had met Decard nearly two years before during an op to the Egyptian-inspired city of Aten hidden within a canyon in the Guadalupe desert. He too was a former Magistrate, but unlike Kane and Grant, he had not chosen to make war on his former masters unless they came looking for him. Barely twenty years old, he had accepted the responsibilities of a wife, an adopted child and an important position in the government of Aten.

"What's happening here, Decard?" Kane asked.

The young man deliberately didn't look at him when he murmured, "I'm going home, sir."

Kane refrained from correcting him. "Not just for a visit, I take it?"

Decard shook his head, dry-scrubbing his short, sandy-blond hair with his fingers. "I've got a wife, a baby on the way and an obligation to the queen."

Kane smiled gently. "And you're thinking you can't fulfill those responsibilities if one of the Nephilim shoot you dead."

Decard sighed. "That's about the size of it. I mean, it could have just as easily been me as Halloran or Garsden. You can call me pussy-hearted if you want but—"

"I don't and won't," Kane broke in. "You've got nothing to prove to me or anyone else. You signed on as a personal favor to me to help with the training of the new recruits. You've done more than your share and you don't have to justify yourself."

Decard smiled gratefully. "Thanks. I know you'll have your hands full, so you can call on me in case of an emergency."

He stepped forward, extending his right hand. "As always, it's been an honor, sir."

Kane clasped his hand and said impatiently, "How many times do have I tell you not to call me sir? It's bad enough that some of the old warhorse Mags are calling me commander."

"That's because you are," Decard retorted firmly. "Whether you like it or not, that's what you are and if you don't accept it, you'll be making a mistake."

Kane's eyebrows drew down to the bridge of his nose. "How so?"

He tried to disengage his grip, but Decard refused to relinquish his hand. "In the situation you have here," the young man stated, "it's a priority for you to inspire confidence. Now that you've recruited a group of ex-Mags, they need and expect the same kind of discipline and chain of command they were used to in the divisions."

"Cerberus isn't the damn Magistrate Division," Kane snapped, reflexively tightening his grasp on Decard's hand.

Decard winced and shot back, "These men don't enjoy independence the way you and Grant and I do. They have to be taught. Being free confuses them, and a confused Mag—"

"Makes for an untrustworthy Mag," Kane finished the old bromide for him, relaxing his grip. "I'll take that under advisement."

Decard smiled ruefully when Kane released his hand. "I think you should do more than that, unless you want to be putting down minirevolts every few weeks, when they test you for top-dog position in the pack. It's an instinct with them, you know."

Kane did not respond, although he knew the youth spoke the truth. Most Magistrates were egotistical, testosterone-saturated thugs who aspired to nothing more than to act as tools in the hands of an authority figure, to be used to batter and terrorize.

He walked Decard to the corridor. As the young man strode toward the ops center and the gateway unit, he called back over his shoulder, "If you need me, just whistle."

"Will do. Take care of yourself."

Decard flashed him a wry grin. "You too—Commander."

Chapter 7

Rather than joining a group of scientists in a poorly ventilated and windowless work room to mutter over an artifact, Kane opted for a breath of fresh mountain air. He strode along the main corridor, the vanadium-alloy walls and floor gleaming softly. Great curving ribs of metal and massive girders supported the high rock roof.

The multiton vanadium security door was already folded aside, accordion fashion, and a cool breeze wafted in from the plateau, carrying with it a whiff of tobacco smoke. He passed the illustration of Cerberus on the wall beneath the door controls. Although the official designations of all Totality Concept-related redoubts were based on the phonetic alphabet, almost no one who had ever been stationed in the facility referred to it by its official code name of Redoubt Bravo. According to Lakesh, the mixture of predark civilian scientists and military personnel simply called it Cerberus and the name stuck.

Kane stepped out onto the sprawling plateau. It was broad enough for the entire population of the redoubt to assemble without getting near the rusted remains of the chain-link fence ringing it. The flat expanse of tarmac was bordered on one side by a grassy slope rising to granite outcroppings and on the other by an abyss plunging straight down to the tumbling waters of the Clark Fork River nearly a thousand feet below.

Without much surprise, Kane saw Grant standing in the shade cast by the great gray peak overhead, smoking a cigar with a single-minded intensity. The bright midafternoon sun felt uncomfortably hot. Grant's face was wreathed by clouds of blue-gray smoke, and his eyes concealed by sunglasses, but Kane could easily guess his thoughts.

"You got another one of those?" he asked.

Without looking at him, Grant removed a thin cigar and a box of wooden stick matches from a flapped pocket of his camo pants. Setting the cigar alight with a match struck against the sec door, Kane slowly inhaled the smoke.

Casually, Kane commented, "Decard went back to Aten. He doesn't want to take the risks, not with Mavati expecting a child in a few months."

"Don't blame him," Grant replied, allowing the smoke to dribble out of his nostrils in fitful spurts. "We were damn lucky not to have lost more people than Garsden."

Grant could relate to Decard's choice, since he was torn between forging a new life with Shizuka on New Edo and his duty to his fellow exiles in Cerberus in their struggle to keep the overlords from reasserting their ancient claims on Earth.

But his heart was pledged to Shizuka, despite her responsibilities to the people of the island-kingdom of New Edo. They were still determined to spend a couple of days together a month, despite their respective duties that kept them apart most of the time. A couple of years ago, it had been Grant's intent to leave Cerberus altogether and live in the little island monarchy of New Edo with Shizuka, particularly after the arrival of the Manitius base personnel. He felt—or had hoped—the new recruits would alter the balance of the struggle against the barons.

But after being captured and tortured by the sadistic Baroness Beausoleil, Grant realized the struggle remained essentially the same—there were just new players on the field. The war itself would go on and would never end, unless he took an active hand in it, regardless of his love for Shizuka.

"Like I told Decard," Kane stated, "we took the probability of casualties into account…we didn't hide anything from any member of the team."

"I know…I just don't like leaving anyone behind."

"We didn't have much choice. I gave the order, so it's not your responsibility."

Grant shook his head in weary exasperation. "I'm not holding you responsible. I guess I just got used to putting a smaller number of personnel at risk over the past few years. The fewer people in the field, the fewer the casualties."

"And the larger the stakes," Kane interjected, "the

bigger the risks. With the way things have changed, there's no way the three of us—four, if you count Domi—could stay on top of overlord activity world-wide. The away teams aren't a perfect solution, but since they're the only options we've got, they're the best we've got."

As Magistrates, he and Grant had served together for a dozen years and as Cerberus warriors they had fought shoulder to shoulder in battles around half the planet, and even off the planet. Grant had been through all of it covering Kane's back, patching up his wounds and on more than one occasion, literally carrying him out of hellzones.

At one time, both men enjoyed the lure of danger, courting death to deal death. But now it was no longer enough for them to wish for a glorious death as a pay-off for all their struggles. They had finally accepted a fact they had known for years but never admitted to themselves—when death came, it was usually unex-pected and almost never glorious.

Kane puffed reflectively on the cigar for a silent mo-ment, then inquired, "She's still out there?"

Grant grunted, rolling the stub of his cigar from one corner of his mouth to the other. "With Beta Team on a drill. There's a couple of Mags among 'em and you know how Domi just *loves* Mags."

"Yeah, just like I know how Mags love taking orders from outlanders, too...women especially." Kane snorted. "Everybody is going to have to accept the fact we're on a new playing field with new rules. Domi included."

Grant scanned the far side of the plateau, where it de-bouched downward into a road. The two-lane blacktop leading down from Cerberus to the foothills was little more than a cracked and twisted asphalt ribbon, skirting yawning chasms and cliffs. Acres of the mountainsides had collapsed during the nuke-triggered earthquakes nearly two centuries ago. It was almost impossible for anyone to reach the plateau by foot or by vehicle, so it was easy for Lakesh to list the facility as irretrievably un-salvageable on all ville records.

When Lakesh had reactivated the installation some thirty-plus years before, the repairs he made had been minor, primarily cosmetic in nature. Over a period of time, he had added an elaborate system of heat-sensing warning devices, night-vision vid cameras and motion-trigger alarms to the plateau surrounding it. He had been forced to work in secret and completely alone, so the upgrades had taken several years to complete.

Following an attack on the redoubt staged by Over-lord Enlil, a network of motion and thermal sensors surrounded the Cerberus installation, expanding in a six-mile radius from the plateau.

Although a truce had been struck, a pact of noninter-ference agreed upon by Cerberus and the nine over-lords, no one—least of all Lakesh—trusted Enlil's word, and so the security network had been upgraded over the past year.

Planted within rocky clefts of the mountain peak and concealed by camouflage netting were the uplinks to the orbiting Vela-class reconnaissance satellite, and a Comsat. It could be safely assumed that no one or nothing could approach Cerberus undetected by land or by air—not that there was much reason to do so.

The few people who lived in the region held the Bitterroot Range, colloquially known as the Darks, in superstitious regard. Due to their mysteriously shadowed forests and deep, dangerous ravines, a sinister body of myths had grown up around the Darks. Enduring myths about evil spirits that lurked in the mountain passes to devour body and soul was a form of protective coloration that every exile in the redoubt went to great pains to maintain.

Grant suddenly cocked his head, as if he were listening for something more than the trilling of birds and the sigh of the wind through the fir trees. Faintly, the two men heard the steady tramp of running feet and a sharp, female voice chanting profane, rhyming doggerel: "Three, four, kick the whore, five, six, pick up your dicks, seven, eight, I'll make your ass ache!"

Up over the incline and onto the plateau jogged a group of six people wearing T-shirts and sweatpants. A small white wraith led them. Domi was small, barely five feet tall, and although petite enough to be childlike, she was exquisitely formed. Her flesh was the color of a beautiful pearl, and her ragged mop of close-cropped hair the hue of bone.

Eyes like polished rubies gleamed on either side of her thin-bridged nose. She wore a spandex sports bra and a pair of high-cut khaki shorts showed off her gamin-slim legs. Although she often went barefoot, this day she wore a thick-soled pair of laced boots and knee-high, bright red socks. Born a feral child of the Outlands, there was a primeval vibrancy, an animal-like intensity about her.

As Cerberus Away Team Beta jogged to the center of the plateau, Domi came to a halt, gesturing for the others to do the same. Kane and Grant could easily differentiate between the ex-Mags and the Manitius base émigrés—the pair of former Magistrates breathed hard and their faces shone with sweat, but they did not appear to be as winded as the three other people.

The two women and one man gasped and panted loudly, leaning forward to rest their hands on their knees, perspiration dripping from their flushed faces.

Domi acknowledged the presence of Grant and Kane with a fleeting smile, then turned to face her team, small hands on her hips. "Not bad," she announced in her high voice. "For toddlers. At least only one of you puked this time. How do you feel now, Mariah?"

Dr. Mariah Falk struggled to raise her head, summoning a feeble grin. Staring meaningfully at Grant, she stated hoarsely, "Like I'm getting too old for this shit."

Kane stifled a chuckle and cast a sidewise glance at Grant, who affected not to notice. In truth, he reflected, Mariah Falk might indeed be too old for the rigors of an away team. A former geologist from the Moon base, Mariah wasn't particularly young or particularly pretty, but she had an infectious smile and a relaxed, easy manner. Her short chestnut-brown hair was threaded with gray at the temples.

Deep creases curved out from either side of her nose to the corners of her mouth. Brown eyes bracketed by laugh lines looked out from beneath long brows that hadn't been plucked in years, if ever. Like the other lunar colonists, Mariah had been born in the twentieth century but spent almost all of the twenty-first and twenty-second centuries in a form of cryogenic stasis.

Edwards, the shaven-headed ex-Mag from Samariumville, snorted disdainfully. "I think you are, too. We don't need no dried-up old bitches slowin' up the rest of the squad."

Kane stiffened at the man's contemptuous tone, but his attitude was characteristic of most hard-contact Mags. However, Mariah Falk was well-liked and respected among the Cerberus staff, and he knew Domi wouldn't allow the insult to pass unchallenged.

The albino girl marched up to Edwards, nearly treading on his toes. She glared up at the much larger man, her face as immobile as if chiseled from marble. "I didn't quite catch that, Edwards," she snapped even though it was obvious she had.

Edwards glowered down at her with eyes of glacial blue. "Only talkin' to myself."

"Do it louder," Domi suggested, dropping her voice to almost a whisper. "I want to hear it."

Edwards exchanged a supercilious glance with Brady, his fellow expatriate Mag. "Never mind."

"Repeat it," Domi said coldly, enunciating every syllable like a gunshot.

Everyone watched the tableau of the small white-skinned girl and the big bald man. Edwards shrugged. "I don't think we need techs and old bitches on a hard-contact squad, is all. You can't count on them under fire."

Domi kept her disconcertingly crimson gaze fixed on the man's face. "What about outlander bitches? Can you count on them?"

Edwards folded his arms over his broad chest. "Not in my experience."

Domi nodded as if she had expected the response and took a step back. Then, moving in an eye-blurring explosion of speed, she dropped flat to the tarmac. Balancing herself on her right arm as if it were an axis, she spun in a circle, slamming a reverse-heel kick into the backs of the big man's knees. Bellowing a curse, arms windmilling, Edwards went down heavily.

Domi expertly turned her leg sweep into a shoulder roll and bounced to her feet. A taunting smile stretched her lips. "This should be a new experience for you, then."

Edwards pushed himself to a sitting position, examined a scraped elbow and bared his teeth in a silent snarl. He began to heave himself to his feet, then caught himself, as if suddenly becoming aware of the presence of Kane and Grant. He cast a surreptitious glance in their direction.

Grandly, Kane gestured with his cigar. "By all means, Edwards. All new experiences are learning experiences, as they used to tell us in the academy."

Edwards came to his feet in a bull-like rush, a growl humming in his thick throat. He crowded Domi, swinging his fists at her head in a one-two-three combination. The blows, had they connected, would have put Domi down, since the man outweighed her by a minimum of one hundred pounds. Just one of his bulging biceps was nearly as large as her entire head.

Domi's lightning-fast reflexes allowed her to dodge and duck and back pedal, the mocking smile on her face never faltering. She shifted position, leaned diagonally away from Edwards and delivered a roundhouse kick, planting the toe of her boot into the man's diaphragm just below his breastbone. Edwards jackknifed at the waist, wheezing, his features squeezing together like a fireplace bellows.

Reaching forward, Domi jammed two hooked fingers into Edwards's nostrils and gave his nose a hard, vicious twist. "Gotcher nose!"

Scarlet sprayed from the man's nostrils and he uttered a gargling, snuffling cry and stumbled backward, clapping one hand over his nose. Blood oozed between his fingers as he listed from side to side, still doubled up.

Domi watched the man's pain-racked contortions with satisfaction. Kane almost called a warning to her. As a former Magistrate, Edwards was not an opponent who could be so easily incapacitated.

Even as the notion registered, Edwards side-kicked
Domi in the midriff and all the air shot from her lungs
in an agonized whoof. She bent in the middle and staggered, nearly falling to her knees. With a snarl of blood-
thirsty gratification, Edwards whirled and swept her up
in a crushing embrace, hugging her from behind. His
fingers roved over her body, mixing pleasure with the
business of humiliation.

Grant made a move to intervene but subsided when
Kane said quietly, "She brought this on herself—let's
see if she can finish it."

Domi sagged in Edwards's arms, then flung her head
back, the rear of her skull smashing against his already
throbbing nose. The man howled as his head snapped
back, and his grip loosened, but not enough for Domi
to fight completely free.

However, she wriggled her right arm out of the pri-
son of the man's embrace, groping down and behind her,
at the junction of his thighs. By the time Edwards realized what she was doing, she had secured a grip on the
ex-Mag's testicles.

The man roared in maddened agony and released the
albino girl, but she did not relinquish her grip. Dropping
to her knees, Domi maintained her grasp, applying the
hold Kane had taught her, who in turn had learned it during training at the Magistrate Academy. The martial-arts
instructor called it Monkey Steals the Peach.

Edwards's scream climbed to a high-pitched shriek,
and only when his legs began to buckle did Domi open

her hand. Edwards fell onto his left side in a fetal position and clutched at his crotch, eyes squeezed shut.

Breathing hard, Domi climbed to her feet, kneading her bare belly over which a bruise was beginning to spread, a livid purple against the stark white of her complexion. She was unaware of Brady stepping up behind her, hand reaching out for the back of her neck.

The man froze in midmotion when Grant announced loudly but dispassionately, "Touch her and you're one dead son of a bitch."

Brady swung furious eyes in his direction and then lowered his arm, stepping back from the albino girl. Although Grant presented a dour, closed and private persona, even Brady knew that when he was provoked, his ruthlessness was unstoppable. The man had no doubt that if he disobeyed Grant, the big man would think nothing of pitching him headfirst off the plateau into the abyss.

Mariah Falk and the other members of Beta Team moved around Domi, breaking out into a smattering of spontaneous applause. Domi affected not to notice. She turned toward Brady. "Get Edwards on his feet."

The ex-Mag refused to make eye contact with her, turning away toward the sec door as if he intended to stomp inside the redoubt.

Kane casually stepped in front of it and said, "She gave you an order, Brady."

The man's shoulders slumped and he turned. "Yes, sir."

Kane opened his mouth to voice a profane correction, thought better of it and kept silent. He even refrained from commenting how Edwards had been exceptionally fortunate that Domi wasn't armed with her signature weapon—a combat knife with a nine-inch-long serrated blade.

The knife was the girl's only memento of the six months of sexual servitude she had been forced to endure at the hands of Guana Teague. The former Pit Boss of Cobaltville, Teague had found Domi in the Outlands and smuggled her into the Tartarus Pits with a forged ID chip.

In exchange, she gave him six months of service. When seven months passed without him releasing her from their agreement, she terminated the contract by cutting his throat—and saved Grant's life in the process.

At the sound of an apologetic, attention-getting cough behind them, Grant and Kane turned to see Nguyen, one of the Manitius personnel, leaning out of the entrance.

"Sirs?" the pudgy Asian woman ventured. "You're wanted in ops."

Grant arched an eyebrow. "By who?"

"By everybody." The woman sounded very regretful.

Kane took a final puff of his cigar and crushed it out against a vanadium door panel. Grant flipped his smoldering stub toward the rim of the precipice. To his surprise, Domi deftly snatched it out of the air and jammed it at a jaunty angle between her teeth.

"We'll carry on," she declared. "Drill ain't over yet."

When the squad groaned in dismay, Domi only grinned.

Chapter 8

As Grant and Kane strode down the corridor, they noticed the heads of men and women turning toward them, the glances respectful and even embarrassingly admiring. Kane, Brigid, Grant and Domi were considered something special among the personnel for various reasons, the least of which was quite literally saving the world from destruction.

Although Cerberus had been constructed to provide a comfortable home for well over a hundred people, it had been virtually deserted for nearly two centuries. For a long time, shadowed corridors, empty rooms and sepulchral silences outnumbered the Cerberus personnel.

Over the past couple of years, the corridors had bustled with life, the empty rooms filled and the silences replaced by conversation and laughter. The immigrants from the Manitius Moon base had arrived on a fairly regular basis ever since the destination-lock code to the Luna gateway unit had been discovered. Only a handful of the émigrés expressed a desire to make separate lives for themselves in the Outlands.

With the fall of the baronies and the constant threat

of the overlords, most of the immigrants had shown a disinclination to wander too far from the Cerberus redoubt. As the installation became more crowded, Kane felt less content to stay there for any length of time. The pull of adventure, of exploring the remote places, grew stronger with every passing day.

Despite the sense of danger, he also experienced a profound sense of peace while in the wild regions. Regardless of his growing sense of claustrophobia, he still considered the Cerberus facility his home.

The corridor ended at a T junction. The two men walked through an open door into the central command center, the brains of the redoubt. Two aisles of computer stations divided the long, high-ceilinged room. The operations complex had five dedicated and eight shared subprocessors, all linked to the mainframe behind the far wall. Two centuries before, it had been one of the most advanced models ever built, carrying experimental, error-correcting microchips of such a tiny size that they even reacted to quantum fluctuations. Biochip technology had been employed, protein molecules sandwiched between microscopic glass-and-metal circuits.

A huge Mercator relief map of the world spanned the entire wall above the door. Pinpoints of light shone steadily in almost every country, connected by a thin glowing pattern of lines. They represented the Cerberus network, the locations of all functioning gateway units across the planet.

The overhead lights in the long, vault-walled room

automatically dimmed at sunset and came back on to full brightness at dawn. They were bright now, causing Kane to squint at the consoles that ran the length of the walls. Indicator lights flickered red, green and amber, circuits hummed, needles twitched and monitor screens displayed changing columns of numbers.

On the opposite side of the operations center, an anteroom held the eight-foot-tall mat-trans chamber, rising from an elevated platform. Slabs of brown-tinted armaglass enclosed the six-sided chamber. All of the official Cerberus gateway units in the mat-trans network were color-coded so authorized jumpers could tell at a glance into which redoubt they had materialized.

Despite the fact that it seemed an inefficient method of differentiating one installation from another, only personnel holding color-coded security clearances were allowed to make use of the system. Inasmuch as their use was restricted to a select few units, it was fairly easy for them to memorize which color designated what redoubt.

Armaglass was manufactured in the last decades of the twentieth century from a special compound that plasticized the properties of steel and glass. It was used as walls in the jump chambers to confine quantum energy overspills.

According to Lakesh, this particular unit was the first fully debugged matter-transfer inducer built after the prototypes. It served as the template for all the others that followed.

Only half a dozen people were present in the control center proper, and three of them stood around a computer station. Brigid Baptiste, Lakesh and Brewster Philboyd were clustered around Donald Bry, who sat hunched over the keyboard, manipulating a mouse. The monitor screen displayed a CGI bar graph. Emanating from the machine itself came a faint voice, so shot through with static it was nearly incomprehensible.

"It's still distorted as hell, Donald," Philboyd declared.

"Let me patch in another filter," Bry replied waspishly. A slightly built man of short stature, he thrust his copper-curled head very close to the screen. His expression was always one of consternation, no matter his true mood. "But I think I caught 'Redoubt Papa' this time around."

"What's going on, Baptiste?" Kane asked as he approached.

She cast a glance over her shoulder. "Donald picked up an anomalous signal on the voyeur channel."

Brigid employed Bry's own personal vernacular for the eavesdropping system he had developed through the communications linkup with the Keyhole Comsat. It was the same system and same satellite they used to track the telemetry from the subcutaneous biolink transponders implanted within Cerberus personnel.

Bry had worked on the system for a long time and finally established an undetectable method of patching into the wireless communications channels all of the baronies used. The success rate wasn't one hundred percent, but he had been able to listen in on a number of baron-sanctioned operations in the Outlands. He monitored different frequencies on a daily basis, but ever since the fall of the baronies, all of the villes had been in states of anarchy, with various factions seizing power, then being dispossessed by other factions. The radio transmissions were equally chaotic.

"So what?" Grant demanded. "I thought picking up anomalous signals was the whole point of the channel."

Lakesh leaned forward, scrutinizing the monitor screen and the jagged wave sliding back and forth across the CGI scale. "Very true, friend Grant. But this signal was directed specifically at us."

Startled, Kane echoed, "*At* us?"

Bry nodded, tapping a pair of keys on the board. "Here, I'll replay it again. It should be cleaner this time around."

Kane found himself leaning forward almost unconsciously as a flat, colorless male voice floated from the computer's speaker. The hash and buzz of static wasn't quite as thick, but it still hissed and popped over certain words.

"Calling Cerberus," the voice intoned. "Calling Cerberus. If you receive…transmission…must listen closely."

Kane strained to hear as the voice continued to drone: "Offer informa—in exchange for asylum. Rendezvous. Repeat, offer information for asylum. Rendezvous. Redoubt Papa eight-ten. Urgent…doubt Papa eight-ten.

Information *Tiamat* mem…buffer. Have info…memory buf…*Tiamat*."

The voice dissolved in a wash of static. Kane's nape hairs tingled in apprehension. He, Brigid and Grant exchanged wary, expectant glances.

Philboyd caught the looks that passed among the three people and asked, "Redoubt Papa means something to you?"

Kane nodded. "Kind of."

Lakesh tugged absently at his long nose. "Redoubt Papa was the only Totality Concept-linked installation in the vicinity of Washington, D.C."

"D.C.?" Philboyd echoed. "That's the place you call Washington Hole now, right?"

"Right," Grant said grimly. "Also known as the hellzone of hellzones."

Lakesh nodded. "But the redoubt itself was of extreme importance as an escape route for politicians and high-ranking members of the military and intelligence community."

"In other words," Bry said sourly, "it was built to protect a select few from the very war they started."

"Of course," Brigid put in dryly, "they were misconceived enough to believe the Totality Concept would somehow save everything."

"Idiots," Grant grunted dispassionately.

No one disagreed with his one-word assessment. The umbrella designation for American military supersecret researches into many different arcane and eldritch sciences, the Totality Concept delved into everything from Project Cerberus's method of hyperdimensional matter transfer, to the temporal dilation of Operation Chronos.

Most of the overprojects had their own hidden installations, like Overproject Excalibur's biogengineering facility in a subterranean complex in New Mexico or the Anthill in South Dakota, which was by far the most extensive Continuity of Government facility. Built inside Mount Rushmore using advanced digging and tunneling machines, the layout of the complex resembled a vast ant colony. All of Mount Rushmore was honeycombed with interconnected levels, passageways, stores, theaters and even a small sports arena.

Since the military and government personnel in charge had no choice but to remain in the facility, it took them awhile to realize they were just as much victims of the nuclear holocaust as those whom they referred to as the "useless eaters" of the world. Even now Lakesh couldn't help but smile over the grim irony. He well remembered how a fringe movement called survivalism had gained popularity, primarily among ex-military and rural people with various political axes to grind.

They trained and indoctrinated themselves so thoroughly to survive Armageddon, some of them actually began to look forward to it. They deluded themselves into believing a nukeholocaust world would be better than the one they lived in. They aspired to have a world where the romance of the frontier spirit would be revived, free of government regulations, laws and moral obligations, where a human being's worth would be measured only in how willing he or she was to kill a child for a crumb of food.

Most of the government people in the Anthill viewed survivalists as brain-damaged paranoids. But as the second anniversary of the nukecaust passed, it became patently obvious the men who knew in advance about the atomic megacull were just as stupendously ill-informed as the survivalists at whom they had once sneered.

Like their less educated counterparts, they had no real grasp of the scope of the global devastation. None of their painstaking calculations regarding acceptable losses, destruction ratios and the length of the nuclear winter bore any resemblance to the terrifying reality.

After the implementation of the Program of Unification and the baronial system, the Anthill became not so much a forgotten installation as a feared installation. The oligarchy of the barons viewed it as both a threat and an untapped treasure trove. But inasmuch as all the villes were standardized, equally matched in terms of technology and firepower to maintain a perfect balance of power, none of the barons dared mention what unclaimed wonders lay within Mount Rushmore.

Even a word of wonder about it might be construed as evidence of ambition, a prelude to a territorial war. Because such ambitions were strictly forbidden by the tenets of the Archon Directorate, the Anthill became a taboo subject, a no-baron's land.

"What's with the numbers?" Kane inquired. "Eight-ten?"

"Month and day," Brigid answered curtly. "Tomorrow's date, in fact. Someone wants us to go to Redoubt Papa tomorrow."

Bry swiveled his chair, blinking his eyes in confusion. "Who and why?"

Brigid shrugged. "I won't even hazard a guess as to the who, even though I have a suspicion. But the why is fairly easy to postulate—someone wants to trade information about a memory buffer from *Tiamat* for asylum here."

"Another crystal skull, you figure?" Grant asked, voice heavy with skepticism.

"Probably," Brigid answered.

Lakesh snorted. "A nice bit of bait to dangle."

"You think it's a trap?" Philboyd inquired.

Lakesh gestured to the computer screen. "Of course it's a trap. Whoever transmitted the message hopes we'll bring the crystal skull to a rendezvous at Washington Hole tomorrow. It's no great mystery about who is orchestrating the trap. Nergal is behind this."

Philboyd frowned at him. "How did you come to that conclusion?"

Lakesh met the astrophysicist's frown with a scowl of his own. "Washington Hole fell under the jurisdiction of Baron Sharpe, who was actually the chrysalis form of Overlord Nergal who, you might remember, was in Pakistan just yesterday laying waste to the city of Harappa to recover a crystal skull."

Bristling at Lakesh's patronizing tone, Philboyd argued, "Even so, Nergal isn't stupid enough to think an anonymous radio signal transmitted over the old baronial operations frequency would entice anybody from Cerberus to bring the skull to the redoubt there."

Before Lakesh could respond, Grant said flatly, "No, Nergal isn't that stupid. And even though he's an Annunaki overlord, I don't think he believes any of us are that stupid, either."

"Not to mention," Bry interposed, "that it's highly unlikely Nergal is even aware we're able to eavesdrop on the frequency."

Kane glanced over his shoulder at the Mercator projection map. No lights blinked anywhere in any of the represented countries. "It doesn't look like the mat-trans network is being used."

"Not lately, no," Bry agreed. "There's been no registered activation signature of the unit in Redoubt Papa."

Lakesh narrowed his eyes at the man's matter-of-fact statement. "Are you certain?"

"I can review the log, but I don't think I'll find anything. In fact, I don't think anybody has gated there in the last couple of years."

Kane wasn't surprised. He repressed a shudder at the memory of his first visit to Redoubt Papa several years before. It had been as grimly depressing a place as he ever imagined, haunted by the ghosts of a hopeless, despairing past age. Even the walls seemed to exude the terror, the utter despondency, of souls trapped there when the first mushroom cloud erupted from Washington on that chill January noon.

"We can always ignore the message," Grant suggested.

"That might be tactically unwise," Brigid declared. "It just doesn't track that Nergal is trying to lure us to the vicinity of Washington Hole on the off chance he'll get the drop on us."

"So what do you think it's all about?" Philboyd demanded.

Brigid sighed and shook her head. "There's no way to be sure, unless we go there. Whoever transmitted the signal provided just enough information to make us curious, to whet our appetites. I'm sure that strategy was deliberate."

"Which may indicate a familiarity with us," Lakesh commented uneasily.

Comprehension suddenly glinted in Kane's eyes. "Maybe whoever wants us to meet them there has inside knowledge about overlord activities."

"That's what I'm thinking," Brigid ventured. "A long shot, I know."

"Which is par for our damn course," Grant rumbled.

"So it's agreed?" Kane asked. "Tomorrow we gate to Redoubt Papa?"

Philboyd and Lakesh stared at him in confusion, then alarm. "I didn't hear anyone agree to that!" the lanky astrophysicist exclaimed.

"Indeed not," Lakesh concurred vehemently.

Brigid folded her arms over her breasts. "It's patently

obvious someone with a working knowledge of *Tiamat* and her operating systems wants to meet with a Cerberus representative to ask for asylum."

"A long shot, like you said," Lakesh pointed out. "It's most likely a snare."

With a feigned weariness, Brigid said, "If this is a trap, then it's a very poorly conceived one, since the person in question is gambling that we even heard the message, much less will abide by their request."

Although Grant's brows knitted at the bridge of his nose, he said, "Pretty desperate ploy. A trap wouldn't be this dependent on chance."

After a thoughtful moment, Lakesh said reluctantly, "I see your point. Our own operations have been hampered by a distinct lack of hard intel about overlord activities. It's been based primarily on guesswork and extrapolation."

"That's why I think we should make the rendezvous," Kane said. "Any chance to hook up with an insider shouldn't be ignored because of a little risk."

Lakesh smiled bleakly. "In this instance, I fear there's more than a 'little' risk."

Grant lifted the wide yoke of his shoulders in a shrug. "I was about to ask when have we ever let that stop us, but I figured after all this time, everybody here knows the answer."

Kane nodded once in understanding. "Of course we do."

Chapter 9

Kane stepped away from the sheltering rock overhang and glanced at the shaft of late-morning sunlight slanting down from a partially overcast sky. The sere and sterile plain was interrupted only with outcroppings of dark, flinty rock. The only deviation was southward, where he could barely make out a vague black line rising slightly above the horizon, a mere hint of the rim of the vast crater that had replaced Washington, D.C., over two centuries earlier.

The acidic air irritated his sinus membranes and coated his tongue with a foul, sulphurous tang, making him want to spit. Washington Hole hadn't changed much since his last visit, nor had he expected it to.

Only a vast sea of fused black glass occupied the tract of land that once held the seat of American government. Seen from a distance, the crater lent the region the name by which it had been known for nearly two centuries. Washington Hole, the premier hellzone of the country, was still jolted by ground tremors and soaked by the intermittent flooding of Potomac Lake.

A volcano, scarcely an infant in geological terms, had

burst up from the rad-blasted ground. The peak dribbled a constant stream of foul-smelling smoke, mixing with the chem-tainted rain clouds to form a layer of stinking sulfur and cloying chlorine.

The shantytowns, which once ringed the outskirts of Washington Hole, had been razed nearly a century ago, during the first year of the Program of Unification. Most of their inhabitants had succumbed to rad sickness many years before. Although the former District of Columbia had once fallen under the jurisdiction of Sharpeville, the barony itself was located many miles away, in the former state of Delaware.

Rubbing his nose, Kane turned around to face Brigid and Grant, who sat on rocks on either side of the open sec door, a massive slab of metal recessed beneath a shelf of granite. "How long has it been, Baptiste?" he demanded.

Brigid sighed wearily and looked up from the open book in her lap. "Twenty minutes since the last time you asked. We've been here for five hours and forty-one minutes."

Grant carefully placed the big Barrett sniper rifle, snugged inside its felt-lined leather case, on the ground beside him. Stiffly, he pushed himself to his feet and stretched, hands pressed against his lower back. "After we've been here for five hours and forty-*five* minutes, let's gate back home, how about."

Brigid smiled wanly. "It's so peaceful and quiet out here, don't tell me you're bored."

"Why the hell would I be bored?" Grant shot back. "Sitting out here on a big comfy rock in such a lovely climate?"

Kane's chuckle turned into a growl of annoyance when the collar of his shadow suit chafed the underside of his jaw. Tugging at it, he announced, "You may find this place relaxing, Baptiste, but I've had my limit."

All three people wore high-necked, midnight-colored coveralls that absorbed light the way a sponge absorbed water. Although the material of the formfitting garments resembled black doeskin, and didn't appear as if it would offer protection from fleabites, the suits were impervious to most wavelengths of radiation.

Upon finding the one-piece garments in the Operation Chronos facility on Thunder Isle, Kane had christened them shadow suits. Later they learned that a manufacturing technique known in predark days as electrospin lacing had electrically charged polymer particles to form a single crystal metallic microfiber with a dense molecular structure.

Kane maintained the shadow suits were superior to the polycarbonate Magistrate armor, if for nothing else but the internal subsystems. Also, they were almost impossible to tear or pierce with a knife, but a heavy-caliber bullet could penetrate them and, unlike the Mag body armor, they wouldn't redistribute the kinetic shock.

Flat, square ammo pouches were attached to the small of their backs by Velcro tabs. Long combat knives, the razor-keen blades forged of dark blued steel, hung from scabbards at their hips.

Grant and Kane wore their Mag-issue Sin Eaters secured in bulky power holsters strapped to their right forearms. The Sin Eaters were big-bored automatic handblasters, less than fourteen inches in length at full extension, the magazines carrying twenty 9 mm rounds. When not in use, the stock folded over the top of the blaster, lying perpendicular to the frame, reducing its holstered length to ten inches.

When the weapons were needed, Grant and Kane tensed their wrist tendons and sensitive actuators activated flexible cables within the holsters and snapped the pistols smoothly into their waiting hands, the butts unfolding in the same motion. Since the Sin Eaters had no trigger guards or safeties, the blasters fired immediately upon touching their crooked index fingers.

Stepping over to their pile of gear, Kane opened an equipment case and removed a bottle of distilled water. "Nobody's coming to meet us. This has been a waste of time."

Uncapping the bottle, he took a long swallow, then washed his mouth out, turning to spit over the rim of the ledge. Grimacing, he muttered, "I can still taste this place."

Grant snorted. "And I can smell it, believe it or not."

Kane and Brigid reacted to the big man's remark with appreciative smiles. Grant's nose had been broken three times in the past and always poorly reset. Unless an odor was extraordinarily pleasant or virulently repulsive, his sense of smell was so impaired that he couldn't detect subtle aromas unless they were right under his nostrils. A running joke during his Mag days had been that Grant could eat a hearty dinner with a dead skunk lying next to his plate.

Kane's Commtact buzzed and the voice of Wolverton, one of the two members of CAT Alpha who had gated in with him, Grant and Brigid, said, "Wolverton here—just making my quarterly check-in, Commander."

Kane made a conscious effort not to correct him. "Status?"

"Same as it's been every quarter hour I've reported since we gated in here, sir." Wolverton sounded bored and a little irritable. Kane didn't blame him. "I think Cohen has gone into a coma."

The five Cerberus personnel materialized in Redoubt Papa's gateway chamber a few minutes shy of dawn. Wolverton and his companion, Cohen, stayed behind to guard the unit just in case their mysterious contact entered the installation by that route, although Brigid didn't find that likely. The destination-lock codes for the Cerberus network units in specific redoubts were not widely known, even though some of that data had been circulating via various back channels for the past couple of years.

"Nothing to report here either," Kane said. "Stand by, Wolverton. And wake up Cohen. We'll be moving out in a couple of minutes."

"Yes, sir. Thank you, sir."

Stepping to the lip of the ledge, Kane surveyed the

heap of stone rising around him and his two partners. Evidently the massive slabs and chunks of rock had once been the upper floors of a multilevel complex. Even being located some thirty miles away from ground zero had not spared the exterior of the place from taking severe damage.

Sheared-away reinforcing rods jutted like gnarled, skeletal fingers. Two centuries of hell-weather had scoured the rock mercilessly, rounding the jagged edges, smoothing the corners, filling in cracks with grit. Scraggly thorn brush hung by tenacious roots over the rockfall.

He glanced into the sky again. Thick, fleecy clouds always overlay Washington Hole, casting it into a form of perpetual twilight. For a time, following the nuclear Armageddon of two centuries earlier, the entire Earth lay beneath a canopy of clouds.

Massive quantities of pulverized rubble had been propelled into the atmosphere, clogging the sky for a generation, blanketing all of Earth in a thick umbrella of radioactive dust, ash, debris, smoke and fallout.

The exchange of atomic missiles did more than slaughter most of Earth's inhabitants. It distorted the ecosystems that were not completely obliterated and resculpted the face of the planet into a perverted parody of what it had been.

Suddenly filled with angry revulsion, Kane whirled away from the ledge, gesturing to their gear and then to the open sec door. "Let's wrap it up and gate the hell out of here. Nobody is coming. This has all been a major waste of time."

He started picking up their equipment, then froze, his ears catching a new sound borne on the breeze. The faint drone resolved itself into a rhythmic, steady swish, distantly underscored by a familiar crack-sizzle. Heart pounding, Kane pivoted, scanning the sky with narrowed eyes. He shivered as a jolt of adrenaline shot through his system.

A tiny fleck of jet-black outlined against the vast tapestry of gray appeared in the sky. Brigid and Grant joined him at the rim of the ledge. Brigid raised a pair of compact binoculars to her eyes. The two ex-Magistrates did not need binoculars to identify the waspish configuration of a Deathbird swooping in on a direct course with the redoubt.

They were surprised to see the black chopper, although they knew they shouldn't have been. The Deathbirds were the only form of air transportation to make a return after the nukecaust, and they were the sole property of the Magistrate Divisions of the various baronies. Painted a matte, nonreflective black, the choppers' sleek, streamlined contours were interrupted only by the two ventral stub wings. Each wing carried a pod of missiles. The multiple barrels of the chin-mounted Chain gun in its swivel turret winked dully in the diffused sunlight.

Kane and Grant exchanged a quick, grim glance as the chopper drew closer. Even though the two men were intimately familiar with them, neither one could deny the Deathbird attack helicopters were frighteningly efficient pieces of machinery. Modified AH-64 Apache attack gunships, most of the Deathbirds in the Magistrate Division fleets had been reengineered and retrofitted dozens of times.

Thirty feet long, fifteen feet high, the maximum speed of the insectlike choppers was 185 mph. At the hands of an experienced pilot, they could maneuver like hummingbirds, up, down, sideways, backward, all very swiftly and fairly quietly.

As the Deathbird arrowed in a straight course at a steadily decreasing altitude, Kane glimpsed a brief flash of distant silver. It was high and moving as fast as the chopper, coming in behind and above it. The shape grew larger until he caught a reflective glint of a shimmering, domed surface.

Grant snarled, "An Annunaki disk! It *is* a trap!"

Even as he snapped out the words, threads of white light lanced downward from ship. The three people heard the characteristic crack-sizzle of a plasma fusillade and then the boom of an explosion.

Fire-laced smoke erupted from the Deathbird's tail assembly. The chopper lurched, then slid sideways at a swiftly decreasing angle. The vanes continued to fan the air sluggishly, which turned its plummet into a somewhat controlled vertical landing.

The Deathbird dropped violently on its belly within a few yards of an outcropping. The landing gear collapsed and its nose tipped up. The blades chopped into the rocky ground with semimusical chimes, bending backward at forty-five-degree angles and digging up bucketfuls of dirt and pebbles.

As Brigid, Grant and Kane watched in wide-eyed silence, the port-side cockpit hatch flew open and a small body plunged out through the billows of smoke, falling to all fours only a few feet away.

The body appeared to have been dyed jet-black from the neck down but after a half-second of staring, the three Cerberus exiles realized the figure wore the same kind of formfitting bodysuit as they did.

Brigid Baptiste, still gazing through the ruby-coated lenses of the binoculars, managed to break the spell of shock that paralyzed all of their vocal cords. She blurted, *"Sindri!"*

Chapter 10

Brigid and Kane bounded down the face of the rockfall, jumping from concrete slab to basalt boulder. The footing wasn't treacherous, but it wasn't particularly trustworthy, either. Twice, stones turned beneath Kane's feet and he nearly pitched headlong to the barren ground below. Trying to keep his eyes on his feet, the smoke-belching chopper and the sky-disk all at the same time did not make for a swift or easy descent.

The Deathbird, its tail assembly canted up, continued to burn, the boiling smoke completely obscuring the black-clad figure Brigid had identified as Sindri. Kane didn't doubt her, but at the moment he wasn't overly concerned about who it was, either.

The silver disk hovered a hundred feet above the wreck, the smoke rising from below curling up in tendrils around its rim. Despite its configuration, Kane was irresistibly reminded of a vulture trying to determine whether its potential prey still had some life in it.

Brigid leaped lithely from a cluster of reinforcing rods, landed on the balls of her feet and sprinted toward the Deathbird, her TP-9 autopistol gripped in her right fist. Kane followed a few seconds later, pausing only long enough to cast an over-the-shoulder glance up at the ledge. Although he couldn't see him, he knew Grant had the stock of the heavy Barrett rifle jammed firmly in the hollow of his right shoulder with his finger resting on the trigger guard, gazing steadily through the twenty-power telescopic sight.

Chambered to take .50-caliber ammo, the weapon possessed massive recoil, which only made sense, since it had been introduced two centuries before to take out armored targets and blast holes through concrete walls. Still and all, both men realized the rounds would inflict little damage on the smart-metal-alloy hull of the sky disk.

"You set?" Kane asked as he ran after Brigid, his Sin Eater in hand.

"The ship's in my sights," Grant responded over the Commtact.

Kane caught up with Brigid, and together they dashed across the hundred yards behind the base of the rubble and the site of the chopper crash. Their feet kicked up little puffs of dust from the arid, powdery soil.

When they came within a dozen yards of the downed Deathbird, the throat-abrading, eye-stinging clouds of smoke forced them to halt. Crouching, they warily approached, all too aware of what would happen when the fire ignited the various incendiaries and explosives contained within the machine's stub wings.

Drawing a breath, struggling not to succumb to a coughing fit, Kane shouted, "Sindri!"

Heard faintly over the crackle of the flames, a male voice replied urgently, "Here, over here! Hurry!"

Brigid and Kane exchanged quick, frowning glances. The voice did not sound like Sindri's, but they crept in the direction from which it had come. The spreading umbrella of smoke blotted out the feeble sunlight, and they could barely see more than a couple of feet ahead of them.

"Here," the voice called again.

The pair of Cerberus warriors moved toward the granite outcropping rising from the ground.

"The disk is coming down, about fifty yards left of your position," Grant suddenly announced,

"Acknowledged," Brigid responded in a whisper.

She and Kane eased around the outcropping, their backs against the stone. They abruptly halted, blinking their watering eyes, both surprised into silence. Two men huddled together at the base of the rock, together a study in sharp contrasts.

A shaved-headed middle-aged man lay on his belly in the dirt. He coughed into his fist, allowing them glimpses of the thick calluses covering his elbows. His bare, pale legs trailed behind him, like a pair of boneless tentacles. He wore a leather, chrome-studded harness and velvet loincloth. The harness displayed his exceptionally well developed upper body. His torso looked to be all knotted muscle from the neck down to his hips.

Whereas the harness showed off his bulging biceps

and dinner-plate-sized pectorals, the loincloth did nothing to disguise his shriveled, atrophied legs. They stretched out behind him like flaccid, flesh-colored stockings half-filled with mud. Even in the dim light Brigid and Kane could make out the red scars bisecting the back of his knees.

"Crawler," Kane snapped.

"What?" came Grant's puzzled inquiry. "I thought Brigid saw Sindri."

"I did," Brigid said, sinking down to her knees beside the two men. "Crawler is here, too. We couldn't see him because of smoke."

Sindri's eyelids fluttered and he forced a grin to his face. "Miss Brigid, Mr. Kane," he said in a strained, hoarse voice, "For a time there, I doubted we would ever see each other again."

Except for the blood streaming from a laceration at his hairline, Sindri looked exactly as he had the last time Brigid and Kane had seen him, nearly three years before. He was extraordinarily small, a few inches over three feet tall, but his proportions were extraordinarily perfect. There was much about Sindri that was perfect. If he had been three feet taller, a hundred or more pounds heavier, he would have been one of the most beautiful men ever born.

His thick, dark blond hair was swept back from a high forehead, tied in a foxtail at his nape. Under level brows, big eyes of the clearest, cleanest blue, like the high sky on a cloudless summer's day, regarded them sharply.

Beneath his finely chiseled nose, a wide, beautifully shaped mouth slowly stretched in an engaging grin, displaying white, even teeth.

"Help us," Crawler said, but it was less a plea than a demand.

"Why should we?" Kane demanded.

"I sent the message," Crawler replied.

"Terrific," Kane said coldly. "And why should we care again?"

Wiping at the scarlet streaming down the side of his face, Sindri sat up and groped inside a crack at the base of the outcropping. He dragged out a bulging backpack. "We have something that several parties are interested in. We thought we'd offer you the chance of first refusal."

"We'll discuss business later," Brigid stated curtly. "Can you travel?"

Setting his teeth on a groan, Sindri pushed himself to his feet, fingering the laceration on his scalp. "Do I have a choice?"

"Not unless you prefer to stay here and die."

Sindri picked up the backpack and slid his arms through the straps. "The Nephilim are less interested in killing us than recovering this item."

Grant announced, "The disk is opening. I suggest you start moving."

"Let's go," Brigid said, pointing toward the rockfall. "Double-time it."

Sindri squinted through the veils of smoke in the direction her finger indicated. "That's an awful lot of open and exposed ground."

"Grant will give us covering fire if we need it," Kane commented. "Unless he decides it's in our best interests to shoot your slagging ass dead."

Sindri glared up at him, eyes blazing with a malevolence that was quickly veiled as if a curtain had been dropped over them. "That's not very funny, Mr. Kane."

"That's because I wasn't trying to be. Now move, both of you."

Kane kicked himself into a sprint, bursting out of the shifting planes of smoke. The air tasted only a bit cleaner, but his vision was no longer blurred. He glanced toward the grounded disk. A section of the hull split wide in a triangular shape, as if it were cloth slit open by an invisible blade from within.

A ramp extended outward, the smart metal of the ship forming a long walkway, as if the ship itself were sticking out its tongue.

From within the ship emerged a contingent of burgundy-armored Nephilim, jogging down the ramp, holding their right arms straight out from the shoulder. Red energy pulsed in the gullets of the stylized adder heads of the ASP emitters.

"Nephilim of Nergal," Grant drawled sardonically over the Commtact. "No big surprise there."

Kane didn't expend any breath on a reply. The armored soldier in the lead swung his arm directly toward him. Triple streams of eyeball-searing yellow light spit from the serpent mouths, joining together to form a coruscating globule of plasma that jetted forth like a fireball launched from a catapult. He dodged to one side and the bolt punched a hole in the ground less than a yard from his right foot.

A sound like a sledge striking an anvil was followed an instant later by the hard, flat crack of the Barrett. Punched in the breastplate by the .50-caliber, depleted-uranium-core round, the Nephilim flew backward nearly half the length of the ramp. His arms and legs flailed like those of a disjointed puppet's, and blood foamed from his mouth in a crimson fountain.

He struck the metal with a gonging chime, his armored body twisting and writhing, legs kicking feebly. Two of the soldiers went down with him in an awkward sprawl of metal-shod limbs.

"One down," Grant said calmly.

Kane, Brigid and Sindri ran as fast as they could, their feet churning up the dry soil. Crawler wriggled along behind them, propelling himself forward by his elbows with a speed that came of long practice. If nothing else, because of his almost prone posture, he presented the most difficult target.

The ASP bolts of the Nephilim stabbed at the four people like lightning flashes, bursting around and ahead of them in searing sparks. Kane heard Sindri gasping, wheezing and cursing as he tried to keep up. A sudden concussion thumped heavily against their ears, the air shivering with a shock wave.

Kane hazarded one quick backward glance just as a roiling, expanding fireball engulfed the downed Deathbird. A tidal wave of orange-yellow flame and concussive force poured out, bowling over half the Nephilim like stalks of wheat blasted by hurricane-force winds.

When the four people reached the foot of the rock tumble, they took a moment to catch their breaths and look behind them. The chopper was gone, just bits and pieces of smoking debris scattered over the ground. A puddle of oil burned, the fire whipped by the wind.

Four Nephilim trudged onward, oblivious to the flames, the smoke and the deaths of their fellow soldiers. Their ASP emitters sparked at the ends of their extended arms.

Kane, Brigid, Sindri and Crawler clambered up the rock face as the energy bolts blew fist-sized craters in the stone all around them. Crawler dragged himself very efficiently along and over the most jagged of stones without injury. Brigid lagged behind to help Sindri along, weighted down as he was by the backpack and half-blinded by the blood flowing from his head wound.

When they reached the ledge, all of them panted from exertion, faces sheened with sweat. Grant rose, snatching up the Barrett's carrying case and sliding the rifle into it. "Cutting it close," he rumbled. His gazed dropped to Sindri. "Long time, pissant."

Sindri showed the edges of his teeth in either a defiant grin or a grimace of pain. In between gasps, he retorted, "I can't say the absence of your company has made my heart grow fonder, Mr. Grant."

"What a coincidence," Kane husked out, stepping toward the open sec door. "I feel the same way about you…pissant."

Moving quickly and methodically, Brigid took a square pressure bandage from the medical kit and handed it to Sindri. "Just hold it there for the time being," she instructed him.

The five people entered the redoubt, and Grant pulled down on the locking lever on the wall beside the door. The multiton portal dropped with a crunching thud. "I don't think the Nephilim can shoot their way in, but let's get to the gateway fast."

They trotted swiftly down the corridor, noting the cracks and splits riven deep into the concrete walls and ceiling. Most of the overhead neon light strips were completely dark.

Over the Commtact, Kane raised Wolverton. "You and Cohen prep the jump chamber. We'll be leaving in a hurry."

Wolverton responded with a crisp "Yes, sir!"

Jogging beside him, Brigid asked, "You don't think the Nephilim know how to get the door open, do you?"

Sounding half-strangled, Sindri gasped out, "If Nergal gave them the entry code, sure they can. They're not completely mindless. Only the higher cognitive functions of their brains are impaired."

"How do you know that?" Grant demanded.

Sindri gestured behind him at Crawler slithering along the floor. "We've been living among them for two years."

"Apparently you didn't make many friends," Kane observed snidely.

"I might surprise you, Mr. Kane," Sindri countered, tone silky and slightly mocking.

Brigid swung her head toward him, green eyes widening in surprise. She opened her mouth to demand clarification, but Kane murmured, "Later, Baptiste."

They reached the first of four stairwells slanting sharply into the subterranean command center of Redoubt Papa. The four people went down them swiftly and surefootedly. Sindri clung to the banister as if he were ninety years old.

The double sec doors that separated the mat-trans section from the rest of the installation were open, and they ran between them. The control room was a shambles of broken plaster and tiles that had spilled from the ceiling. Everything bore a film of gray-white, powdery dust. Long black cracks spread out in a jagged pattern from the corners, and through the ruptures vanadium alloy gleamed dully.

But the main console still flickered with power, lights on boards and panels blinking and glowing. The arma-glass walls enclosing the jump chamber were a beautiful shade of clear, cerulean blue. As per Kane's orders, Wolverton and Cohen were already in the jump chamber. The two men wore desert camo BDUs and they peered curiously out at Sindri and Crawler, their H&K XM-29 assault rifles held at the ready.

Brigid opened the medical kit and treated Sindri, sponging away the blood seeping from a shallow laceration. From an areosol can, she sprayed a thin, film-like layer over the wound. The liquid bandage contained nutrients and antibiotics that the body absorbed as the injury healed.

Sindri tolerated her ministrations silently, but he winced and grimaced a time or two. After she was done, he said with a seductive smile, "It's been a long time since I felt your touch, Miss Brigid. It brings back pleasant memories."

Face impassive, she smacked the injury with the fingers of one hand, drawing from him a cry of pain. He recoiled, staring up at her in reproach. "How about that touch? Does that bring back memories?" she asked.

Holding a hand over the injury, he replied sullenly, "Yes, it does. Thanks for the reminder."

She closed the medical kit. "My pleasure."

Kane repressed a laugh and asked, "How did you know that if you transmitted a message on that particular frequency, we'd hear it?"

Sindri shrugged. "I remembered you got a message to Baron Sharpe that way the last time I was in Cerberus."

Kane nodded and gazed out through the sec door toward the stairwell. After a moment of straining his ears, he turned away. "Nothing."

Grant shouldered the Barrett and looked distrustfully at the jump chamber. "I don't think we need to make such a big rush out of gating back."

"Are you sure of that?" Crawler asked, a slight smirk creasing his lips.

Grant frowned down at him. "Are you sure we should?"

Crawler shrugged and his smirk widened. Then a globe of seething plasma blazed between the open doors and impacted with a kaleidoscopic flare of sparks and spurts of smoke against a wall of the jump chamber.

Everyone crowded into the chamber very quickly, Brigid pulling the heavy door closed on its counterbalanced pivots. ASP bolts blossomed into miniature novas against armaglass, leaving ugly black scorch marks against the blue.

The sealing of the door automatically engaged the dematerialization cycle circuitry. The familiar yet still slightly unnerving hum arose from the array enclosed within the platform. The hum climbed in pitch to a whine, then to a cyclonic howl. The hexagonal floor and ceiling plates shimmered with silver. A fine, faint mist gathered at their feet and drifted down from the ceiling. Thready static discharges, like tiny lightning strokes, arced through the vapor.

Sindri grinned lopsidedly up at Kane, Brigid and Grant. "This is a lot like old times, isn't it, ladies?"

"Yeah," Kane growled. "Can't you tell that's why we're all so damn happy at the moment?"

The mist thickened, blotting out everything, even Sindri's grin.

Despite the passage of several years since they last encountered him, Kane had never doubted he and his partners would cross paths with Sindri again. The little man truly enjoyed acting in the role of the proverbial bad penny, turning up when he was least expected. Sindri delighted in unpredictability.

The Cerberus warriors hadn't seen him since he sought sanctuary with Baron Sharpe. Over the past couple of years, they had discussed what might have become of their old enemy when the barons evolved into their true forms, but they had not explored the matter beyond casual conversation.

Now Sindri was back and, true to character, the little man had returned in a very big way. Even in the twilight state between existence and nonexistence, Kane knew Sindri's big return would mean very big trouble for him and everyone in Cerberus.

Chapter 11

Lakesh had just stripped and turned on the water of the shower when his wall trans-comm buzzed. He tried to ignore it, adjusting the knobs to balance the water temperature. He liked it very hot, whereas Domi preferred tepid.

He had been born in the tropical climate of Kashmir, and he often felt that his internal thermostat was still stuck there. Lakesh spent nearly a century and a half in cryonic stasis, and though he conceded it made no real scientific sense, he had been very sensitive to cold ever since.

Standing naked before the full-length mirror attached to the wall, Domi examined the purple bruise spreading lividly across her midriff. "Want me to answer it?" she asked.

Shaking his head, Lakesh gusted out a profanity-salted sigh. "No, I'm sure it's just Mr. Bry with the latest crisis du jour."

Padding naked out into the living room, he called in the direction of the voice-activated trans-comm, "What is it now?"

He didn't even try to soften the hard edge of impatience in his tone. To his surprise, it wasn't Bry's voice that responded from the comm but that of Conrad, the security officer for the shift.

"Sorry to disturb you, Dr. Singh, but you asked to be notified when the away team made its return jump. We received a demat signal from Redoubt Papa less than a minute ago."

"Their conditions?"

"Except for blood-pressure and heart-rate spikes, their transponders indicate their vitals are well within the normal range."

All permanent residents of the Cerberus redoubt had been injected with subcutaneous biolink transponders that transmitted heart rate, respiration, blood pressure and brain-wave patterns. Based on organic nanotechnology, the transponders were composed of nonharmful radioactive chemicals that bound themselves to an individual's glucose and the middle layers of the epidermis. The constant signal was relayed to the redoubt by the Comsat, one of the two satellites to which the installation was uplinked.

The Cerberus computer systems recorded every byte of data sent to the Comsat and directed it down to the redoubt's hidden antenna array. Sophisticated scanning filters combed through the telemetry using special human biological encoding. The digital data stream was then routed through a locational program to precisely isolate an individual's position and current physical condition.

"There's one other thing," Conrad added, then fell silent.

Lakesh pictured the man staring in puzzlement at some sort of enigmatic warning on a computer screen and he prodded, "And what is that?"

"The automatic scan verification registers one unknown pattern. Should I initiate the shunt to the confinement buffer?"

Despite his impatience, Lakesh knew Conrad's question was a sound one.

Every piece of matter, whether organic or inorganic, that had ever been to or from the Cerberus gateway left a computer record in the database. The image processor scanned for patterns corresponding with those in the record and allowed for materialization unless the pattern was physically locked out and redirected to a holding buffer.

After a few thoughtful seconds, Lakesh reached a decision. "No, Mr. Conrad. Allow for the materialization, but make certain a security detail is present."

"Yes, sir. I have one standing by."

"I'll be there in a few minutes," Lakesh replied.

Returning to the bathroom, Lakesh saw that Domi had tired of waiting for him and entered the shower alone. She stood under the spray of water, soaping herself. His eyes roved her compact body, realizing again that he had never met a woman so unconscious of her body. She had a way of wearing nudity as if it were clothes.

Before arriving at the redoubt, Domi hadn't been accustomed to wearing much in the way of clothes at all unless circumstances demanded them, and then only the skimpiest concessions to weather, not to modesty. Born a feral child of the Outlands, she was always relaxed being naked in the company of others, and if those others didn't share that comfort zone, she couldn't care less.

Even now, she was very much a creature driven by the impulse of the moment, displaying the free style and outspoken rough manner acquired in the scramble for existence far from the relative luxury of the baronies.

She didn't miss the short and often brutal life in the Outlands. She had quickly adapted to the comforts offered by the Cerberus redoubt—the soft bed, protection from the often toxic elements and food that was always available, without having to scavenge or kill for it.

Despite the scars marring the pearly perfection of her skin, particularly the one shaped like a starburst on her right shoulder, Domi was wild, maverick beautiful. With droplets of water sparkling on her arms and legs, her skin looked opaque, its luminosity heightened by an absence of color.

As his body responded to her naked, wet proximity. Lakesh swiftly pulled on a bodysuit, announcing loudly to be heard over the drumming of water against tiles, "I have to go, darlingest one. The demands of duty and all that."

"What else is new?" she retorted, blinking back streams of water flowing down her face.

Lakesh zipped up the coverall. "Perhaps we can have early dinner together."

Domi frowned unhappily. "More drills with the team this afternoon. Small arms."

Lakesh heaved a weary sigh as he adjusted the tabs on the boot-sox. "I find myself wishing for the grand old days around here when the entire staff consisted of a baker's dozen of misfits. Then—"

"Then," Domi broke in with an impish grin, "you were an old fart and couldn't get it up with a derrick." Leaning out of the shower, she traced the outline of his erection through the fabric of his bodysuit. "Like it better this way."

Lakesh presented the image of seriously pondering Domi's comment before nodding in agreement. "On second thought, so do I, even we do have three times as many misfits to deal with."

They kissed quickly and Lakesh left their quarters, walking along the side passageway that led to the main corridor. He repressed a grin, reflecting on how Domi never tired of reminding him of how decrepit his physical condition had been when they first met, five years ago now.

Then he resembled a spindly, liver-spotted scarecrow, with a gray patina of ash-colored hair that barely covered his head, his eyes covered by thick lenses, a hearing aid inserted in one ear. Overall, he appeared to be fighting the grave for every hour he remained on the planet.

His complexion was leathery, crisscrossed with a network of deep seams and creases that bespoke the anguish of keeping two centuries' worth of secrets. For a long time, Lakesh could take consolation only in the fact that though he looked very old indeed, he was far older than he looked.

Even though he had not been able to demonstrate his feelings, Lakesh had been fond of Domi since the day they first met. In the interim, during shared dangers and joys, that affection had grown to love. She had risked her life to save him when he was imprisoned in Cobaltville and was grievously wounded during the rescue. The starburst-shaped scar on her right shoulder was a lasting memento of the incident, when a Magistrate bullet had shattered her corticoid bone.

And then, not quite four years ago, Sam the self-professed imperator, had laid his hands on Lakesh and miraculously restored his youth. At the time, Sam claimed he had increased Lakesh's production of two antioxidant enzymes, catalase and superoxide dismutase, and boosted up his alkyglycerol level to the point where the aging process was for all intents and purposes reversed.

Sam had indeed accomplished all of that, but only in the past couple of years did Lakesh learn the precise methodology—when he laid his hands on Lakesh, Sam had injected nanomachines into his body. The nanites were programmed to recognize and destroy dangerous organisms, whether they were bacteria, cancer cells or viruses. Sam's nanites performed selective destruction on the genes of DNA cells, removing the part that caused aging. For a time, he had felt he was living in the dream world of all old men—restored youth, vitality and enhanced sex drive, as Domi could attest.

It had been a great source of joy to Lakesh when he learned Domi reciprocated his feelings and had no inhibitions about expressing them, regardless of the bitterness she still harbored over her unrequited love for Grant. In any event, he had broken a fifty-year streak of celibacy with her and they repeated the actions of that first delirious night whenever the opportunity arose.

However, the nanites in his body became inert after a time. He and DeFore feared that without the influence of the nanomachines, he would begin to age, but at an accelerated rate. But so far, that gloomy diagnosis had not come to pass. True, he was sporting new gray hairs and he noticed the return of old aches and pains, but so far, the aging process seemed normal. He was cautiously optimistic that he would not reprise the fate of the title character in *The Picture of Dorian Gray,* and he hoped Domi shared that optimism.

Entering the ops center, Lakesh strode up the aisle between the computer stations. He glanced casually at the main mat-trans control console, noting that all the indicator lights shone green. Upon standard gateway activation, a million autoscanning elements committed to memory every feature of the jumpers' physical and mental composition, even, he supposed, down to the very subconscious. The data filtered through the system's built-in memory banks, where it was matched it with a variation range field.

Once the autoscanning sequence was complete, the translation program of the quincunx effect kicked in, a process by which lower dimensional space was translated, phased into a higher dimensional space along a quantum path. The jumpers traveled this path, existing for a nanosecond of time as digital duplicates of themselves, in a place between a relativistic *here* and a relativistic *there*.

Conrad, a tall, deeply tanned man with prematurely gray hair, stood near the door of the mat-trans ready room. His relaxed posture told Lakesh that, as yet, nothing untoward had happened.

As Lakesh passed him, he commented wryly, "The away team came back with some interesting guests, sir."

Lakesh acknowledged the man's remark with a wry smile. "That's not unusual, Mr. Conrad."

Three men in white bodysuits stood at various positions along the ready room's walls, all aiming compact SA-80 subguns in the direction of the jump chamber, making it the apex of a triangulated crossfire if one was necessary.

After the mad Maccan's murderous incursion into the installation, it had become standard protocol to have at least one armed guard standing by during any gateway materializations. The anomaly reported by Conrad necessitated a security complement.

To simplify matters, a weapons locker had been moved into the ready room. All of the Cerberus personnel were required to become reasonably proficient with small arms, and the lightweight "point and shoot" sub-guns were the easiest for the novice to handle.

Brigid, Kane, Grant, Wolverton, Cohen and two small figures Lakesh did not immediately recognize stood before the elevated platform of the gateway chamber. They all appeared a bit disoriented, eyes slightly glassy. A hyperdimensional trip via the mat-trans units was considerably more stressful on mind and body than stepping through an interphase point.

"Stand down, gentlemen," Lakesh told the security squad.

As the three men lowered the weapons and moved aside, Sindri flashed Lakesh a grin. "You're looking as spry as ever, Dr. Singh."

Lakesh couldn't help but grin in return. Despite their repeated clashes, Lakesh admired the little man who, in Brigid's words, had ambition enough to challenge God.

"Thank you, Sindri," he replied. "And what have you been up to since we last met?"

"We're still trying to find that out," Brigid said wryly, gesturing to the figure crouched beside Sindri.

The shaved-headed man was nearly as extraordinary looking as Sindri. Lakesh guessed his identity, but before he could speak, Kane interjected, "You might remember me talking about Crawler."

Lakesh nodded to the crippled man with the overdeveloped upper body and grotesquely shriveled legs. "I do indeed. You're Baron Sharpe's former high councelor. I've wanted to make your acquaintance for a long time, sir."

Crawler favored him with a suspicious, slit-eyed stare, his brow furrowing. Lakesh sensed a wispy touch against his mind, and his heart began to pound, despite the fact he knew the crippled man was a psionic, with telepathic abilities. In the Outlands they were called doomseers or doomies, their mutant precognitive abilities feared and hated.

Most of the mutant strains spawned after the nuclear holocaust were extinct, either dying because of their twisted biologies or hunted and exterminated during the early years of the unification program. Doomseers weren't necessarily mutants, but norms with true telepathic abilities were rare.

Extrasensory and precognitive perceptions were the most typical abilities possessed by mutants who appeared otherwise normal. Almost every human who exhibiting warped genetics had all but vanished. From what he understood, Crawler was one of the last of that particular precog breed.

A broad smile suddenly creased Crawler's face. "Yes, you have, haven't you?"

He extended a big flat hand. "I'm very pleased to meet *you*, Dr. Singh."

Stepping forward, Lakesh clasped the proffered hand, a little surprised by the softness of the man's palm, yet dismayed by the strength in his grip. "You scanned my thoughts to ascertain if I was lying to you."

Crawler nodded, pumping his hand formally. "A useful talent that has saved me on more than one occasion."

"Saved us both," Sindri said dourly, wriggling out of the straps of his backpack. He laid it on the long table with a very audible thud, and sighed in relief.

"You never did say what you were carrying, only that several parties were interested in it," Grant rumbled.

Sindri nodded, undoing the buckles of the covering flap. "Very much so."

As he reached inside, Kane remarked warningly, "Careful there now, Sindri."

The little man cast him a contemptuous glance over his shoulder. "Do you think I went to all of this trouble, shed my own blood in order to get here, just so I could blow it—and me—up with a bomb or something?"

Kane lifted a shoulder in a negligent shrug. "I'm just saying."

With both hands, Sindri removed an object that glinted in the light. He placed it on the table and stepped back, murmuring, "And I'm just saying—*behold.*"

A life-size human skull crafted from purple amethyst grinned at him, a silvery sheen in the eye sockets glimmering in the fluorescent lights shining down from overhead.

Their eyes widening, Brigid and Lakesh leaned forward reflexively to scrutinize it. Kane and Grant uttered weary, exasperated groans.

"My, isn't this a surprise—not," Kane muttered.

Sindri whipped his head around. "What do you mean?" he challenged.

Grant waved toward the door. "We've got a skull

made out of quartz crystal. Picked it up in Pakistan the day before yesterday."

Sindri's blue eyes lit up with excitement. "Really? Oh, this is better than I hoped! Two at hand...only eleven more to go. And as fortune would have it...I know *just* where they are."

Kane folded his arms over his chest and blew out a disgusted breath, rolling his eyes ceilingward. "I had a feeling you were going to say something like that. Next you'll be convincing us why we should care."

Sindri's grin was broad, but held all the genuine humor of a predator baring its teeth. "Mr. Kane, why else do you think I'm here?"

Chapter 12

Sindri insisted that neither he nor Crawler required medical attention, but Brigid and Lakesh were just as insistent that an examination was part and parcel of Cerberus security protocol.

Sullenly, the little man stated, "You're not interested in our health—you just want to make sure we're not smuggling weapons or nanites into your sanctuary here."

Fixing an accusatory gaze on Lakesh, he added, "Like some people in this room."

Lakesh felt the back of his neck flush with angry heat at Sindri's not-so-veiled reference to the events surrounding his last visit to the redoubt. He had exposed Lakesh's miraculous restoration as being due to nanomachines injected into his body by Sam.

"Things have changed around here," Lakesh stated firmly. "We run a much tighter ship."

Sindri sighed. "Don't wind it so tight you sink to the bottom. All right, then. I'll let your resident sawbones poke and prod me."

Crawler hesitated before commenting, "I'm not enthusiastic about an examination either, but I'll abide by your rules. We are, after all, your guests."

Kane gestured to the security squad. "Escort our guests to the dispensary, please."

"And bring them to the workroom when DeFore is done," Brigid interjected. "That's where we'll be."

Sindri reached for the translucent skull on the table, but Grant laid a big hand over it. "You won't need this where you're going, Sindri."

The little man bared his teeth in a ferocious scowl. "It's my property!"

"Nobody is going to steal it from you," Lakesh said coldly. "But we'll take it to the workroom and subject it to a spectroscopic test like the other skull we have in our possession."

Sindri changed his scowl to a rueful grin. Even Crawler chuckled. "Test away," the crippled doomseer said. "You won't learn anything."

"What makes you so sure?" Brigid asked.

Reaching inside the backpack again, Sindri withdrew a flat compact laptop. "Everything I've learned about the crystal skulls and their history is in this...and it's not much."

Brigid picked it up, tucking it under an arm. "We'll take a look at your data and decide for ourselves."

Bracketed by the subgun-wielding guards, Sindri and Crawler left the ready room. When they were out of earshot, Lakesh lifted the skull and hefted it in his right hand, frowning at it. "An extraordinary confluence of events."

"They would be if they were random," Brigid said.

"Which they're not," Kane declared. "Nergal is behind this."

"Behind what?" Lakesh inquired, holding the skull up before his face and staring into the eye sockets. "You haven't debriefed me."

"If you'll stop your 'Alas, poor Yorick' performance piece," Brigid said, laughter lurking at the back of her throat, "I will."

Lakesh laughed shortly in appreciation, although Kane and Grant exchanged mystified glances. Kane was accustomed to her enigmatic remarks after all these years, but could still be irked by them, particularly since they all seemed to target dead zones in his education.

He always felt like he was playing straight man to one of her academic performances. Brigid Baptiste wasn't quite the ambulatory encyclopedia she appeared to be, since most of her seemingly limitless supply of knowledge was due to her eidetic memory, but her apparent familiarity with an astounding variety of topics never failed to impress and frequently irritate him.

She retained just about everything she ever read, particularly during her years as an archivist. A vast amount of predark historical information had survived the nukecaust, particularly documents stored in underground vaults. Tons of it in fact, everything from novels to encyclopedias, to magazines printed on coated stock that survived just about anything. Much more data was digitized, stored on computer diskettes, usually government documents.

Although her primary duty as an archivist was not to record predark history, but to revise, rewrite and oftentimes completely disguise it, she learned early how to separate fiction from the truth, a cover story from a falsehood and scientific theory from fact.

As the four people walked through the ops center and out into the main corridor, Brigid swiftly told Lakesh everything that had transpired at Redoubt Papa. His eyebrows rose toward his hairline.

"I tend to agree with you, friend Kane," Lakesh said. "It doesn't seem likely the events in Pakistan and Washington Hole are unconnected."

"It's definitely some kind of scam," Grant declared matter-of-factly.

Brigid cast him a challenging glance. "Like what?"

"I don't know, but Sindri has run cons on us before, remember? He, Nergal and Crawler probably cooked this one up together."

Lakesh smiled sourly. "He's apparently been living comfortably in what used to be Sharpeville for the last couple of years. Some intense incident drove him from there."

Kane nodded. "We'll get the story out of him one way or the other."

When they entered the workroom, they saw Philboyd seated at a table, chin propped up by a hand, eyes darting over several sheets of hard copy containing dense columns of text. He glanced up casually at their approach, but upon spying the purple skull in Lakesh's right hand he performed an almost comical double-take, his eyes popping wide behind his glasses.

"Oh, for the love of—" he groaned. "Not another one."

"Yep," Kane announced with mock satisfaction. "Sindri brought it so we could have a matched set of really ugly bookends."

Philboyd's face registered surprise. "He's the one who transmitted the signal on the voyeur channel?"

"No, but he was responsible for it," Kane replied. "We need you to spectroscope out this one, too."

The astrophysicist shook his head. "It's a waste of time." He hooked a thumb in the direction of the crystal skull resting on the center of the trestle table. "Guess what the spectroscopic analysis showed that thing really is?"

"What?" asked Grant, then he instantly regretted falling for Philboyd's gambit.

"It's a skull made out of quartz crystal…just like I told you yesterday."

Before anyone could voice an objection or ask a question, the lanky man continued in a peevish rush, "I found absolutely no unusual properties about its specific gravity, its reflective and diffraction values or its characteristic density. In other words, it's exactly what it looks like…a lump of sculpted quartz crystal."

Brigid smiled in amusement at the scientist's agitation. "Brewster, it's not what the skull is made of but what it reputedly can do."

"Which is what again?" Philboyd retorted sarcastically. "I did a little reading last night and today about the sort of the things crystal skulls supposedly could get up to, and I'm telling you right now there's no scientific basis for the legends."

"Perhaps not our science," Brigid said genially, as if she were speaking to a cranky child on the verge of a tantrum. "And not even the scientific principles you were trained to work with in the twentieth century."

Gruffly, Kane demanded, "What the hell are you talking about?"

Philboyd uttered a scoffing sound. "What was known in my day as New Age claptrap."

Brigid's eyes and tone turned cold. "And what has been known in our day to have a foundation in fact." She shot a challenging glance at Lakesh. "Not even you can deny that."

The man nodded, replying reluctantly, "Although I wish I could."

"What was that Sindri said about eleven more skulls?" Grant asked.

"According to legends among certain South American Indian tribes," Brigid answered, "there are thirteen crystal skulls in existence. These skulls represented twelve planets, and were originally kept in a Mayan pyramid within a circle formation. A thirteenth larger crystal skull represented the collective consciousness of the twelve, and was placed in the center of the circle. This circle formation of the twelve crystal skulls with one larger crystal skull in the center was known as the Throne of Ascension."

Philboyd shook his head in disgust. "A skull throne, in other words."

Brigid did not respond to his comment. "The key crystal skulls were supposedly scattered over the world, and it was prophesied that one day they would be re-united back into the circle formation and trigger a planet-wide raising of consciousness."

"That's the claptrap part, right?" Kane inquired dourly.

Brigid shrugged. "Who knows? A number of South American tribes have a twelve-plus-one configuration as part of their history. For example, the Mayan peoples of Central and South America spoke of a mysterious leader with twelve followers that visited them.

"Some called him Quetzacoatl, others called him Votan, others Kukulkan and yet others Viracocha. Yet all these individual legends from each of the individual native Indians tribes bear very close similarities to one another, as if the different versions and names originate back to the same source. It's the same with the legend of the thirteen crystal skulls."

"The operative term is legend," Lakesh pointed out.

"Even so," Brigid retorted, gesturing to the amethyst sculpture in Lakesh's hand, "the crystal skulls *do* exist. They've been studied and the general consensus of scientific opinion was that it would have taken genera-tions to construct just one of them by grinding or rub-bing methods."

"Even if all that's true," Grant said, "it doesn't follow they contain information that can be accessed."

"The three of us saw the crystal skull on *Tiamat*," Brigid replied reasonably. "Balam himself claimed it corresponded to a memory buffer. Experiments were performed with the terrestrial skulls and there's nothing about them that would preclude them from containing encoded, digitized information.

"I think it's highly likely that they have data of a certain kind stored, possibly even optical information, like some computer hard drives, that are read with special lasers. Regardless of any unearthly properties the crystal skulls may or may not possess, the question still remains—where did they come from?"

Philboyd extended a hand toward Lakesh, who placed the purple-tinted skull in the astrophysicist's grasp. "This one looks like amethyst."

"That's because it is," Brigid said.

Philboyd's lips twisted as if he tasted something sour. "I read about an amethyst crystal skull that was discovered in a cache of Mayan artifacts in Mexico in the early 1900s."

"I imagine this is the same one," Lakesh stated.

Picking up a sheet of printout, Philboyd scanned the text, then examined the skull, turning it this way and that in the light. "According to what I read, the identifying features are circular indentations in the temples and a white squiggly line that follows the circumference of the skull."

He squinted, nibbled on his underlip, revolved the skull between both hands and then said in a hushed voice, "It has them. It's the genuine article."

"Was there any doubt?" demanded Sindri's sonorous voice. He and Crawler entered the workroom, followed closely by the three-man security squad who held their subguns in a passable imitation of a "present arms" position.

"When you're involved," Grant growled, turning toward him, "there's *always* doubt."

Brigid regarded him with a slit-eyed stare. "Surely you don't expect us to take anything you say on faith alone."

Sindri fluttered a dismissive hand through the air. "All faith must have a pinch of doubt mixed in—otherwise it's just flabby sentimentality. Don't you agree, Crawler?"

Dragging himself along beside the little man on his elbows, the crippled doomseer chuckled. "If I didn't, we'd both be dead, wouldn't we?"

Oliff, one of the security detachment, said, "DeFore gave them both clean bills of health."

The man addressed Kane and he couldn't help but notice how Lakesh bristled slightly.

"Thanks," Kane told him. "You're all dismissed."

"Yes, sir."

As the three men left the room, Sindri angled an interrogative eyebrow at Kane. "'Sir' now, is it? My, you *have* become a lot more spit, polish and anally retentive since the last time I was here."

"Not everything has changed," Grant rumbled menacingly. "We still have the same holding cell we gave you back then."

"Thank you, no," Sindri retorted with breezy insouciance. "Being your prisoner again isn't the reason we escaped from Sharpeville and sought you out."

Philboyd, who had met Sindri on his previous visit to the redoubt, demanded, "What are your reasons, then?"

Sindri turned toward the astrophysicist, a smile tugging at the corners of his mouth. "Dr. Philboyd, isn't it? What do you think of my little prize there?"

Philboyd hefted the skull in his hand as if trying to gauge its weight. "As far as I'm concerned, it and the other one are just ugly conversation pieces."

"The other one?"

Philboyd nodded toward the quartz skull resting in the center of the table. Sindri's breath came fast and harsh. He stepped closer, his blue gaze rapt. "Have you put the two of them in proximity?"

Philboyd's brow furrowed. "No, I haven't. Why?"

"Could you do so?"

Philboyd lifted a knobby shoulder in a shrug. "Sure, why not."

Kane's sixth sense, what he called his point man's sense, howled an alarm. The skin between his shoulder blades seemed to tighten and the short hairs at the back of his neck tingled. His point man's sense was really a combined manifestation of the five he had trained to the epitome of keenness. Something—some small, almost unidentifiable stimulus—had triggered the mental alarm.

Loudly, he said, "I don't think that's a good idea, Brewster."

Philboyd, in the process of putting the purple-hued skull on the trestle table, regarded him blankly. "Why not?"

Kane groped for a reason, then said, "Since Sindri made the suggestion, we should probably think it over for a couple of weeks."

Sindri exhaled a long, aggrieved sigh. "Mr. Kane, I can assure you that I would not undertake any action that would put me at risk."

"What will happen if the skulls are close together?" Brigid asked.

"I'm not sure. That's why I asked him to do it."

"Let me put this another way," Lakesh said impatiently. "What do you think will happen?"

"More than likely, nothing at all," the little man replied. "However, if the legends about the skulls containing encoded information have even the smallest shred of veracity, then it stands to reason they would have been designed to work in tandem."

Brigid nodded thoughtfully, then cast a quizzical glance at Kane. "Makes sense. Since the thirteen skulls are supposed to function in a circle formation, then logically each one forms an interdependent component of a larger whole, much like a parallel computer processor."

Grant eyed the skulls doubtfully. "What's the worst that can happen?"

"Only that we waste more of our time," Philboyd said snidely.

"I can't foresee anything dangerous coming of it," Lakesh commented.

"Those sound like the proverbial famous last words to me," Brigid replied dryly.

"Don't they just." Kane hestitated, then said, "All right, Brewster. Put them close together and we'll see what kind of interaction we'll get."

"I can tell you right now the kind we'll get," Philboyd said acidly. "The zero kind."

Moving with exaggerated, mocking caution, the lanky astrophysicist placed the amethyst skull on the tabletop about a foot away from the one made of quartz crystal. He stepped back and said stentorously, "Wait for it, wait for it…"

He faced Kane and Brigid, his lips curled in a sneer. "Wait for…absolutely *nothing*. Gee, isn't this magical?"

Kane couldn't help but grin, but then he heard a startled intake of breath from Sindri. The eye sockets of the two skulls began to glow, softly and dimly at first. The carved hollows pulsated with muted flares of variegated color.

"What the hell?" Grant murmured, reflexively stepping back.

Philboyd's mouth fell open in astonishment. Suddenly, the two skulls slid across the surface of the table as if drawn by a powerful magnetic force. The occipital regions of the craniums slammed together with a solid clack.

Kane felt the fine hairs in his nostrils and on the back of his neck tingle, his skin prickling as if a hundred thousand ants crawled over his body. At the edges of his hearing, he sensed a distant, muffled roar, a sound he could not focus on or even really be sure he heard.

The air in the room seemed to thicken, to swell in the lungs, making respiration labored and difficult.

Drawing in a deep, raspy breath, Lakesh muttered, "Sindri, what is happening?"

The little man did not respond. He stood at the edge of the table, eyes fixed unblinkingly on the pair of skulls. Lines of consternation creased Brigid's smooth forehead. "Some sort of power generation is going on, almost a surge."

A softly glowing funnel of light fanned up from the skulls as if emanating from within the crystal craniums. It looked like a cone made of a diffused veil of flame, with tiny shimmering pinpoints of light dancing within it. It expanded into a swirling aurora of incandesence several feet above the table, spreading out along the ceiling. The overhead lights flashed on and off and on again.

Heads back, the people in the room gaped up as the wreath wavered and billowed and coalesced. Geometric shapes appeared to swim through the glowing funnel, sliding, joining and coalescing into definite forms.

Sindri stared at the display, electrified by the sight, eyes full of wonder.

Then, without warning, the funnel of light writhed and coalesced into an image of a very tall, four-sided, white stone building. It towered above a grassy plaza, surrounded by what appeared to be miles of green rain forest. The structure rose in a series of steplike tiers, a succession of progressively smaller stone rectangles laid atop one another, to an enclosed temple at its pinnacle. A stairway slanted up the side facing them. The image rotated slowly, allowing them a three-dimensional view of all sides of it.

At the base of the pyramid stood a colonnade made of square blocks of white stone, flanked by the heads of two carved serpents.

From the roof of the temple atop the multiterraced structure shrugged the stone shoulders and neckless carved head of a monstrous figure that stared straight into the souls of the people in the room with the black, bottomless eyes of a demon. Its grinning face was skeletal, resembling those of the crystal skulls. The ziggurat was surrounded by half a dozen smaller versions of itself, all giving the impression of strength and imperishability.

Sindri stared at the images silently, then he hugged himself as if he were cold. His body trembled and he bit his lips. Tears swam in his eyes. Pulling a great sob of air into his lungs, he husked out, "It's all true…all the skulls are hidden there…in the lost city of Z."

Chapter 13

Philboyd grabbed for the skulls, exclaiming, "There's got to be a control or something—"

As his hands touched them, the wreath of light vanished with the suddenness of a candle flame being extinguished. In the silence that followed, the overhead lights flickered, then came back on.

"What the hell was all of that?" Grant demanded, trying to cover his apprehension with a veneer of angry impatience.

"Holography," Lakesh declared, his voice sounding eerily calm. "Using some sort of light-amplification process like a laser."

"A hologram of what, though?" Philboyd asked, sounding shaken.

"It looked like a Mayan pyramid," Grant stated. "Me and Kane had to fight our way out of one a few years back."

"If we saw a location in Brazil, that doesn't seem likely," Brigid said, although she sounded doubtful. "The Mayans never penetrated so far south."

Kane repressed a shudder at the memory of battling

a huge constrictor wearing a feathered headdress the natives had believed was an incarnation of Kukulkan.

"The architecture definitely looked Central American," Lakesh said, "The temple roof atop the pyramid was crafted to represent Ah Puch, the Mayan god of death. That's supposed to be marking the point at which our world and the underworld, Xibalba, meet."

Sindri swung his head sharply toward him, his blue eyes alight with excitement. "Very astute, Dr. Singh. Presumably to pass through the temple is to pass through a portal and enter the realms of the Lords of Darkness."

Philboyd gingerly poked at the skulls with a forefinger. They were no longer connected, and they slid easily apart. "Nothing now, not even a static electricity charge."

He turned his perplexed gaze toward Sindri. "What just happened?"

Sindri smiled in a patronizing fashion. "According to my research, when two or more of the skulls touch, their combined stored energy produces a visual record."

Philboyd's expression was skeptical but he asked, "A record of what?"

"Apparently a record of what we saw," Sindri answered condescendingly.

"What was that you said about the lost city of Z?" Lakesh demanded.

Sindri glanced up at him. "Have you heard of it?"

Lakesh frowned. "It rings a faint bell, I confess, but I can't place it."

Brigid stepped close to the table, eyeing the skulls dubiously. "Surely two of the skulls were in close contact at some time or another in the past, since they went through so many hands. Why didn't this phenomenon happen before?'

"Who said it didn't?" Sindri countered.

Brigid stared at him, eyes narrowed suspiciously. "I don't recall reading any reports about such a thing."

"As far as I know," Sindri stated, "only one other person ever experienced this kind of phenomenon with the skulls."

"Who was that?" Kane asked.

"An Englishman named Colonel Percy Harrison Fawcett."

Lakesh's shoulders stiffened in surprise, and Sindri observed dryly, "I take it that name rings a faint bell, too?"

Lakesh nodded. "Yes, it does…and now I know why the lost city of Z seemed so familiar."

A BRIEFING WAS CERTAINLY called for, but they didn't go to the officially designated briefing theater on the third level. Big and blue-walled, it came equipped with ten rows of theater-type chairs facing a raised speaking dais and a rear-projection screen. It was built to accommodate the majority of the installation's personnel, back before the nukecaust when military and scientific advisers visited.

The miniauditorium hadn't been used for its official function since the last installation-wide briefing a couple of years before. Generally, the big room served as a theater, a place where the personnel watched old movies on DVD and laser disks found in storage.

Generally, briefings were convened in the more intimate dining hall. When Lakesh, Kane, Grant, Brigid, Sindri and Crawler entered the cafeteria, they saw Farrell and Wegmann seated at a table near the main serving station.

Farrell was a rangy, middle-aged man who affected a shaved head, a goatee and a gold hoop earring after watching an old predark vid called *Hell's Angels on Wheels*.

A balding, sharp-featured, slightly built man under medium height with dark hair caught back in a ponytail, Wegmann served as the Cerberus redoubt's engineer, tending to the nuclear generators and the reactor buried deep within the stony bosom of the mountain.

Normally taciturn while in the best of moods, he glared at Sindri with undisguised contempt and surveyed Crawler with revulsion. The crippled man speared him with a frosty gaze and said, "I feel the same way about you."

Farrell and Wegmann recognized Sindri from his last visit to the redoubt, but they did not greet him with anything other than glowers.

As they took seats around a table, Lakesh asked, "Does anyone care for coffee?"

Sindri shook his head. "No, thank you. I never acquired much of a taste for it."

"This is the real article," Lakesh stated proudly. "Not the swill that's been passed off as coffee in the baronies."

One of the few advantages of being an exile in Cerberus was unrestricted access to genuine coffee, not the bitter synthetic gruel that had become the common, sub-par substitute since the skydark, the generation-long nuclear winter. Literally tons of freeze-dried packets of the real article were cached in the redoubt's storage areas. There was enough coffee to last the exiles several lifetimes.

"In that case, I wouldn't mind a taste," Crawler announced.

Grant fetched a carafe from a serving station and poured him a cup. Sitting in his chair, his shriveled legs dangling, the shaved-headed man sipped experimentally, then drained the contents of the entire cup in a couple of swallows. Smacking his lips with relish, he said, "I haven't tasted real coffee in nearly a hundred years."

Kane stared at him distrustfully. "A hundred years?"

Crawler nodded and pushed his cup toward Grant who obligingly refilled it. "I'm 126 years old."

No one disputed his statement. Some muties were reputed to possess remarkable longevity, and the Cerberus warriors had encountered more than one human of vast age.

"Baron Sharpe didn't care much for coffee, either," Crawler went on. "Absinthe was his beverage of choice."

"That figures," Brigid commented wryly, placing Sindri's laptop on the table in front of her. "An addiction to it might go a long way toward explaining his behavior."

Crawler smiled thinly, lifting the cup to his lips. "Not really."

The Cerberus warriors had encountered Crawler on several occasions in the past and had learned a bit about his history with the former Baron Sharpe. Part of Sharpe's legacy from his human great-grandfather was a small private zoo of creatures that had once crept and slithered and scuttled over the postnuke shockscape. The monsters had been fruitful and multiplied, and one of them was a doomie called Crawler.

It was more of a title than a name, bestowed upon him after his leg tendons had been severed. The psi-mutie had displayed a great cunning and propensity for escape from his compound, no doubt employing his mental talents to find the most opportune time and means to do so. After his leg tendons had been severed, his psi-powers availed him nothing, inasmuch as his ambulations were restricted to dragging himself around his cell by fingers and elbows.

After recovering from a near fatal illness, Baron Sharpe visited Crawler one sultry summer midnight, revulsed by the human face staring back at him from a wild, matted tangle of gray beard and long, filthy hair.

"I have a question," Baron Sharpe announced. "About my death."

In a high, whispery voice, Crawler said, "That question has no meaning, my lord baron. You have died and crossed back. You no longer need fear death, for it is behind you, not ahead of you."

Baron Sharpe was so delighted, he came close to bursting into tears of gratitude. His hopes had been realized, his fear of death proved groundless. That very night, he ordered the release of Crawler from his cage, saw that he was bathed, fed, shaved, cropped and pampered. He installed him as a high councilor, ignoring the outraged reactions of his personal staff.

For many years, Crawler was the only creature he trusted, even though the doomie had tried to orchestrate his murder at one point. Crawler had duped Sharpe into accompanying a squad of Magistrates to Redoubt Papa. Sensing Kane's presence there, the doomie conceived a plan whereby Sharpe would be assassinated and thus he could avenge himself for the wrongs done to him by Sharpe's great-grandfather.

When Kane refused to cooperate, to be used as a pawn, Sharpe attempted to kill Crawler and Kane shot him. He assumed he had dealt the baron a mortal wound, but Sharpe recovered, nursed back to health by the doomseer who had sought his death.

After that, both hybrid baron and mutie doomseer realized they were linked in some fashion and knew that if one died, so would the other. The notion made no real sense and couldn't be tested without incurring lethal results, so they decided to trust each other implicitly from then on.

Filling a cup from the decanter, Kane commented, "This is probably the best time to tell us what've you been up to for the past couple of years, particularly after Baron Sharpe underwent his makeover into Overlord Nergal."

Sindri shrugged. "Not too much changed, actually."

Lakesh's eyebrows curved down to meet at the bridge of his nose. "I find that exceptionally hard to believe, Sindri. *Everything* has changed. Nothing is as it was and nothing will remain as it was."

The nine barons, as venal and as vicious as they had been, were at least fairly predictable. They had needed the complex support system of the villes, the Magistrate Divisions, the forced labor supplied by the Tartarus Pits to remain in power.

Once the barons evolved into overlords, they had turned their backs on the villes and all of their territories.

Crawler and Sindri exchanged a meaningful glance, then Crawler nodded curtly, as if granting his permission for Sindri to speak.

Matter-of-factly, Sindri declared, "By the time of Baron Sharpe's transformation, Crawler and I had been running the ville for quite a few months. The baron was a figurehead who saw to the implementation of our plans."

Kane uttered a short, scoffing laugh. "I can't say I'm surprised that you usurped his authority."

"On the contrary," Crawler said smoothly, "the baron gladly ceded his authority to us. He was grateful that we removed the burdens of decision-making. He was more than willing to delegate all the tedious details of governing the ville to trusted subordinates like us."

"A baron who trusted his subordinates?" Grant rumbled skeptically. "That's a first."

Crawler favored him with an insipid smile. "Baron Sharpe was rather unique among the baronial hierarchy, as you know."

No one argued with the doomseer's statement. Of all the oligarchy, Sharpe had displayed the most human emotional characteristics—he could be capricious, ridiculous and unpredictable.

"Anyway," Sindri continued, "by the time the baron left the ville, Crawler and I had our own subordinates so thoroughly insinuated within the ville's infrastructure, there was no power vacuum to fill. Actually, Sharpeville became the most efficient and peaceful it had ever been."

Crawler interposed, "There were a couple of members of the Trust who objected to us running things, but we saw to their removal. The others accepted us."

Every ville in the network had its own version of the Trust, a secret society that allowed the only face-to-face contact with the barons.

With a sardonic smile, Brigid asked, "Then why did you leave the little pocket utopia you had built?"

Sindri swallowed hard and his face paled by a shade. "We had no choice."

"Why?" Lakesh pressed.

Crawler exhaled slowly. "The baron came back—as Nergal. And he wasn't at all happy to find us still there."

Chapter 14

"He came back?" Lakesh demanded raggedly, incredulously.

Sindri nodded, saying nothing.

"Ever since the barons evolved into the overlords, there have been no reports of any of them returning to their former territories, let alone the villes themselves. Why would Nergal do it?"

In unison, Crawler and Sindri intoned, "The skull."

Kane's eyebrows rose like dark wings. "The amethyst skull was in Sharpeville?"

"Yes," Crawler answered. "It was part of a collection owned by Sharpe's human grandfather, the one who imprisoned me so long ago."

"Apparently as Sharpe, he had forgotten all about it," Sindri put in. "But as Nergal, he remembered it—and a purpose for it."

"When did he return?" Brigid asked.

"A little over two weeks ago," Crawler replied, his tone resentful. "He was cold, distant, imperious, but he talked about the ancient sites of his people, the Annunaki, and how they concealed their vaults when their empire collapsed. He'd been competing with his family, seeking them out, reclaiming the technology so one or the other of the overlords could exert mastery over the council and the rest of the Earth."

Grant knuckled his chin thoughtfully. "And he thinks one purple skull will help him accomplish that?"

Sindri shook his head impatiently. "No, he thinks one purple skull will lead him to twelve more, and all thirteen will be the means to accomplish his goal."

"Which is?" Brigid inquired.

"A force that almost conquered the entire planet aeons ago," Sindri explained, "but it can't be used by only one member of the Supreme Council."

Kane stirred restlessly. *"Tiamat."*

"Exactly," Sindri said. "Nergal believes that with all the crystal skulls in his possession, he and he alone can use *Tiamat* to his own ends, without the participation or the knowledge of the rest of the council."

"How do you know about *Tiamat?*" Grant challenged.

Crawler regarded him with a pitying smile and tapped the side of his head with a forefinger.

"Oh," Grant said, comprehending. "You read Nergal's mind."

"Not precisely," the doomseer replied, "but I received sufficiently detailed mental impressions to understand his desires and goals….and why he so covets the thirteen crystal skulls."

Brigid's eyes widened. "With them, Nergal thinks he

can gain control over *Tiamat*'s neuronic systems, her main memory core."

Sindri nodded dolefully. "And once he has *Tiamat* under his thrall, he will dominate the Supreme Council, including Enlil himself...and thus Earth."

Despite Sindri's flight into melodrama, chills crept up the spines of Brigid, Kane and Grant. Their memories flitted back to their experiences on the sentient spaceship that the ancient Annunaki had created and worshiped as the creation-mother, *Tiamat.*

With *Tiamat* in permanent orbit, hanging over the world like a dark angel of doom, the Cerberus warriors knew they had no chance of emerging victorious from a head-on confrontation with the overlords, even if they managed to kill all of them.

The giant ship was capable of dispatching remote probes, essentially smaller versions of herself, to blanket the planet with fusion bombs, biological and chemical weapons and defoliants of all kinds.

As a result, the seas would be rendered toxic, the atmosphere contaminated, starvation and exposure to radiation would kill anyone who was unlucky enough to survive the initial onslaughts. Within a fortnight, humanity as the dominant species on Earth would cease to exist.

"Is gaining control over *Tiamat* even possible?" Lakesh asked uneasily.

"Nergal certainly thinks so," Sindri answered. "He put me to work, searching through the ville archives for any historical record pertaining to the skulls, the Throne of Ascension and their whereabouts."

"I presume you found…something," Kane drawled.

Sindri smiled wolfishly. "You know me so well, Mr. Kane. Yes, I indeed 'found something,' as you put it." He tapped the laptop with a forefinger. "It's all in there. While Nergal was in Pakistan following up a lead I provided, Crawler and I planned our escape. But we knew we needed allies to further our objective so—"

"So that's where Cerberus figures into this," Grant interrupted brusquely.

"As astute as always, Mr. Grant," Sindri responded, his voice brittle with sarcasm. "I remembered your eavesdropping channel from my last visit here, and Crawler transmitted a recorded message to you on that frequency."

Lakesh eyed him distrustfully. "That was quite the gamble, friend Sindri. A true shot in the dark that we would receive the message or heed it."

"Under the circumstances," Crawler stated gloomily, "all we could do was gamble. If we did not, then Nergal very well might be the master of all humanity in less than a month."

"So you absconded with the data and skull," Brigid interposed, "by appropriating a Deathbird from the Magistrate Division. Which one of you was the pilot?"

"That would be me," Sindri replied, tapping his chest. "I'm a quick study, as I'm sure you remember. Flying the chopper was far less difficult than piloting the Aurora."

"Maybe so," Kane commented. "But your landings sure could use some work. And you definitely need a brush-up on evasive manuevering."

Sindri glowered at Crawler. "My associate here miscalculated the amount of time we would have before Nergal returned and realized what we had done."

"The future is malleable," Crawler responded in a detached tone, "the outcome of events always in flux. I explained that to you."

"Nergal dispatched a pursuit ship," Sindri went on, as if he hadn't heard Crawler's defense, "and the rest of the story you know."

Lakesh folded his arms over his chest and stared steadily at the little man. "I must take issue with you on that score. We barely know the prologue, much less the 'rest of the story.' What did you find in the archives?"

Sindri tugged the laptop toward him, thumbing open the latch. As he raised the cover, the computer juiced up automatically, emitting a soft, musical chime. The screen flashed.

"Everything we need to know about the crystal skulls," he stated, "where they are and who found them before, is contained in this. The only mystery is how to stop Overlord Nergal from laying claim to them."

Chapter 15

The screen displayed a black-and-white image of a man with a stern face and a long, ringleted beard usually associated with pictures of Assyrian kings. Beneath the brim of a pith helmet, the man's eyes held a critical stare, as if he examined everyone's mental and spiritual credentials and almost always found them wanting.

A huge spread of khaki-covered shoulders and a chest like a barrel were the only other parts of him visible in the photograph.

"Colonel Percy Harrison Fawcett," Sindri announced. "One of the preeminent eccentrics of the twentieth century." He cast a sly glance at Lakesh. "Other than yourself, of course."

Kane didn't even bother repressing a grin, particularly when Lakesh scowled. "What was so eccentric about him?" he asked.

"He was a celebrated explorer for one thing," the little man answered. "He worked for the Bolivian government to survey its frontier with Brazil, and he made several expeditions deep into the interior of the Mato Grosso. He was also something of an occultist."

"So?" Grant grunted.

"So, in 1925, at the age of fifty-eight, Fawcett set out with his eldest son and his son's friend, Raleigh Rimmell, to look for a hidden city known in local mythology as Z. The last word was heard from the group as they crossed the Upper Xingu, a southeastern tributary of the Amazon. The party vanished without a trace after that. Repeated rescue missions followed, as did rival theories about Fawcett's demise.

"Either he had been eaten by jaguars, was living as a native, had starved or been killed by the indigenous people, the Kalapalo. Bones unearthed in 1951 proved on examination not to belong to Fawcett, and the mystery continued to grow over the decades."

"Once again," Brigid said, "so? Fawcett was like any number of English explorers of that era. The most likely solution is that he ended up living with one of the local tribes."

Lakesh nodded. "Very possible. Fawcett himself wrote, "The English go native very easily…there is no disgrace in it. On the contrary, in my opinion it shows a creditable regard for the real things in life.'"

Sindri's eyes narrowed with annoyance. "If you know that much about him, do you know where he got the idea about a lost city called Z?"

"I'm sure you're going to tell us," Kane said diffidently. "Just as I'm sure you'll tell us it has something to do with a crystal skull."

"Very good, Mr. Kane," Sindri retorted with a mocking smile. "Your mental agility seems to have improved since we last associated with each other. Yes, according to private personal papers that weren't unearthed until the late 1990s, it appeared that Fawcett had no intention of ever returning to Britain. He claimed a spirit guide who contacted him through the Mitchell-Hedges crystal skull—and probably the one made of amethyst, as well—lured him to the city of Z.

"Having no idea of the nature of a hologram, Fawcett interpreted his experience as a supernatural vision. Afterward, he planned instead to set up a commune in the Mato Grosso jungle, based on a bizarre cult."

Grant arched a questioning eyebrow. "What kind of cult?"

When Sindri didn't immediately reply, Crawler interposed, "That was never made clear in the records we found. However, it had something to do with the then-fashionable credo of Theosophy."

Lakesh rolled his eyes ceilingward. "I should have known. Edwardian-era Britishers not only went native easily, but they also fell for crackpot occult beliefs."

"What's Theosophy?" Kane asked, stumbling slightly over the pronunciation.

"A doctrine that was popular in the early part of the twentieth century," Brigid replied curtly, "following occult principles laid down by a Russian mystic named Helena Petrovna Blavatsky. Her Theosophical Society believed in the spiritual unity of all things."

"Yes," Lakesh said sarcastically. "She rejected the

idea of a God existing outside nature. Her so-called theosophy spoke of an all-pervading divine essence, an infinite ocean of consciousness, from which all things are born and to which they ultimately return. The human kingdom was one of the phases of experience that each god-spark must pass through during its long evolutionary journey through the worlds of matter."

"That's no crazier than the belief system of the Lakota," Kane pointed out.

Lakesh chuckled, but there was no humor in it. "Perhaps not, but much of the actual content of the Theosophical Society appealed to racists, occultists and even to Satanists, like Aleister Crowley. It postulated that certain races—the Aryans, of course—were inherently superior to all the others. The most popular forms of western occultism owed a great deal to Theosophy. And in the mid-twentieth century, much of the theosophical tenets were adopted by various UFO sects, like the Heaven's Gate cult."

"In which case," Brigid remarked, "Blavatsky and her sect might have been influenced by Balam's people. We know that his father, Lam, had contact with Crowley's cult."

Lakesh smiled wearily. "Yes, I was about to get to that. The same notion occurred to me…long before you were born."

Brigid returned his smile but did not reply. She knew that after Lakesh's resurrection from stasis, more than fifty years earlier, he had made a study of ancient history, scanning old texts for clues to nonhuman involvement in human evolution.

However, with the revelations supplied by Balam and even the Supreme Council of overlords, Lakesh had finally solved the enigma that had perplexed not only him, but his Hindu ancestors. Lakesh had once believed the solution to both the riddle of the so-called Archons and humanity's mysterious origins lay in ancient religious codices. He had finally come to accept that he could not penetrate the convoluted conspiracy of secrecy that had been maintained for twenty thousand years or more.

The few surviving sacred texts contained only hints, inferences passed down from generation to generation, not actual answers. Millennia-old documents that might have held the truth had crumbled into dust, or were deliberately destroyed. Regardless, historical records of nonhuman influence on Terran development ran uninterrupted from the very dawn of humankind to the present day.

Always it was the same—human beings as possessions, with a never-ending conflict bred between them, promoting spiritual decay and perpetuating conditions of unremitting physical hardship. And always, secret societies were created by human pawns to conceal and to protect the true nature of humanity's custodians—or masters.

"The Theosophist's bible so to speak, *The Book of Dzyan,*" Lakesh continued, "contained a tale about a group of beings who came to Earth many thousands of years ago in a huge craft that orbited the world—very possibly that's an account of Annunaki colonization."

"Can we get back to the matter at hand?" Sindri asked peevishly. "It's not really relevant whether Fawcett was a Theosophist or not."

"I disagree," Lakesh replied, "but pray continue."

"More than thirteen separate expeditions failed to discover what happened to Fawcett," Sindri went on, "and over a hundred people died in the attempts. But by deciphering clues in Fawcett's correspondence it appeared the rescue expeditions were all looking in the wrong direction."

"And you," Grant inquired dourly, "think you've found the right direction?"

Sindri nodded smugly. "That I do, Mr. Grant. Fawcett not only wanted to find the city of Z, but to establish a secret community there. He had scores of like-minded associates who were planning to go out and join Fawcett to live in a new, freer way. I think they succeeded, their movements protected by bribes to government officials. They created a society hidden deep in the rain forests of Amazonia."

"Assuming that's the truth," Kane said, "what the hell was this 'Z' place?"

"Actually, we think Z was simply a diversionary code word," Crawler said. "It's our opinion Fawcett meant X."

Grant snorted derisively, "Yeah, X is so much better than Z. Everything is a lot more clear now, thanks."

"X stands for Xibalba," Sindri intoned.

"Xibalba?" Lakesh echoed skeptically. "The Mayan underworld?"

"In this instance, an actual place in the jungle named after the underworld," Sindri said. "Where most of the sacred relics and artifacts of the Mayan religion were taken and hidden from the conquistadores."

"That's quite the stretch, even for you," Brigid said dryly. "You have evidence to support this theory?"

Sindri favored her with a prideful smile. "Of course I do, Miss Brigid. You should know that about me, by now."

"Get on with it," Kane grated impatiently.

Uttering a brief laugh, Sindri tapped the keyboard of the laptop and the image of Fawcett was replaced by an image of a yellowed, chip-edged piece of parchment. The faint words printed on it made no sense to Kane, but over the past five years he had come in contact with enough dead languages to recognize Latin even if he could not read it.

Sindri stated, "The Catholic church of sixteenth-century South America was as much an educating force as an evangelizing one, although its main purpose was propagation of the faith. Shortly after the final Mayan conquest of the 1600s, Spanish monks and friars set about teaching them to read and write their own language. They adapted the Latin alphabet to Mayan, innovating where necessary to cover sounds foreign to the romantic languages.

"The new form of writing was intended for Christian

purposes only, but the Maya, no strangers to writing, were quick to see the script's potential. They recorded everything from prophecies and rituals to petitions to the Spanish crown. But of all the manuscripts created in this manner in the century following the conquest, the *Books of the Chilam Balam* were the most important."

When he saw the startled reactions among the people at the table, Sindri chuckled. "Yes, I rather thought that name would get a rise out of you."

Balam was the last of the so-called Archons, the descendents of the First Folk, the last of the children created by two races who had turned Earth into a battleground millennia ago, and who had directly influenced many of humankind's belief systems.

"The name probably means something completely different in Mayan," Kane said, although he didn't believe it.

"Could be," Sindri replied. "But I doubt that very much. The Chilam were native priests, shamans or seers. 'Balam' means 'jaguar' and is used here as a title of rank, or to bestow respect. The original Jaguar Priest may have been a real personage whose greatness prompted the use of his name for these texts.

"Whoever—or whatever—he was, Chilam Balam was believed by the Maya to be a seer or a prophet. He supposedly foretold the coming of the white men and even gave details of the diseases and wars they would bring, and gave the dates of great disasters that actually came true, according to his calculations on the Mayan calendar."

"It certainly sounds like our Balam," Lakesh murmured contemplatively.

"Perhaps," Sindri agreed. "The narratives contain a lot of information on life in colonial Brazil, but basically, they reflect the religious and mythological traditions of the Maya. A given community's narrative was written and maintained by its leader, usually a sage or priest. He wrote the name of the community in the book for identification purposes: thus we have the *Chilam Balam of Chumayel.*"

With a forefinger, Sindri traced a line of text on the screen. "Now if you read this description here, and account for a couple of translation discrepencies, you'll—"

Kane reached out and slammed down the cover of the laptop, the edge scraping Sindri's knuckle. He yanked his hand away, uttering a yelp of surprise and pain. Nursing his finger, Sindri glared at Kane with pure, almost homicidal fury.

"What the fuck do you think you're doing?" he half shouted.

"Nothing," Kane shot back, "and that's the problem. This is all so much yadda-yadda. Bottom-line it for us, Sindri."

"That's what I thought I was doing," Sindri argued petulantly. "Do have I to spell it out?"

"Yes," Grant stated in a monotone. "Yes, you do."

Sindri sighed deeply, as if obnoxious children were pestering him to the point of madness. "The so-called lost city of Z, of X, of Xibalba, is not just a hiding place

Get FREE BOOKS and a
FREE GIFT when you play the...

LAS VEGAS
GAME

*Just scratch off
the gold box with a coin.
Then check below to see
the gifts you get!*

YES! I have scratched off the gold box. Please send
me my **2 FREE BOOKS** and **gift for which I qualify**. I understand
that I am under no obligation to purchase any books as
explained on the back of this card.

DETACH AND MAIL CARD TODAY! ▼

366 ADL EF6L   **166 ADL EF5A**
                                                    (GE-LV-07)

FIRST NAME   LAST NAME

ADDRESS

APT.#   CITY

STATE/PROV.   ZIP/POSTAL CODE

7	7	7	Worth TWO FREE BOOKS plus a BONUS Mystery Gift!
🍒	🍒	🍒	Worth TWO FREE BOOKS!
🔔	🔔	♣	TRY AGAIN!

Offer limited to one per household and not
valid to current Gold Eagle® subscribers.
All orders subject to approval. Please allow
4 to 6 weeks for delivery.

Your Privacy - Worldwide Library is committed to protecting your privacy. Our privacy policy is available online at
www.eharlequin.com or upon request from the Gold Eagle Reader Service. From time to time we make our lists
of customers available to reputable firms who may have a product or service of interest to you. If you would
prefer for us not to share your name and address, please check here. ☐

©2001 WORLDWIDE LIBRARY
® and ™ are trademarks owned and used by the trademark owner and/or its licensee.

The Gold Eagle Reader Service™ — Here's how it works:

Accepting your 2 free books and free gift places you under no obligation to buy anything. You may keep the books and gift and return the shipping statement marked "cancel." If you do not cancel, about a month later we'll send you 6 additional books and bill you just $29.94* — that's a savings of 10% off the cover price of all 6 books! And there's no extra charge for shipping! You may cancel at any time, but if you choose to continue, every other month we'll send you 6 more books, which you may either purchase at the discount price or return to us and cancel your subscription.

*Terms and prices subject to change without notice. Sales tax applicable in N.Y. Canadian residents will be charged applicable provincial taxes and GST. Credit or debit balances in a customer's account(s) may be offset by any other outstanding balance owed by or to the customer.

If offer card is missing write to: Gold Eagle Reader Service, 3010 Walden Ave., P.O. Box 1867, Buffalo NY 14240-1867

BUSINESS REPLY MAIL
FIRST-CLASS MAIL   PERMIT NO. 717-003   BUFFALO, NY

POSTAGE WILL BE PAID BY ADDRESSEE

GOLD EAGLE READER SERVICE
3010 WALDEN AVE
PO BOX 1867
BUFFALO NY 14240-9952

NO POSTAGE
NECESSARY
IF MAILED
IN THE
UNITED STATES

for the Maya's sacred relics, but was also used as a remote transmission station."

Lakesh cocked his head quizzically. "What?"

Crawler said flatly, "The crystal skulls are data-transfer interfaces with the computer systems aboard *Tiamat*, much like a wireless communication network that processes electronic and telemetric signals."

Brigid Baptiste's green eyes gleamed with sudden comprehension. "And the pyramid in the city is a transmission tower…that's why Nergal has been seeking out all the skulls, so he can reactivate it!"

Sindri slitted his eyes, favoring her with an exasperated frown. "Well…*duh*."

Chapter 16

In the center of the verdant valley towered a pyramid. The sides were absolutely smooth except in the center, where a long series of steps had been carved. At the top stood a temple with a flat stone roof supported by square pillars adorned with skull-faced men and writhing serpents.

It was a series of plazas, each surrounded by small stone buildings from south to north, conforming with mathematical precision to a rising ridgeline.

Lakesh nodded to the image on the big VGA display screen in the ops center and said, "Just like I thought. The hologram we saw resembles the Mayan settlement of Lubaatum."

Brigid, Kane and Grant stood around him, staring at the picture Lakesh had found in the main database. That the images were there was not surprising—the information contained in the main database may not have been the sum total of all humankind's knowledge, but not for lack of trying. Any bit, byte or shred of information that had ever been digitized was only a few keystrokes and mouse-clicks away.

"Resembles," Grant repeated, fingering his chin. "But not identical?"

Lakesh shook his head. "The holographic projection showed a much smaller city but the architectural features are very similar to those at Lubaatum. It was unique among Mayan settlements for having been built out of precision-cut stones and fitted without mortar. The pyramid there had rounded corners, a characteristic shared by the one in the hologram."

"But Lubaatum is in Belize," Brigid objected. "Fawcett allegedly disappeared in Brazil. That's a very long way off."

The four people had left Sindri and Crawler in the dining hall to eat, under the watchful eye of a security guard, while they checked on his story and discussed it privately.

"Actually," Lakesh replied, "Fawcett is thought to have gone missing on the eastern fringe of the Serra de Huanchaca, between Brazil and Bolivia."

"Is that significant?" Kane asked.

Lakesh shrugged. "It's certainly desolate, known as the land of mists and mirage. Old topographical reports described it as a region of fog, weird weather patterns and deep mountain valleys that were never explored."

"Are you suggesting that the Mayan empire penetrated that far from the Yucatán peninsula?" Brigid inquired skeptically.

"Why not? Think how far the Roman Empire expanded from the Mediterranean Basin. The Maya certainly reached as far as Costa Rica. They were a very remarkable people, after all. With innovations in art, mathematics and astronomy—not to mention the discovery of chocolate—the Mayan civilization was one of the most advanced in ancient Mesoamerica. But calling them an empire is a misnomer."

"Why?" Grant wanted to know.

"The Maya were not united under a single empire," Lakesh answered, "but rather lived in various groups and tribes in a number of sovereign states bound together through cultural, mythological and religious ties. In ancient times, Mayan territory stretched along the length of the Yucatán peninsula into southern Mexico and northern Guatemala, with large colonies extending into parts of Belize and Honduras.

"The Mayan civilization was governed by a hereditary monarchy, with the ruling class legitimizing their power through claims to divine heritage. Because kings were thought to be descended from the gods, political leaders also served as the heads of spiritual and religious matters, as well, performing rituals and leading ceremonies."

Kane grunted. "That sounds familiar…the old Annunaki god-king setup."

"There was a difference between the way it was practiced among the Maya and the Sumerians," Lakesh stated. "Because there was no separate priesthood within Mayan class society, there was accordingly no segregation between the spiritual and the secular in Mayan culture. Nor was there a distinction between the spiritual and the scientific, for their many advances in mathematics and astronomy were investigations that served both practical and religious purposes."

Brigid nodded thoughtfully. "The Sumerian god-king system tried to keep the rank-and-file citizenry as ignorant as possible, to make it easier to rule them. But the Maya are credited with the discovery and use of the value of zero and the creation of a complex and accurate astral calendar."

Lakesh threw her an appreciative smile. "Exactly. The calendar, known as the Tzolkin, was based on the discovery that the cosmos operated in cycles, and was calculated and created in order to track the movements of large heavenly bodies, such as the moon or the planet Venus. Archaeologists projected that the Maya began measuring time with this astral calendar on approximately August 31, 3114 B.C. All dates began there, with each age consisting of thirteen cycles lasting a period of four hundred years.

"Because of their fragmented political structure, the Mayan civilization withstood the destructive campaigns of the Spanish conquistadores better than that of the Aztecs, who fell quickly once their capital, Tenochtitlan, was conquered. The Mayan people survived the turmoil of those first years of European colonization and settlement. However, much of their land and their traditional way of life was either lost or had to be abandoned or altered as increasing assimilation with dominant cultures became unavoidable."

Lakesh's smile widened and he added, "Even as late as the twentieth century, there were lonely mountain settlements where the inhabitants spoke almost pure Mayan—or they did until radio and television broadcasts reached them. Over the centuries, the Mayan people persevered against exploitation and domination."

Brigid nibbled at her underlip reflectively. "I suppose it's possible the Maya established a colony or outpost in Amazonia and during the Spanish invasions moved their most sacred relics there. Perhaps they hid them underground, beneath the pyramid, and that's what they called the place Xibalba."

"That makes a certain amount of sense," Grant conceded.

"More than you know, friend Grant," Lakesh declared. "There were many legends of secret vaults hidden beneath Mayan temples, of repositories of ancient wisdom in the form of crystals."

From the nearby enivro-ops station, Bry snorted disdainfully. Lakesh swiveled his chair and said reprovingly, "Just as we use magnetic tape, lasers and microprocessors as recording and playback devices, some ancient peoples could have used quartz crystals for encoding and storing information."

"And if Balam was in contact with the Maya as Sindri implied," Brigid interjected, "then he very well might have taught them the techniques of doing so, and even supplied the necessary technology. He might have been responsible for the smuggling of a few skulls out into the world, the ones containing holographic information."

"Speaking of which," Kane said, "could there be any validity to the crystal skulls and the pyramid operating in tandem to form some kind of direct transmission tower to *Tiamat?*"

Lakesh tugged at his nose absently. "Theoretically, I suppose it's possible, but it would all depend on the actual technologies in use. They'd have to be supported by a number of transmission and channel assignments, including time and code division multiple access, spread-spectrum multiplexing and other multicarrier systems."

Bry stated flatly, "It's not just technologies, but the actual hands-on know-how to achieve a lock with a space-based receiver."

"Like what?" Grant asked.

Bry lifted his knobby shoulders in a shrug. "Spatial transmission techniques mainly, notably space-time coding and beam-forming to exploit spatial diversity, and space-time processing to jointly blend temporal and spatial properties of the signaling environment."

"Ah." Grant nodded as if a mystery that had long vexed him had finally been solved. "I didn't understand a goddamn thing you just said, Donald."

Bry frowned. "In layman's terms, there's a lot more to turning a pyramid into a transmission and data-trans-fer station than just a bunch of crystal skulls arranged in a certain way. There's got to be some kind of computer there, too, one that can interface and network with *Tiamat*'s systems."

Kane cleared his throat. "Well, this is all very interesting in a techno-babbly sort of way, but the evidence to support it is pretty damn slim. Besides, taking into account from whom we got this story in the first place—"

He trailed off, but there was no need to elaborate. Everyone shared his mistrust of Sindri.

"After what we've seen of overlord activity in the past couple of years," Brigid said, "we can't afford to altogether discount what Sindri claimed...although I wish we could."

"Yeah, me too," Grant agreed fervently.

Lakesh eyed the three people. "We shouldn't assume Sindri is lying or running a scam and reject his story outright. If Nergal or any of the Supreme Council manage to alter *Tiamat*'s programming, then the Annunaki empire will be reborn virtually overnight."

Kane's imagination suddenly reeled with scenes of carnage, of megadeath and fire. Monstrous pillars of white-hot flame roared mile-high into the sky, men, women and children fled howling in terror as the gargantuan black shadow of *Tiamat* fell over the Earth. Columns of hell-light sprang from her underbelly, flattening settlements, boiling the seas, wrenching mountains from their beds.

Armored, dead-eyed Nephilim marched through the smoke-shrouded streets of the villes, trampling bodies with the flesh seared down the bone, using their ASP emitters to burn down anything that caught their attention.

Shaking his head to drive out the visions and repressing a shudder, Kane stated grimly, "We don't have any choice."

"Do we ever?" Brigid asked bitterly.

Grant said, "We'll have to take Sindri with us, you know. And I'm sure he'll insist on Crawler going along. So how do we get to Amazonia? Is there a mat-trans gateway in the vicinity?"

"No," Lakesh answered. "The nearest one is hundreds of miles from your destination, so the interphaser seems to be the best bet. I'm sure a set of parallax points can be activated."

The interphaser had evolved from the Project Cerberus. Several years before, Lakesh had constructed a small device on the same scientific principle as the mat-trans gateways, a portable quantum interphase inducer designed to interact with naturally occurring hyperdimensional vortices.

The first version of the interphaser had not functioned according to its design, and was lost on its first mission. Much later, a situation arose that necessitated the construction of a second, improved model.

During the investigation of the Operation Chronos installation on Thunder Isle, a special encoded program named Parallax Points was discovered. Lakesh learned that the Parallax Points program was actually a map, a geodetic index, of all the vortex points on the planet.

This discovery inspired him to rebuild the interphaser, even though decrypting the vortex index program was laborious and time-consuming. Each newly discovered set of coordinates was fed into the interphaser's targeting computer.

With the new data, the interphaser became more than a miniaturized version of a gateway unit, even though it employed much of the same hardware and operating principles. The mat-trans gateways functioned by tapping into the quantum stream, the invisible pathways that crisscrossed outside of perceived physical space and terminated in wormholes.

The interphaser interacted with the energy within a naturally occurring vortex and caused a temporary overlapping of two dimensions. The vortex then became an intersection point, a discontinuous quantum jump, beyond relativistic space-time

Evidence indicated there were many vortex nodes, centers of intense energy, located in the same proximity on each of the planets of the solar system, and those points correlated to vortex centers on Earth. The power points of the planet, places that naturally generated specific types of energy, possessed both positive and projective frequencies, and others were negative and receptive.

Lakesh knew some ancient civilizations were aware of these symmetrical geo-energies and constructed monuments over the vortex points in order to manipulate them. Once the interphaser was put into use, the Cerberus redoubt reverted to its original purpose—not a sanctuary for exiles, or the headquarters of a resistance against the tyranny of the barons, but a facility dedicated to fathoming the eternal mysteries of space and time. Unfortunately, Interphaser Version 2.0 had been lost during a mission to Mars to unlock a few of those mysteries.

Brigid Baptiste and Brewster Philboyd had worked feverishly to construct a third one, but with expanded capabilities. They had completed Interphaser Version 2.5 a couple of years before.

Brigid turned toward a computer station. "I'll review the Parallax Points log and look for a set of coordinates that correspond with our destination."

"If Xibalba was a sacred site," Lakesh said, "then there should be vortex points all over the vicinity."

She pulled out a chair and sat down, saying, "This could take a while, so you might as well go brief Sindri and his pal."

"I'm sure the sawed-off son of a bitch will be overjoyed to know that he's made suckers out of us again," Grant muttered darkly.

Chapter 17

They tumbled through a writhing tunnel made of ribbons of raw energy. For a long, terrifying moment, they felt their bodies dissolve, then re-form.

A raging torrent of light, wild plumes and whorling spindrifts swirled like a whirlpool, glowing filaments that congealed and stretched outward into the black gulfs of space.

Streaks of gray and dark blue became interspersed with the colorful swirls. Bursts of light flared in garish displays on the tunnel walls. They felt themselves plummeting through an alternately brightly lit and shadow-shrouded abyss, an endless fall into infinity. They were conscious of a half instant of whirling vertigo as if they hurtled a vast distance at blinding speed.

Then, the sensation of a free-fall lessened. Slowly, as if veils were being drawn away one by one, the darker colors on the tunnel walls deepened and collected ahead of them into a pool of shimmering radiance.

Brigid, Kane and Grant stepped out of the energy field. Sindri and Crawler stumbled out of it, lurching awkwardly across a broad stone surface.

The cascade of light whirled and spun like a diminishing cyclone, shedding sparks and thread-thin static discharges. As quickly as it appeared, the glowing cone vanished, as if it had been sucked back into the apex of the interphaser.

Kane and Grant automatically dropped into crouches. Pungent smoke caught them by the throat and set them to coughing. Kane's eyes stung and watered. He blinked repeatedly. Clearing his vision with the heel of his left hand, at first he saw only flames and for a wild, disoriented moment he feared the interphaser had malfunctioned and dropped them into the gullet of a volcano. Despite his shadow suit, he felt intense heat. He glimpsed his four companions gaping around in stupefied shock. Even Brigid looked bewildered, which was unusual for her.

Due to her many years as an archivist in the Cobaltville Historical Division, Brigid had worked hard at perfecting a poker face. Since archivists were always watched, she had worked diligently to develop a persona that was cool calm, unflappable and immutable. She looked anything but cool and calm at the moment.

Trying to tamp down his confusion and to keep from succumbing completely to a coughing fit, Kane looked around and concluded they had phased onto an elevated stone altar beneath an arching, wooden-beamed roof. Shaped much like the geodetic marker in Harappa, the stone was elaborately engraved.

Through the veils of smoke he glimpsed square columns on either side of the altar, deeply inscribed with relief carvings of people and animals.

The fierce heat drew sweat out of all of them. Kane almost felt as if the exposed skin of his face shriveled under its touch. If not for the shadow suits all of them wore, including Crawler, they would have incurred second-degree burns within seconds of completing the transit.

"Where the fuck are we?" Grant demanded hoarsely.

Brigid snatched up the interphaser but didn't waste time putting it in the carrying case. "We'll only find out once we leave this barbecue pit!"

Kane stepped down from the altar, working his shoulders beneath the straps of the backpack. He heard a shout from somewhere in the roiling vapors and his Sin Eater popped up from its holster, the butt slapping solidly into his waiting palm. He husked out, "I think we're in a temple."

Covering his mouth a black-gloved hand, Sindri coughed and half gasped, "A temple where?"

Kane moved forward, not answering. Smoke, thick and suffocating, swirled around him, blinding him for a moment. His left boot struck something on the floor and he glanced down, wiping at his stinging eyes. A dead man lay at his feet. He was copper skinned, and a wool cloak lay over his shoulders like a poncho. His face looked strangely aristocratic, and his black hair was bound with double twist of gold wire. Between the strands glinted the beads of fire opals. His eyes were open and staring sightlessly up at the smoke-shrouded and flame-wreathed ceiling timbers.

The man's chest bore a gaping cavity surrounded by a spattered pattern of blood. Kane leaned down, looking into the wound. Brigid's voice, raised in a frightened outcry, commanded his attention. "Look out!"

He glanced up just as half of a burning rafter sagged, splintered and fell from the ceiling. He skipped aside as the timber crashed down with a thunderous explosion of smoke and a sleet-storm of orange embers, forming a flaming barrier between him and his companions.

In the echoes of the crash, a woman screamed. Kane peered through the shifting wreaths of smoke and barely made out a square opening a score of yards away. Shadows flitted to and fro on the other side of the portal. At the same time, he became conscious of a loud tumult— the clash and clangor of metal against metal, men howling in pain and fury, children shrieking and women weeping. Male voices bellowed orders in a language Kane thought sounded like English, but he couldn't be sure.

The woman screamed again, her outcry full of anger, the word "Itzaman!" repeated over and over.

Heeling around, throat feeling raw from inhaling the smoke, Kane saw two people writhing on a small stone altar on the far side of the temple. By squinting through the eye-stinging haze, he barely made out the form of a woman bent half over the flat top, a long, lacy robe of filigreed gold and silver flung up over her upper body.

The face she turned over a shoulder was locked in a grimace, tears glistening on her cheeks.

A man stood behind her, clutching her hips with blood-wet fingers. At his feet lay a bronze-hued helmet, a kilt-like garment and a plaited leather belt. Although short, he was strongly built; he easily held the woman down.

Kane did not stop to think. Reaching the altar in one long-legged bound, he raked the barrel of his Sin Eater against the back of the rapist's black-haired head, where his skull joined his nape. The thudding of metal against bone was very loud, even over the crackle of flames.

The man grunted only once before toppling backward like a felled tree. Kane pulled the woman to her feet, considerately arranging her torn mantle to fall over her lower body. She stared up at in him in terror, then wild bewilderment as if she doubted her sanity. Kane stared a little himself. She was as lovely a young woman as he had ever seen.

She was under medium height, her complexion coppery, her dark almond eyes very wide, her lips full. A tousled mane of black hair, thick and lustrous, spilled over her shoulders. On her brow she wore a twin of the golden wire and fire opal diadem as the dead man.

The woman wore no other jewelry, but golden bracelets encircled her slender wrists. They were connected to golden chains, which in turn connected her to the altar by a thick metal staple driven deep into the stone surface.

The woman opened her mouth either to speak or to

scream, then shut it again when Grant, Brigid, Sindri and Crawler appeared out of the billowing smoke, materializing like night-colored apparitions. All of them were soot-streaked and laboring for breath. Crawler, being closest to the floor, displayed little respiratory distress, but he looked genuinely frightened. Sindri, however, maintained a neutral expression.

"Who the hell is that woman?" Sindri demanded with impatient asperity.

"I have no idea," Kane retorted. "We just met."

Experimentally, he tugged on the chains, pulling them taut against the staple. Leveling his Sin Eater at it, he said, "Watch your eyes" before realizing the woman would not understand him.

To his surprise, she did as he said, turning away and shielding her face with her hands. Kane took careful aim and tapped the trigger stud. The 245-grain round punched a crater in the altar's surface, knocking loose the staple with a spurt of rock dust. The woman quickly reeled in the chain's slack, wrapping them around her bracelets.

"Thank you," she said, speaking not just in English but with the crisp and ear-pleasing enunciation of the well-educated British.

Brigid stared at her in surprise, but before she could respond, a burning rafter crashed down close by, spattering them with sparks. The young woman flinched instinctively, pressing up against Kane. A second later a great stone fell from the ceiling and smashed into several pieces on the floor.

"Time to be going," Grant announced curtly, fanning floating sparks away from his face.

"This way," the woman said, wrapping the chains around her wrists and forearms. Before plunging into the smoke, she pursed her lips and spit on the slack, up-turned face of her would-be rapist.

As the five outlanders followed her, the smoke became thinner and the visibility improved. The heat seemed to sear their lungs with every inhalation, so all of them tried not to breathe deeply. Brigid cradled the interphaser within her arms.

Suddenly, they felt a touch of fresh air from their right and they moved toward it, pushing through a cloud of smoke and into a narrow passage that led to an open doorway. Beyond it the sound of strife and the clangor of battle could only dimly be heard, as if the conflict had moved out of earshot.

The woman paused, apparently hesitant about exiting a temple on fire into a war zone. Behind them the ceiling stones and support beams began crashing down with eardrum-compressing impacts and whooshes of flame. Whipping tongues of fire lashed through the passageway toward them, and Crawler cried out in pain and fear.

"Can't we get the hell out of here?" he squawked.

Kane pushed past the woman to take the lead. During his years as a Cobaltville Magistrate, he almost always assumed the position of point man. When stealth was required, he could be a silent, almost graceful wraith. In a dangerous setting, his senses became uncannily acute, sharply tuned to every nuance of any environment. It was a prerequisite for survival he had learned in a hard school.

The sound of steel ringing on steel faded. Kane cautiously edged out, glancing first to the left, then to the right, then up. He saw a narrow band of star-speckled night above a treeline and felt a clammy hint of a humid breeze against his exposed face. After the blast-furnace intensity of the temple, it felt as bracing as a sharp polar wind.

Kane stood in a narrow lane between the rear of the temple and a structure made out of woven reeds and wooden latticework. Half a dozen bodies lay on the ground, fresh blood streaming into a flagstone gutter.

The woman sidled around him, announcing brusquely, "We cannot stay here. We must take our chances. Come."

She turned right and, after gesturing for his companions to follow, Kane fell into step behind her. Within a handful of seconds, the roof of the temple collapsed with a shuddering crash, turning the entire temple into a pyre of blackened stone and blazing wooden timbers. The breeze snatched up the floating embers and cast them like a swarm of fireflies onto the straw-thatched roof of the adjacent building. The bright red sparks instantly ate at the reeds, smoke crawling upward.

As the six people navigated the lane, Kane gave the bodies quick visual examinations, noting they had died brutally by bladed weapons. Thick blood, black in the dim light, still streamed from deep stab wounds and slashes. Two of the corpses wore bronze-hued helmets and strange vests over black leather jerkins. The vests resembled collections of flat wafers made of volcanic glass or murky crystal to form a type of body armor. Swords of the same substance lay near their bodies. All their fingers looked to have been dipped in red dye to the second knuckle.

One of the men seemed to have died under a heavy ax. It had sheared through his helmet, splitting it in two and cleaving the skull beneath very nearly to the man's chin. The halves of the helmet still clung to the blood-matted and brain-clotted hair. On impulse Kane picked up the forepiece, pulling it free with a sticky smack.

The faceplate, made of a layer of thin, flattened bronze, was fashioned to resemble a skull. The crest sported a plume of blue feathers and the sides were adorned with elaborate, curlicue-spiral designs. Little inlaid white enamel tiles represented bared teeth.

Kane passed it behind him to Brigid. "What do you make of this, Baptiste?"

She gave it a swift appraisal. "Definitely Mayan influence. Old Empire."

The robed woman paused briefly to bend over a man's body, then she moved on, shaking her head in regret. Kane noted his chest was mutilated in a manner similar to the corpse he had seen in the temple. He wore a pleated kirtle but no helmet, only a short woolen mantle similar to that worn by the dead man in the temple.

A small shield was strapped to his right forearm. Despite the dim light, Kane saw how the metal boss was embellished with a curious design. It resembled a ziggurat topped by a grinning human skull but possessing a pair of staring eyeballs.

As the woman continued walking quickly down the lane, they passed rows of dark adobe houses with overhanging roofs. All of the buildings looked deserted, some with broken-down doors and rattan furniture scattered around outside. Kane figured the occupants had either been slain in an attack or managed to flee.

The lane opened up at a small plaza surrounded by the straw-and-latticework buildings. Pure white stones formed a path to a fountain in the center. It looked very much of out of place.

A statue of a nude, slender young woman poured water from a carved representation of a basket into a stone reservoir. The sides were decorated with glyphs and pictograms that resembled those Kane had seen during his first visit to Amazonia years before. Parrotbeaked, winged animals crawled in chiseled relief over the surface. A pair of stelae carved with fantastic leering faces rose on either side of the fountain.

Staring at the sculpture of the girl, Kane realized the similarity between it and the flesh-and-blood woman standing before him was uncannily exact. As she started to step out into the square, she hesitated and murmured, "Something is not right."

"That's a fairly sound assessment of the situation." Kane commented lowly.

The young woman swung her head up and around, staring at him over a bare shoulder. "Just who are you?"

The tone of her voice was not overtly hostile, but it sounded a far cry from friendly, much less grateful. Despite her youth, the woman carried herself with an aristocratic maturity that reminded him uneasily of the Devi Juballah's manner.

Kane pointed to himself, then to his companions. "My name is Kane. This is Brigid Baptiste, Grant, Crawler and Sindri."

As the introductions were made, the woman's brown eyes flitted to each face, rested on them momentarily as if to commit them to memory, then moved on. "Unusual names, but then you are a very unusual group. Outlanders, I presume."

Brigid, who had taken advantage of the pause to pack away the interphaser in its cushioned carrying case, acknowledged her observation with a smile. "You presume correctly. And you are?"

"My name is Ixchel."

Brigid's eyes widened. "And you say our names are unusual? I don't believe I've ever met anyone named after the Mayan goddess of weaving, fertility and childbirth before. How is it you speak English?"

Ixchel frowned slightly. "How is it that you do, with such a flat tonality?"

"It's the tongue of our land," Grant rumbled.

"As it is mine...or at least the tongue of my father who named me."

"Father?" Kane echoed.

With an impatient toss of her head, Ixchel turned away. "Yes…my full name is Ixchel Isabella Fawcett."

Chapter 18

They entered the plaza, Ixchel looking around alertly, her movements careful and stealthy. Kane couldn't help but admire her firm rear end beneath the thin fabric of her robe.

"Can you tell us where we are?" Brigid asked.

The woman gestured autocratically, impatiently, the length of chain clinking against her bracelets. "Later we will talk," she whispered. "Now is not the time."

Ixchel reached the fountain first, scanned the ground, picked up a large stone and slammed it against the rim of the reservoir in a one-two, one-two-three rhythm.

Alarmed and confused, Kane demanded, "What are you doing?"

Ixchel whirled on him, face contorted in grief, anger and fear. "*Later,* I said!"

Underscoring her fierce whisper, Kane detected a note of hysteria. He realized she was younger than he first guessed and maintained a semblance of self-control by the most fragile of threads. Her torn, low-cut robe nearly exposed her full breasts. When she saw Kane's glance, she hastily gathered it around her shoulders and spun away.

Moonlight, blurred by ash and drifting smoke, provided an unreliable source of illumination, but it was sufficient for the five outlanders to see a slab of cobblestones near the fountain shift sideways with a grating crunch.

Kane began to raise his Sin Eater, but Ixchel stepped away from the reservoir as the thick slab slid aside, pushed from below. Reaching down, she helped people climb up out of the dark opening. Men came first, soldiers by the look of them. They carried small shields, long, black-bladed knives, bows and short-hafted axes that sported razor-edged flakes of obsidian. They were weary men, begrimed and bloody from hard fighting, many of them heavily bandaged. Women and children followed them out of the opening.

All of the people were copper-dark of complexion and of moderate height, the men smoothly muscular, the women slender. The men wore mantles covered in bright geometrical patterns, but the women were naked except for loincloths and beaded anklets. Their features held a grave, stoic cast reminiscent of Sky Dog's band of Lakota and Cheyenne. Kane counted about thirty of them.

When the warriors caught sight of the five black-clad outlanders standing at the fountain, they jerked in surprise, lifting their weapons. Ixchel interposed quickly, "No, they don't mean us any harm—at least I don't think so. I called upon Itzaman right before they appeared. That one—" she pointed to Kane "—saved me from defilement."

The gazes directed at him made him feel distinctly uneasy, even though they lowered their swords and axes. Awe shone in their dark eyes, even glints of fear.

An old man stepped out from the crowd, wearing a long robe of fleece, his white hair gold-banded like Ixchel's. He looked Kane and up and down with a somber expression on his seamed face.

At length he said, "This chap doesn't look like a servant of Itzaman to me." Like Ixchel, he spoke with a cultured British accent.

"That's because I'm not," Kane retorted. "Who might you be?"

The man bowed his head courteously. "I am Metemphoc Rutherford."

The odd juxtaposition of names brought a smile to Kane's lips. "Are you the chief or the shaman?"

The man's wrinkled face creased in a toothless grin. "Oh, heavens no. You might say I'm a...gentlemen's gentleman."

In a voice pitched low to disguise the sob in it, Ixchel laid a hand on the old man's arm. "Metemphoc, your master, Ptalucan, is dead. Murdered at his prayers, his heart torn out."

The man's only reaction was to close his eyes; otherwise, he didn't move.

Sindri pushed himself forward, saying in a loud, aggressively impatient voice, "Since we all speak the same language, will any of you tell us where the fuck we are and what the fuck is going on?"

Brigid hissed, "Shut up!" but the little man affected not to hear her.

Metemphoc, his eyes still closed, intoned, "You are in the city of Tulixin."

Sindri stiffened. "Not Xibalba?"

Metemphoc's eyes snapped wide. The faces of the people who had overheard the question registered surprise, then outright suspicion. Sword blades lifted and this time, they didn't lower.

Grant sidemouthed to Brigid, "That apparently isn't a very popular place to go to or be from around here."

Ixchel's relentless eyes bored in on Sindri. "How do you know that word—how do you know of that place?"

Sindri sidled swiftly between Brigid and Kane, then took up a position behind Grant's tree-trunk legs. Grant glanced down at the little man disdainfully. "Hell of a time for you get shy, pissant."

"I command you to tell me!" Ixchel cried, voice ragged. "Are you of the League of Cizin, in service to the lords of Xibalba?"

Kane opened to his mouth to answer, realized he really didn't understand the question and cast a glance at Brigid. "Do you know what she's talking about, Baptiste?"

Brigid stepped forward, standing beside Kane. In a strong, clear voice, "We're explorers from another country, not emissaries from the land of the dead. We came here to—"

Before she could say more, the dark lanes between the houses erupted with a cacophony of shrill screams and disgorged a horde of skull-faced men. For a wild, chaotic instant, Kane couldn't understand how Ixchel could have confused him and his companions with *real* emissaries from the land of the dead.

THE HOWLING WARRIORS who swarmed from the shadows wore feature-concealing helmets fashioned to look like macabrely grinning skulls, blue feathers streaming from the crests. Light glinted dully from vests of crystalline body armor over black jerkins. Most of them brandished swords that were double-edged with saw-tooths of crystal, and others wielded short-hafted spears and fist-sized glass spheres held in the pouches of leather slings.

The soldiers of Tulixin milled around uncertainly as the civilians screamed and began to run. They unlimbered their bows and let fly with only a few arrows into the ranks of the attackers, and the wooden shafts splintered against crystal-plated vests. The volley was so half-hearted, Kane figured they knew how ineffective the arrows would be against the body armor of the attackers.

He couldn't tell how many attackers there might be, but he knew the soldiers were outnumbered. Although reluctant to choose sides with so little information on which to base a decision, Kane doubted that adopting a neutral stance would accomplish anything. He knew from experience that declaring themselves noncombatants would most likely make them targets of both factions.

Pulling Ixchel toward him with his left hand and putting her behind him, he sighted swiftly with his Sin

Eater, achieved target acquisition and tapped the trigger stud.

The report of the pistol sounded like the breaking of a tree branch, many times amplified. The round caught a skull-helmeted man dead center in the chest, shattering several crystal wafers and crushing the clavicle beneath. The man left his feet, catapulting backward into several of his comrades, bowling them over.

The citizens, rather than being gratified by the death of an enemy, clapped hands over their ears and fell into a mindless panic. They raced pell-mell in all directions, jostling their own soldiers, knocking weapons from their hands, leaving terrified children to fend for themselves.

A flurry of lances arced through the air, and although they didn't find flesh and blood targets, Kane saw that the projectiles were little more than javelins, short-shafted with razor-sharp blades. They were fitted loosely into long wooden sleeve sockets and when thrown, the lancer retained the socket in his hand.

The village square filled up with running, screaming people. The defense put up by the Tulixin soldiers was disorganized and sporadic. They retreated toward the far side of the square without watching one another's backs or even taking the time to aim the arrows they let fly. One of the shafts passed so close by Kane's head, the vanes whipped his ear.

Kane and his friends instinctively drew together, forming a wedge. Kane took the point of the wedge,

Grant the left side and Brigid the right. Crawler, Sindri and Ixchel crouched down behind the fountain.

Simultaneously, the three Cerberus warriors opened fire, Grant and Kane with their Sin Eaters, Brigid with a Copperhead jammed against her shoulder.

A helmeted soldier's war cry became a gargled grunt as the 9 mm blockbusters from Grant's Sin Eater tore blood-bursting gouges in his throat and knocked him backward.

A dozen death's-head warriors rushed to the attack, still uttering wild screams. They apparently had a grasp of tactics. They spread out across the area, some trying to cut their quarry off from a retreat.

Three of the attackers paused to whirl the slings around their heads. They showered the Tulixin soldiers with a flurry of the small glass spheres, which burst with a semi-musical tinkle. Where each globe shattered, sheets of flame cascaded down.

The soldiers of Tulixin shrieked and fled, some of them beating desperately at the flames on their clothes. Kane instantly understood the means of setting the temple ablaze and felt a second's worth of admiration for the weapon's simple effectiveness. Another glass sphere broke, spreading a blanket of fire near the soldiers.

They milled around, bowling one another off their feet before turning en masse to stampede for the far side of the square. Bodies slammed into Kane, Brigid and Grant, forcing them out of formation and very nearly trampling them underfoot.

Kane felt a lance pluck at his hair, ripping a few strands out by the roots. Cursing, he leaped behind one of the stelae, his finger depressing the trigger of his Sin Eater. Three bullets hammered through the skull-face of the lancer, who was busily fitting another projectile into the throwing socket. The subsonic rounds cored easily through metal and bone, blowing out the back of his helmet in a gout of blood and brain matter. The man rocked back on his heels, dead before he hit the ground.

Grant managed to stay where he was, legs spread wide, feet planted firmly. He extended his right arm, holding his pistol steady by cupping the butt with his left hand. The autopistol hammered in a steady roar. He exercised no mercy, burning down the skull-faced killers, not stopping till the clip cycled dry. Five corpses lay in bloody, limb-twisted heaps.

Grant quickly changed magazines, outfitting the Sin Eater with another clip. It clicked solidly into place, then he shot the bolt and chambered the top round. He twisted his body in a painful contortion as a glass-tipped lance passed very close by him. It sank into the ground beside his left foot and stuck there, quivering.

Raising his pistol, he squeezed the trigger stud and a 245-grain hollowpoint pounded into the abdomen of a skull-helmeted lancer. The masked man went over backward, bent double around his belly wound and voicing a very human howl of agony. The wooden throwing socket spun from his hand.

Brigid dropped to her knees behind the fountain's

reservoir, and her subgun rattled in short, staccato bursts as she chose her targets carefully. A pair of slugs hit a man who charged a weeping child, ripping into his crystal-armored abdomen, sending him sprawling, his sword clattering across the cobblestones.

Ixchel bounded from cover, swept the boy up in her arms and bore him back to the fountain.

A keening death's-head raced directly for her position, whirling his sling over his head. Shifting the barrel of his Sin Eater from his left-to-right pattern of fire, Grant squeezed off a single shot. The round shattered the fire globe in the sling and, for a microsecond, the village square was haloed in a red flash as the contents of the other glass spheres he had about his body ignited. Flying tongues of flame billowed outward and engulfed the man and three warriors near him.

They thrashed in wild, blind agony, screaming as they tried to beat out the flames on their clothes and hair. Grant fired a triburst at them, the impacts knocking them down, their limbs twisting and convulsing. The air reeked with the sweetish odor of seared human flesh.

Brigid looked past the reservoir of the fountain and glimpsed a pair of the helmeted warriors rushing toward Sindri, Ixchel and Crawler's position from the rear, swords held in double-fisted grips.

She stroked the trigger of the Copperhead, her first burst striking a man full in his skull-face. Her next three shots were a little low, blowing a piece out of the thigh of the other man. Instantly correcting her aim, she put another trio of rounds through his forehead. The back of the helmet bulged, a red mist squirting out through the seams of the headpiece.

Brigid didn't allow herself to feel remorse or horror. As always in a combat situation, her mind seemed to disengage from her emotions, her thoughts functioning in a matrix of reaction, observation and analysis. She did what was necessary to protect herself and her companions, no more and no less.

Inspired by the example set by the black-clad outlanders, the soldiers of Tulixin rallied, organizing a counterattack. The bowmen sent a hail of feathered bolts across the square and although the casualties among the enemy were few, Brigid glimpsed one man go down while clutching an arrow protruding from the right eyehole of his helmet.

Over the cracking reports of gunfire and shrill screams, they heard the repetitive bleat of a horn, bawling out a signal. In response to it, the skull-faced warriors began a retreat from the plaza, but a few seemed too stubborn to completely withdraw. Moving in a crouch, Brigid crept to the far side of the fountain. She sighted down the subgun's length, brought a quartet of skull-faced warriors into target acquisition and squeezed the trigger.

The firing pin clicked loudly on the empty chamber. With an inward groan, she recalled dispensing with the Copperhead's extended 30-round magazine, opting instead for the more manageable 14-bullet clip, which could be burned through in nothing flat.

She reached around behind her for the ammo-pouch at the small of her back, then she heard a voice raised in a wordless warning cry. Brigid twisted just in time to block a naked forearm and deflect the flash of a sword with the frame of her subgun. The crystalline blade clanged loudly against metal, tearing the Copperhead from her grasp.

Years of training sped desperate signals through her nerves as the blade looped back around, toward her face. Swiftly she raised her arms, crossing them to protect her eyes, depending on the tough fabric of the shadow suit to blunt the saw-tooth edge of the weapon. She uttered a short cry of shock and pain when the sword slashed a rent through her right sleeve, scoring the flesh beneath with a thin red line.

Catching the sword hand, Brigid fell back against the rim of the reservoir, ramming her leg in the direction of a groin that was only a guess beneath the heavy kilt. Her kick missed and she lost her balance. As she grappled with the death's-head warrior, the back of her head hit the pool of tepid water and a thickly callused, brutal hand clutched her face, pushing her down beneath the surface. She clamped her lips shut, hanging on to the man's wrist and heaved, struggling to lever herself out of the water.

The man held her under with a bullish strength, but he could not shake his sword hand free of Brigid's grip. Her lungs began to burn and she felt the tickle of water entering her nostrils. She knew she had only seconds before her mouth opened in automatic reflex.

Suddenly, the warrior's grasp on her face loosened and slipped away. She felt the man totter, then stagger backward. Still her clinging to his wrist, he inadvertently hauled her out of the reservoir. Raking her soaking hair away from her face, blinking the water from her eyes, she saw the man convulse, his free hand clawing at his back.

He uttered a gargling scream, sounding hollow and muffled beneath his helmet, and toppled forward. His visor struck the edge of the fountain with a gonging chime. Brigid released her grasp, snorting water from her nasal passages.

The pommel and half the length of a crystal-bladed sword protruded from the flesh of man's left shoulder blade, where his vest had been pulled up to expose his flesh, allowing the weapon to plunge into his heart from behind. Swaying, she looked down and saw Sindri standing right behind the warrior, his face locked into a mask of worry.

"Are you all right?" he asked, voice tight with anxiety. "The bastard didn't hurt you?"

Chapter 19

"Nasty goddamn thing," Grant commented gruffly, turning the sword over in his big hands, thumbing one of the crystal teeth protruding from the edge. "Feels as hard and as sharp as diamonds. No wonder it cut through Brigid's suit."

"Which begs the question," Kane asked, "how the things could be made without high-tech means."

Grant didn't reply, instead taking a long swallow from a water bottle he had removed from his pack. Several different kinds of MREs were in there, too, but his stomach fluttered with too much unspent adrenaline. He was, however, parched. As both men had reason to know, killing was thirst-making work.

The big room was dimly lit by burning bundles of reed rushes soaked in grease and clamped to posts set in tiled floor sockets. The walls were of latticework, which allowed the torch smoke to drift out and that from the smoldering remains of the temple to waft in. Sounds seeped in, as well—the piteous weeping of mourning women and the moans of the injured.

Less than an hour before, the skull-helmeted warriors had been routed, withdrawing into the treeline surrounding the village of Tulixin. They left their dead but killed as many of their wounded as they could, presumably so the villagers could not question or torture them.

After organizing a crew to attend to Tulixin's own causalities, Ixchel directed the Cerberus personnel to wait in a building that apparently served as a public meeting house, like a town hall. She had not made a request, but she stopped short of issuing a command.

So the five people sat on benches carved from single pieces of wood, like chipping blocks. Sindri, however, was too agitated to sit. He paced impatiently around the room as Kane and Grant looked over the crystal sword and Brigid performed an inventory on their equipment taken from the three packs.

The little man peered out through the open door at the sky just showing rose-pink hues of dawn and demanded, "Do any of you know where we are?"

"Somewhere in Amazonia," Brigid answered, holding up an electronic sextant. "I have a pretty good idea of exactly where, but we'll have to wait until daybreak so I can get an accurate reading."

Propping his elbows on the end of the bench upon which Brigid sat, Crawler asked calmly, "Can you give me a general idea?"

"I think we're pretty close to where we're supposed to be—on the border between Brazil and Bolivia. There are number of parallax points scattered throughout the Mato Grosso."

Kane hitched around toward her. "These people speak English, not Spanish or even an Indian dialect."

Brigid nodded thoughtfully. "That's not really as puzzling as it seems."

"You have a theory?"

She smiled wanly. "Of course."

"Of course," he grunted in mock exasperation. "Why should I even have to ask?"

He grinned crookedly to let Brigid know he was only joking and meant no offense. For a long time at the beginning of their relationship, it was very difficult for Kane and Brigid not to give offense to one another.

Both people had their individual gifts. Most of what was important to people in the postnuke world came easily to Kane—survival skills, prevailing in the face of adversity and cunning against enemies. But he could also be reckless, high-strung to the point of instability and given to fits of rage.

Brigid, on the other hand, was structured and ordered, with a brilliant analytical mind. However, her clinical nature, the cool scientific detachment upon which she prided herself sometimes blocked an understanding of the obvious human factor in any given situation.

Regardless of their contrasting personalities, Kane and Brigid worked very well as a team, playing on each other's strengths rather than contributing to their individual weaknesses. It had taken her nearly a year to grudgingly admit she learned a great deal from Kane, and from her association with Grant and Domi.

She had learned to accept risk as a part of her way of life, taking chances so that others might find the ground beneath their feet a little more secure. She didn't consider her attitude idealistic, but simply pragmatic. If she had learned anything from her friends, it was to regard death as a part of the challenge of existence, a fact that every man and woman had to face eventually.

She could accept it without humiliating herself, if it came as a result of her efforts to remove the yokes of the barons from the collective neck of humanity. Although she never spoke of it, certainly not to the outwardly cynical Kane, she had privately vowed to make the future a better, cleaner place than either the past or the present. She suspected he knew anyway.

"Since Ixchel claimed Fawcett is her surname," Brigid stated, "then it's apparent Percy and his party made it this far and survived long enough to build a community. They interbred with the indigenous peoples and their influence was so pervasive that English—good old English English—became the primary language."

"Very good," Ixchel announced as she stepped through the door. "I'm gratified that the outside world still remembers my great-great-great-grandfather's accomplishments."

She moved gracefully into the center of the big common room on sandaled feet, her determined eyes looking very hard, like chips of anthracite. Her sleek black hair was pulled back in a thick bun that emphasized her dignified features, her youthful curves sculpted under the flowing drapery of an apricot frock. The plunging neckline displayed a full cinnamon-hued cleavage. A golden chain around her neck swung between her breasts. She still wore the golden bracelets although the chains had been removed.

A pair of soldiers followed her, long hollow tubes held at angles over their chests. The blowguns were decorated with bits of gold and feathers. Their swart faces showed no expression, but their tense postures exuded apprehension, if not outright fear, of the five strangers.

Grant and Kane rose from the bench, nodding toward Ixchel respectfully. She regarded them imperiously. "How did you come to be here, in the temple?"

"That's a little hard to explain," Brigid answered hesitantly.

"I expect you to make the effort, nevertheless," Ixchel said stonily.

Bristling at the woman's tone, Brigid replied, "By way of a miniature quantum interphase transducer, version 2.5." She forced a wry smile to her face. "Is that of any use to you?"

In a low, grim tone, Ixchel said, "Do not seek to mock me, outlander woman."

"I wasn't," Brigid said. "But like I told you, our method of travel is a bit hard to explain. For the moment, just accept the fact we are here and we've come from far away."

Ixchel's lips twisted in a sneer. Imperiously, she de-

clared, "I can accept that, just like I accept you're all
consumed by equal measures of curiosity and greed."

Brigid arched an eyebrow. "You're about half right."

Ixchel shot her a glare. "Which half?"

"What do you have here to make anyone greedy?"
Brigid countered. "I don't see a whole lot of value."

The woman's eyelids fluttered in surprise, but before
she could reply, Brigid continued, "Or could it be that
just because we're outlanders, you conclude we're gold
or gem crazy?"

Ixchel nodded, full lips tight. "My people have been
taught for generations that anyone from the outside
cared only for material goods, such as silver and gold."

"You're not much for this eternally grateful thing, are
you?" Kane challenged.

"Why should I be?" she shot back. "You did what
you did to further your own ends. That's the way of the
outsider. If it would have benefited you to aid our enemies, you would have done so."

Sindri stepped forward, a calculatedly charming
smile creasing his face. "That may have been true once,
madam, but I can assure you it no longer is. Many things
have changed since the nukecaust."

"Nukecaust?" She eyed the people superciliously.
"Since the quickening, you mean? The time of great
purification?"

Kane nodded. "Some of us call it the nukecaust and
the skydark."

Ixchel frowned. "The what?"

"You've never heard of them?" Brigid asked.

Ixchel shook her head. "Those words are not in my people's lexicon of language. It's an arrogant assumption to think we would be familiar with your own local idiom."

Brigid figured that Ixchel and her people had been cut off from the outside world since long before the nuclear holocaust and so hadn't heard the common terms for the war and the nuclear winter that followed. Bleakly, she reflected that for some people and cultures, there wasn't an ending following the atomic Armageddon, only a new beginning.

Survivors and descendants of survivors tried to build enclaves of civilization around which a new human society could rally, but there were only so many people in the world, and few of these made either good pioneers or settlers.

It was far easier to wander, to lead the lives of nomads and scavengers, digging out stockpiles, caches of tools, weapons and technology laid down by the predark government as part of the COG, the Continuity of Government program, and building a power base on what was salvaged. The scavengers knew that true wealth did not lie in property or even the accruing of material possessions.

Those were only tools, the means to an end. They knew the true end lay in personal power. In order to gain it, the market value of power had to stabilize, to be measured in human blood—those who shed it and those who were more than willing to spill it.

Some of the scavengers used what they had found in the stockpiles and elsewhere to carve out fiefdoms, tiny islands of law and order amidst a sea of anarchy and chaos. They profited from the near annihilation of the human race, enjoying benefits and personal power that otherwise would have been denied them if the nukecaust had not happened.

Ixchel Fawcett apparently assumed the Cerberus party was of that same avaricious breed.

"I imagine there are a vast number of things and experiences that aren't in the lexicon of your people," Sindri said autocratically. "But you at least seem intelligent enough to understand new ideas and concepts...or is that an arrogant assumption, too?"

Ixchel's eyes flashed with anger, her lips working as if she intended to spit at him. "You overstep, little man. Who do you think you are?"

"I know that already," Sindri countered confidently. "It's the question of who *you* are that needs to be answered. Without our intervention, your village would even now lie in smoking ruins and you very well could be dead."

No one chided Sindri for his lack of diplomacy. Regardless of what Ixchel Fawcett thought about their true motives, he had spoken the truth.

The black-haired woman inhaled a deep, calming breath, her bosom straining at the bodice of her smock. She said contritely, "You're quite right. My manners have been execrable, but under the circumstances, I beg your understanding. After all, this was my wedding night. Not only was the ceremony disrupted, but my betrothed was murdered before my eyes and many of my family and friends were killed."

Despite Ixchel's crisp, almost matter-of-fact delivery, her eyes brimmed with tears and her underlip trembled with the effort to control her emotions.

Stepping forward, Brigid said softly, "You have our deepest sympathies, but please know that we are not here to bring harm to you or your people."

Ixchel nodded, struggling to compose herself. In a voice so faint it was barely a whisper, she said, "I was so terrified that I called upon Itzaman, our protector god, the god of justice. So when you—" she nodded toward Kane "—appeared, I thought at first you were an emissary, dispatched to save me."

"Only a matter of fortunate timing," Kane said with a reassuring smile. "For all of us, maybe."

Ixchel tried but failed to match his smile. "Perhaps. First tell me why you are here and then we can go back to the subject of how you managed such fortuitous timing."

Sindri turned to one of the equipment packs on the floor. He removed two PVC containers, unlatched the lids and from the foam-cushioned interiors brought forth the crystal skulls. The flickering firelight struck eerie reflections on the smooth quartz and violet amethyst.

Eyes widening in shock, Ixchel stepped back involuntarily. The two soldiers murmured indistinct words, but their tone was fearful. They edged toward the door, gripping the handles of their swords as if they half expected the skulls to fly from Sindri's hands to their throats.

In a strained voice touched by equal measures of awe and fear, Ixchel breathed, "Two tokens from the treasury of Ah Puch."

Her big eyes flitted from the skulls to Kane's face. "Perhaps you are an emissary of Itzaman, after all!"

Chapter 20

The blazing glory of dawn lit up the sky above the tree-line with cloud-mountains of flame. As the sun rose, the atmosphere quickly grew to feel like the interior of a greenhouse, heavy with humidity and overlaid with the rich odor of flowering vegetation.

All around the village loomed the forest, huge hardwood trees towering a hundred feet above the jungle floor. Brigid identified the mahogany tree, the kapok and the chico, the sweet sap of which was made into chewing gum. Flowering lianas hung from every branch and bough, and bright red orchids bloomed between the gnarled buttress roots of the giant trees.

Life swarmed and flapped among the thick canopy of leaves—cawing green parrots, toucans with grotesquely large, yellow and black bills, red-furred squirrels and brown howler monkeys. The trees resounded and echoed with the raucous calls, chitter and chatter of animals greeting the new day.

Ixchel Fawcett led the way up a short flight of steps and through the stone-linteled doorway of the largest building in Tulixin, positioned on the opposite side of the village from the temple. Sindri and Kane walked on her right, Grant and Brigid on her left and Crawler brought up the rear, scrabbling along between two soldiers.

The villagers eyed the procession with disapproval, murmuring truculently among themselves. Kane was glad he and his two friends had not been disarmed, particularly with the scenes of carnage they walked through. Daybreak disclosed the terrible aftermath of the battle. Gutted men and women lay where they had fallen, and flies already hovered above the congealed pools of blood.

Ixchel Fawcett ignored the living, as well as the dead as they approached the building. The structure was flat roofed and straight walled, and Brigid noted that although the stone slabs looked very thick, she could detect no signs of joints and seams in the blocks of dark rock. "How old is this place?" she asked.

Ixchel shook her head. "I have no idea. Its original foundation dates back at least a thousand years, to the time of Pacal Votan."

Brigid frowned. "Who?"

"He is revered as the chief engineer who guided the Mayan mission of inscripting stone monuments with precise astronomical and astrological information during his reign in the tenth *baktun*…which corresponds to the eighth century as Westerners reckon time. He was an acolyte of the Chilam Balam."

Sindri cast a slightly taunting glance at Brigid. "Don't tell me you've finally come across a topic which isn't stored in that photographic memory of yours, Miss Brigid."

Green eyes glinting with annoyance, Brigid snapped, "I never claimed to be an expert on everything, Sindri…unlike you. I suppose you're aware of this person?"

Sindri shrugged. "Pacal Votan was reputed to be a magician of time…even millennia ago, he allegedly put forth the concept that mathematics was a type of language that transcends the subjectivity of human verbal experience. His basic tenet was that all of life is ordered by the same basic, recurring patterns."

Ixchel glanced down at Sindri with new respect in her eyes. "You continue to surprise me."

Grant and Kane snorted at the same time, their wordless utterances echoing hollowly in the passageway. Grant commented snidely, "Yeah, he'll do that, all right…generally just when you start thinking you can trust his slagging miniass."

Sindri glowered at him but refrained from responding.

They entered a low-ceilinged room lighted by flames flickering from spherical stone bowls set at equidistant points about the floor. The chamber seemed bare at first glance, with no furnishings or carvings on the walls, and Kane inquired nonchalantly, "Kind of low-rent for a temple, isn't it?"

Ixchel shook her head. "It is not a temple. It is our museum…and in a way, our library. Our forefather established it."

She waved a hand to the left. Beside a narrow door-

way rose a life-size stone figure of a man, with a bearded
and mustached visage. The outlanders recognized the features and Brigid ventured, "Colonel Fawcett, I presume?"

Ixchel smiled wanly. "Yes, my great-great-great-
grandfather. His bones are interred here. He taught the
Mayan people he found in this place his language, and
he taught them much of the world beyond the village.
It's rather a good likeness of the colonel, don't you
think?"

Recalling the statue of the naked girl at the fountain,
Kane swept Ixchel with a brief, intense gaze. "You have
a very talented sculptor here."

"We do," she said simply and strode through the
doorway past the stone representation of Fawcett.

The five outlanders paused, then followed her into a
room lit by flames burning in half a dozen of the stone
bowls. The light glimmered from life-size golden figures of nude men and women, and although their sexual characteristics were exaggerated to a heroic scale,
their facial features looked far more Western than those
of the Tulixinans.

Ixchel gestured to them. "Our forefathers and moth-
ers who arrived here over 250 years ago."

Cunningly crafted statues of llamas, jaguars, serpents, leering demons and austere gods shone with an
auerate glow that would dazzled the eye if the light had
been brighter. Four statues were thick and blocky in the
old Mayan style. The head of the tallest figure was a
grinning skull, its empty eye sockets glaring at the peo-

ple in the chamber. It was identical to the carving of Ah Puch, the death god that Lakesh had identified two days before. The outlanders stared back, but in admiration of the simple magnificence of the artistry.

Sindri, his eyes wide and staring, husked out, "It looks like… Are they all made from gold?"

"Of course," Ixchel replied indifferently. "What gold the conquistadores didn't steal came here, many hundreds of years ago."

"I was under the impression Cortez and the Spaniards stole all of the Mayan fortune," Brigid said.

Ixchel made a dismissive gesture with one hand. "If so much gold could have been gathered in the years during the conquest by Cortez, then it stands to reason there was far more gold in an empire as far-flung as the Mayan. Our artisans preferred to work in it more than any other metal. Goldsmithing is a tradition among our people. Most of these statues are five hundred or more years in age."

"They're beautiful," Sindri said hoarsely, his tone equal measures of awe and envy. "I never saw anything like them."

"And you without your putty knife," Kane remarked sarcastically.

Grant stepped closer to the figures, and his breath seized in his throat when he spied a glistening sculpture that depicted a slender humanoid creature draped in robes. The facial features were sharp although minimalistic, the domed head disproportionately large and hairless.

The slanted eyes were huge and chilling in their fathomless quality. Cradled in its six-fingered hands was a shape that appeared to be a book. The slit of a mouth curved slightly upward in an insipid smile.

Trying to sound casual, Grant pointed to the statue and asked, "Is that one of your forefathers?"

Ixchel followed his hand and chuckled briefly. "In a way, I suppose. No, it's one of the prophets of Mayan history…the Jaguar Priest, Chilam Balam."

Kane and Brigid moved nearer to the collection of statues and Brigid murmured, "I suppose there's no more question of Balam and the Archons having influenced the cultures of Mesoamerica, is there?"

Kane shrugged. "There never was, as far as I was concerned."

Ultra-top-secret groups within the U.S. military and intelligence agencies applied the word "Archon" to Balam and his people. An old Gnostic term that described the guardians of spiritual planes, Archons were also reputed to be jailers of the divine spark within humanity.

After World War II, a pact was formed between elements in the United States government and the Archons, essentially a trade agreement for high-tech knowledge. Believing Balam and his people to be extraterrestrials, the so-called grays of popular modern legend, part of the exchange allowed the Archons use of technology developed by the Totality Concept.

Following the nuclear holocaust of 2001, Balam,

who claimed to represent the ruling council of his people, the Archon Directorate, intervened to prevent the rebuilding of a society analogous to the predark model.

A few years before, Balam revealed that the Archon Directorate existed only as appellations and myths created by the predark government agencies as control mechanisms. Lakesh referred to it as the Oz Effect, wherein a single vulnerable entity created the illusion of being the representative of an all-powerful body.

Of course Balam and his kind were known as Archons long before being code-named as such by either the military or intelligence agencies. Kane once again reflected that when it came to Balam, the only thing he could be sure of was that he could be sure of nothing.

Ixchel walked to the far side of the room toward a heap of material scattered over a table. It did not gleam or glisten. "This is also part of my people's history," she said bitterly.

She gestured to swords with blades of rusted steel, corroded copper casques from the era of the conquistadores and Spanish matchlocks. The outlanders saw revolvers and rifles manufactured in the past couple of hundred years.

"Some of these weapons were brought here by our forefathers," Ixchel continued. "Most of them are mementoes of my people's battle with the Spanish invaders."

"You said this place was also a library," Sindri stated.

Ixchel nodded and strode through a doorway on the

far side of the statuary collection. The chamber was larger, lit like the other room by flames dancing in stone spheres. The walls were lined with shelves of oversized leather-bound books, and Brigid eyed the bindings closely, barely able to discern the handwritten words, *Chronicles of Xibalba* .

"Who wrote those journals?" She asked.

"Members of my family, mainly," Ixchel answered. "And the descendants of the founding fathers who built the community around Xibalba."

Crawler scuttled closer, peering up at the tomes. "So it *does* exist. The land of the dead."

"Of course," said a quiet male voice.

The outlanders tensed, turning toward a shrouded figure standing in a shadowy corner. The bearded man who called himself Metemphoc Rutherford stepped out into the light.

"You remember Metemphoc," Ixchel said.

"The gentleman's gentleman," Sindri commented sardonically.

"And also something of the keeper of the archives here," the old man replied. "A librarian."

"Then you ought to have a lot of things in common with him," Kane sidemouthed to Brigid.

"How far are we from Xibalba?" Sindri asked.

Metemphoc smiled and said in his cultured voice, "Xibalba actually means 'one who disappears or vanishes.' In ancient Mayan, the derivation of Xibalba is from a root meaning 'to fear,' from which comes the name for a ghost or phantom. Xibalba was, then, the place of phantoms, of mist and mirage."

"Like purgatory?" Brigid inquired.

Metemphoc shook his head. "It was not a place of torment or a hell that served as the abode of a devil who presided over punishment. The idea of sin was weak in the Mayan mind. The entire notion of punishment for sin in a future state was unknown in pre-Christian American mythology."

Kane glanced back at the statues of nude men and women and grinned crookedly. "Which was one reason Fawcett liked it here so much, I imagine. No rules, no strictures, no conventions."

Ixchel smiled knowingly but sadly. "Very true. The Mayan behavior pattern that so attracted people of Colonel Fawcett's era was mercurial, individualistic, sensual and hedonistic."

Brigid eyed the nude statues of women and men with their bounteous breasts and pumped-up penises and asked wryly, "Are you implying that behavior pattern has changed?"

Ixchel glanced over at Kane, her sweeping lashes veiling her eyes. Almost shyly she admitted, "Much has changed, but some things here have not."

"Greed and lust are constants," Metemphoc said dolefully. "As you saw just a few hours ago."

"Who attacked you?" Grant asked. "Another tribe?"

Metemphoc shook his head. "There is no other tribe here. They were our own people."

Kane repressed a groan of weary exasperation. "Don't tell me we've jumped into the middle of another revolution, with one faction trying to take away what the other one has."

Ixchel regarded Kane gravely. "Hardly. Lord Cizin does not wish to overthrow Tulixin…he just wants to lay claim to a small part of it."

"What part is that?" Brigid asked.

Ixchel touched her left breast. "Me…or rather, my heart."

"He's in love with you?" Grant asked skeptically. "That's what the attack was all about… because you were getting married?"

Ixchel gazed at him reproachfully. "I spoke quite literally, Mr. Grant. Lord Cizin wants my heart. As I am a living goddess, he believes it is my holy obligation to freely surrender it during a sacrificial rite."

No one spoke for a long, awkward moment. Then Sindri cleared his throat and suggested, "Maybe you should start at the beginning."

Chapter 21

"The Mayan people," Metemphoc said, "so far as historical records show, were the first civilized people of Central America. They built great cities and two great flowerings of their civilization appeared, the first, or Old Empire, around A.D. 200 to 850, the second, or New Empire, from around A.D.1000 to 1350.

"The stimulus for the civilization of the New Empire was largely due to the influx of Nahuatl-speaking people from central Mexico who were either related to or descended from the Toltecs and had with them the new religion of Quetzalcoatl that translated into Mayan as Kukulkan."

"Heard of him," Kane commented dryly, rubbing his rib cage.

Brigid stood before the bookcases, eyeing the spines. She removed her wire-rimmed spectacles from a small pouch at her waist, slipped them on and reached out for a volume. She paused to cast a glance over her shoulder at the white-bearded man. "May I?"

He nodded graciously. "Please. Perhaps you might

be able to make sense of some of the more obscure passages written there."

As Brigid pulled the heavy tome from the shelf and carried it over to a table, Metemphoc continued, "By the sixteenth century, the Maya had fallen away from religion to a considerable degree, which probably was the main cause of the breakup of their civilization at that time. They were unable to put up a truly organized resistance against the Spanish invaders."

"Divide and conquer," Grant said dourly.

"Actually," Ixchel interjected, "despite the disunity of the city states, the Spanish under Hernando Cortez took several decades to subdue the Maya due to their determined resistance and their use of guerrilla tactics."

Metemphoc nodded, his expression one of deep sadness. "Many of the native peoples actually hated each other more than the Spaniards, whom they were prepared to help against their old enemies, thus contributing to their own subjugation. This happened in Guatemala under Pedro de Alvarado and in Honduras under Cristobal de Olid, both companions of Cortez."

While the old man spoke, Brigid scanned the pages of the big book, turning them over, her jade eyes flitting back and forth behind the rectangular lenses of her glasses.

"De Olid had tried to set himself up as king in Honduras, but Cortez, with only a small number of Spaniards and some Mexican auxiliaries, marched across the unknown interior of Yucatán to put down the rebellion. Cortez then sent Francisco de Montejo to conquer the remaining Mayan tribes of Yucatán and the cities of the north. His army was unsuccessful and so was a fleet sent around the other side of the peninsula, which was driven from its base at Chetumal to Ulua in Honduras with the Maya remaining in control by 1535.

"Montejo's son began a new campaign in 1542, also helped by feuds among the Maya. The northern cities were subdued by 1546 with tremendous slaughter and half a million Maya were sold as slaves."

Metemphoc sighed heavily, stroking his beard. "The Spaniards conquered the Aztecs around 1520, the Incas around 1530 and the Maya around 1550. They razed many native temples and palaces, and used the stones to build their own churches and other houses. The Indian cities that they occupied were rebuilt on a European grid pattern. Small settlements, like Tulixin here, were abandoned in the jungle and forgotten. The last major Mayan state finally fell to Martin de Ursaa in 1697."

Sounding impressed by the old man's font of knowledge, Sindri asked, "That was about the time the prophecies of Chilam Balam were translated into Latin, right?"

Metemphoc smiled fleetingly in appreciation. "Very much so. It was quite evident that Chilam Balam was not only warning the Indians of the bad days they would suffer under Spanish rule, but also giving them hope."

"Hope of what?" Kane asked.

"That one day their ancient glory would come back when an avatar arrived that heralded an event which would bring all the world into harmony."

Brigid glanced up from the open book, her gaze bright and penetrating. "I think I know who the avatar was…when Percy Fawcett found this little overlooked piece of the Mayan empire, the people naturally associated him with the prophecy."

Ixchel gave her a direct, challenging stare. "Shouldn't they have?"

Brigid tapped a yellowed page of parchment. "The colonel certainly thought so."

To Kane, the fountain-pen handwriting, cursive and florid, looked exceptionally difficult to read, but Brigid had apparently employed her speed-reading skills to whip through many pages of text. A surprisingly realistic sketch of two skulls caught his attention.

"What do you mean?" Grant asked.

"According to Fawcett's account, written a number of years after the fact, when the Mitchell-Hedges skull and the amethyst skull touched during a private showing to the Theosophist Society while he was in London, he received a vision."

"The hologram?" Crawler inquired.

"Apparently," Brigid said. "This is what he wrote—' The room seemed to vibrate and light and mist swirled in the air above the skulls. My fellow Theosophists flung themselves to the floor, as if they were plunged into the midst of some terrible natural disaster.

"The mist and light built to a crescendo of beauty and the spirit residing within the skull, perhaps that of the Jaguar Priest himself, showed me a holy spot where I was to settle and build a community, which would re-shape the world by harnessing the energy of Xibalba. The spirit of the skull had spoken, and I had no choice but to heed.'"

Kane snorted. Metemphoc and Ixchel regarded him bleakly, then the old man said quietly, "Yes, we are familiar with what is written in the chronicles."

"Some of it you may not completely understand," Brigid declared. "Fawcett and his party reached Tulixin first, guided by his so-called vision. The Mayan tribe here feared him at first, but he was just as familiar with the writings of Chilam Balam as their priesthood and he exploited their faith in the avatar prophecy. In fact, when he and his Theosophical Society colonists fully integrated themselves here, Fawcett reorganized the tribe around Mayan prophecy and myth."

"How so?" Grant asked.

Her lips quirked in a rueful smile. "Mainly by subjecting the people here to an intensive program of what amounted to self-esteem therapy. He and his fellow Theosophists taught the villagers they were all incarnations of some aspect or another of the pantheon of Mayan gods. Fawcett lists 166 gods, many of which were probably Mexican imports or alternative names for the same god. That began the tradition of naming the children after gods and goddesses and indoctrinating them to believe their deities manifested themselves in mortal vessels for preordained periods of time."

"Let me guess," Kane ventured. "Fawcett claimed the Big Boss God just happened to manifest inside of him."

Ignoring the flicker of anger in Ixchel's eyes, Brigid's smile widened. "Your guess is correct. He claimed to be the vessel of Itzaman and to curry favor with him was to ensure an exalted place in one of the thirteen heavens…and one of the first edicts of Itzaman was that English would become the native language of Tulixin."

"I think I can guess the second edict," Sindri said, throwing Ixchel a smile that had a hint of a leer in it. "And that was the comeliest lasses of the village would be his wives."

"You're not far wrong," Brigid said. "The Englishmen took native wives, but there were a number of non-Indian women the Theosophists brought with them, basically what were known back then as 'mail order brides.' The polygamous gods and goddesses were fruitful and multiplied, blending touches of Edwardian English culture with that of the traditional Mayan, with a dash of Theosophistical mysticism added as seasoning."

"Quite the con," Sindri commented admiringly.

"Yeah, you'd be the one to know," Grant grunted.

Reprovingly, Metemphoc Rutherford said, "You are casting the motivations of our forefathers in a rather unfavorable light."

Brigid smiled abashedly. "That's not my intent. Actually, I admire what Fawcett and his people managed to accomplish. The fact that you're still here and apparently thriving over two centuries after he began his social experiment shows his basic ideas were sound ones."

She gestured toward the gleaming golden statues in the adjoining chamber. "The colonel and his inner circle of Theosophists thought they did a pretty good job, too, judging by those monuments to themselves. They may have lacked a lot of twentieth-century amenities when they came here, but one thing they didn't have a short supply of was ego."

"What about Xibalba?" Crawler asked impatiently.

Tracing several lines of text with a fingertip, Brigid answered, "Fawcett pushed deeper into the interior, toward a mountainous valley. He writes that the air above it is misty and turbulent, and it was his opinion that's why no aircraft ever spied the pyramid."

"But he did?" Sindri moved eagerly to the table, squeezing himself between Brigid and the book.

"Of course he did," Ixchel said crossly. "I thought that was obvious."

"What's not obvious is why he didn't enter the structure," Brigid retorted.

"My own great-great-grandfather was with him on that mission," Metemphoc declared. "Clarence Rutherford wrote in his journal they could find no door, no manner of egress at all. He decided the pyramid was a holy shrine and not meant to be entered."

"Maybe," Brigid replied. "But Fawcett found what he believed to be a door of some sort, but unfortunately he didn't have the key."

Brigid lifted a page by a corner, preparing to turn it over, but Sindri pressed down on it, saying petulantly, "Wait, I'm not done."

Brigid slapped his hand sharply and he snatched it back with a short cry of outrage, glaring up at her accusingly. "That's a hell of a way to treat a man who saved your life."

"But it's not a hell of a way to treat a man who acts like a spoiled five-year-old," she shot back, turning the page over. "Grant, Kane…take a look at this."

Inscribed on the page in ink was a drawing of a free-standing archway rising from a tangle of undergrowth with carved stones and stelae around it. Kane, Grant and Brigid had seen similar arches before. In general shape, height and width, it resembled the linteled door frame in a predark cathedral.

"An Annunaki threshold," Grant intoned matter-of-factly.

"A what?" Sindri and Crawler demanded in unison.

"A means of point-to-point instantaneous transportation," Brigid said. "Thresholds were used by the Annunaki during their first occupation of Earth. It's possible the devices served as the templates for the mat-trans units of Project Cerberus."

"So you're saying the threshold is the only way into the pyramid?" Crawler asked.

The sunset-haired scholar lifted one shoulder in a shrug. "More than likely, yes. There wouldn't be one on the outside without another installed in the interior."

Her forehead showing lines of confusion, Ixchel glanced at the drawing in the book and said, "I've seen that arch at the Xibalba site, but I just assumed it was the doorway of an outbuilding that had fallen or burned down."

"Until we examine it," Brigid stated, "that's very well what it really might be."

Kane shook his head. "You don't believe that."

"No," Brigid retorted frankly. "But it's possible…not probable, not likely, but possible."

"You said Colonel Fawcett did not have a key," Metemphoc pointed out. "So even if he recognized the threshold, as you call it, for what you claim it to be, it would not have done him any good." He paused and added, "Or you, either."

Brigid pushed her spectacles up on her forehead and smiled at the old man with a trace of triumph on her lips. "I wouldn't say that."

"You have one?" Ixchel challenged.

Sindri suddenly laughed. "To be precise, I believe we have two."

Metemphoc and Ixchel stared at the outlanders with perplexed eyes. The old man opened his mouth to speak, but a sudden commotion of running feet in the adjoining chamber drew everyone's eyes.

One of the torch-bearing soldiers appeared in the doorway, panting heavily, both from exertion and fear. "Oh, my goddess—" He seemed unable to continue, gasping in great lungfuls of air.

Ixchel Fawcett stepped toward him. "What is it, Apol?"

The soldier swallowed hard and blurted, "Lord Cizin has returned. He awaits you outside…to go to him willingly or have your heart taken by force. He bids me tell you those are your only options, the newcomers notwithstanding."

Chapter 22

The citizenry of Tulixin milled about on the steps of the library. Although they maintained a facade of calm, their eyes and postures exuded fear.

A phalanx of soldiers jogged up, pushing through the crowd and forming a protective bulwark between them and Ixchel. A burly warrior, his head bound by a blood-encrusted bandage, announced, "It's Cizin right enough, Goddess. He brought along twenty of his mob with him, and there are probably more of the buggers hiding in the trees."

"Thank you, Lieutenant," Ixchel said. "I presume you saw to the establishment of a defensive perimeter."

The man nodded. "That I have. But so far Cizin hasn't made any hostile moves. He wants to talk to you—" he gestured with his blowgun toward Brigid, Kane and Grant "—and them."

The three Cerberus warriors had accompanied Ixchel, leaving Crawler and Sindri in the care of Metemphoc. "What does the bastard want to talk to us about?" Kane muttered.

Although Ixchel held her head at a regal, defiant

angle, her lips were the color of old ashes. In a voice so faint it was almost a whisper, she said, "I'm sure Cizin also wants to find out if Ptalucan is truly dead."

"Who is that again?" Grant asked.

Ixchel didn't look his way when she answered, "My husband-to-be. The objective of last night's attack was to keep the marriage ceremony from being completed and prevent the consummation upon the Altar of Tomorrow."

She inhaled a shuddery breath. "Metemphoc was Ptalucan's servant and mentor."

Brigid winced in sympathy, noting how young and vulnerable the woman looked at that moment.

Ixchel turned to face the three people. "There's no reason for you to meet with Cizin. I know what he wants...but I will do it if it delays another outbreak of violence even for a few hours. Will you come with me?"

Kane, Brigid and Grant knew they needed the opportunity to size up a potential adversary and nodded.

Ixchel led the way down the steps. As she strode through the village, it appeared as if most of the population lined the street, not speaking or even appearing to move.

"They're scared," Brigid said quietly.

"I don't blame them," Kane replied, checking to make sure the Copperhead hanging from his combat harness held an extended 30-round magazine.

"They're not frightened of Cizin," Ixchel said, still staring straight ahead. "He is a known quantity. They're afraid of you, of what you might bring down on them."

As they walked down the broad avenue, the Cerberus warriors looked around, receiving a better idea of the size and layout of Tulixin. In the distance, between a ribbon of fruit trees, they saw a glimmer of water and orderly fields of crops, cut through by irrigation channels. Split-rail fences contained livestock—pigs, llamas and sheep.

The soldiers marched in formation behind Ixchel and the outlanders. No one spoke and even the birds in the trees fell silent. The only sound was the steady tramp of feet. Once they had a relatively unobstructed view of the horizon, Grant paused long enough to take a sextant reading. The atmosphere, despite the fresh air and sunshine, felt ominously oppressive.

Ixchel spoke so suddenly, her voice startled Kane. "What you said about knowing a way into Xibalba—is it true?"

"We won't know for certain until we get there," Brigid answered. "But I think it's highly probable the archway is a threshold."

"So Xibalba is your ultimate destination?"

"It always was," Grant responded gruffly as he eyed the readouts on the electronic sextant-compass. "I'd judge we're only a day's journey away from it."

Ixchel neither confirmed nor denied his statement. "Why would you enter the pyramid? To loot?"

"The opposite actually," Kane answered irritably. "If the skulls we have came from there, then we'll be returning them."

Ixchel nodded. "Cizin—all of the men who have borne that name—believe that the pyramid is a giant container of the souls of our dead…that within its walls is the physical manifestation of our afterlife. Please do not make mention that it is anything other than that to Cizin."

"What's his connection to you?" Grant asked. "What's his fixation on your heart?"

She exhaled a slow breath. "It's complicated."

"We expect you to make the effort, nonetheless," Kane said sardonically.

Ixchel cut her eyes toward him, anger shining in their dark depths. Then a slow, shamed smile played over her lips. "I deserve that and I apologize for my earlier rudeness. To be blunt, the old Mayan religion practiced sacrificial rites that dealt with the surgical removal of the heart. During times of war, the Maya fought to gain captives, not for slaves but to provide hearts for sacrifices."

"So?" Brigid asked.

Ixchel nibbled nervously at her underlip. "The old Mayan belief is that all of life depends on blood. The Sun, after its nightly descent into the underworld of Xibalba, required blood to recover from the ordeal. And of course, there is no richer source of blood than the human heart."

Brigid's eyes abruptly glinted with comprehension. "Particularly if that heart belongs to the goddess of fertility."

The avenue suddenly ended at a broad plaza surrounding a well. Ixchel came to a halt, gesturing for the soldiers behind her to do the same. Some twenty yards distant a line of figures stood so motionless and silent they could have been statues.

Two dozen Mayan warriors stood shoulder-to-shoulder. In the tropical heat they had dispensed with the skull-shaped helmets, but they wore feathered headdresses, the gaudy plumage bright in the sunlight. Gold bands decorated their dusky arms. In their hands they carried crystal-tipped lances and blowguns. Their dark eyes regarded Ixchel and the three outlanders inscrutably.

A man stepped forward, a brass helmet tucked under his right arm and a polished bull's horn hung by a leather strap from his right shoulder. His bare chest sported dark blue geometric designs. Thick golden bands embedded with tiny ivory skulls encircled his upper arms. A metal collar bound the base of his neck and from it dangled little glass spheres fashioned to look like human eyeballs hanging from red strings. He stared dispassionately at Ixchel and said, "Took you long enough."

She snorted derisively. "I had to make up my mind if you were worth walking this far to talk to, Cizin."

Kane estimated Cizin's age at around forty. He was a little under six feet tall, as wiry as a whip with a hooked nose and unusual eyes of slate-gray. The skin of his face was dark, rough and leathery. A scar bisected his upper lip and several smaller scars marked his right cheek. Straight black hair clung tight to his scalp like a skullcap.

The man's eyes scanned the faces of the Cerberus warriors. "So you are the outsiders who sought to interfere in the affairs of the lords of death."

His voice was surprisingly mild, his tone nearly uninterested, as if he were discussing a topic he found incredibly boring, but he commented on it only to be polite. To Kane's ears, Cizin sounded as if he were imitating the laconic diction of the upper-class British he had heard spoken in old movies.

Adopting a similar tone of ennui, Kane replied, "There's another way to look at it, old boy—the lords of death interfered in *our* affairs."

Cizin's eyes flicked away from Kane and focused again on Ixchel. "You still wear the bracelets of promise…that is sacrilege, unless your marriage to Ptalucan wasn't consummated."

In a voice so thick with loathing it was a nearly incomprehensible snarl, Ixchel said, "You know it was not."

As Cizin's face registered satisfaction, she added venomously, "Nor was my defilement." She indicated Kane with a nod. "He saw to that."

Kane affected a modest shrug and smile. "My pleasure."

Cizin's eyes narrowed to slits. "Just who the bloody hell are you, where did you come from and what do you want here?"

With mock, wide-eyed innocence Brigid asked, "Oh, weren't we introduced? That was a terrible breach of etiquette. You may call me Brigid, and this is Grant and Kane. I believe you've already met Ixchel. Where we're from and what we're doing here isn't really relevant."

Cizin ignored the introductions and the sarcasm. Addressing Ixchel, he said, "You are only prolonging the inevitable outcome, you know."

"The only thing inevitable here is your descent into madness," Ixchel snapped angrily. "It's a part of your own deranged fantasies about your divinity and Xibalba."

Cizin stiffened. "Mind your tongue, woman, else I will have it ripped out before I take your heart. And speak not of Xibalba…you are no longer a goddess and have not the right to mention the sacred site."

Ixchel stared contemptuously at Cizin. "You give yourself away…no, I retract that. You merely confirm two things I and Ptalucan always knew about you—that you're a hypocrite and an opportunistic coward."

"Actually," Kane interjected helpfully, holding up three fingers, "that's *three* things."

Cizin cast him a hate-filled glare. When he replied, there was a deadly sincerity in his tone. "I remind you, Ixchel, that your term of being a goddess is over and I, Cizin, am in supreme authority."

The woman laughed. There was more hysteria in it than genuine defiance, but her effort impressed Kane. "Why do you persist in this farce? No one here has supreme authority! Not even I as Ixchel, the living goddess, has ever wielded that kind of power."

Cizin smiled, but it was a cold, transparent smile.

"We are bound by the destinies of the gods whose essence we bear, and ours are intertwined."

Ixchel's face twisted in revulsion. "It was my destiny as Ixchel to act for the pleasure of Cizin, but all those times I suffered your touch I fought to keep from vomiting! If I believed our destinies were truly intertwined, I would cut out my own heart."

Cizin took a lurching half step forward, lips peeling back from his discolored teeth in a snarl of rage. He came to a halt when three gun barrels, in the hands of Kane, Brigid and Grant snapped up, more or less simultaneously.

Struggling to tamp down his rising fury, he hissed, "Sacrilege, you speak sacrilege, woman."

Ixchel spit on the ground in utter disgust. "You claim to be in supreme authority and you dare to lecture me about speaking sacrilege? You have lied to and manipulated our soldiery so they, like you, can no longer tell the difference between delusion and reality."

Cizin inhaled deeply through his nostrils and bit out between clenched teeth, "I will show you reality, you temple whore."

He gestured behind him with a sweep of his left arm, and two of his feather-bedecked warriors stepped forward, carrying woven reed baskets. They placed them on the ground on either side of Cizin and moved back into line.

The moist flesh of the human hearts seemed to quiver and pulse with faint traces of life. Layers of dark brown, gummy blood covered them. The high humidity had prevented the blood from drying completely.

Kane's stomach slipped sideways, and Brigid uttered a short cry of horror and revulsion.

"These are the hearts of Tulixinian citizens and soldiers," Cizin declared matter-of-factly, "taken because you value your own so highly. Forfeit yours so I may make the proper pilgrimage and sacrifice to the souls within Xibalba. Then the violence will stop. I no more wish to take the hearts of our own people than you wish to see it done—but I have my duty as Cizin to fulfill as you had yours as Ixchel. However, you wish to renege on that final obligation. I cannot allow you to do that, else misfortune will fall upon our people and destroy all which we and our forefathers strove to build here."

In an eerily calm, detached tone, Ixchel said, "For five years I have served as the living vessel of the goddess Ixchel. I have twenty summers now of this incarnation and it is time for me to move on, to give up my divinity to another, which has been our way. It is past time for you to relinquish your role of Cizin, but you have become too besotted with the power of your position. Between the two of us, it is *you* who are reneging on the sacred vows."

Cizin did not seem to hear, or if he did, he did not care. "You have little time to make a decision. Be sure of one thing—I will return again and again and these foreign interlopers with whom you have allied yourself will not be able to stop me from doing what I must do." He pointed to the baskets. "I will add their hearts to those."

Putting the Copperhead to his shoulder and training the barrel on Cizin, Grant switched on the laser auto-targeter. He played a pinpoint of blood-hued light over the man's left pectoral.

"Just say the word," he growled to Ixchel, "and the office of death lord will become vacant."

Ixchel did not respond. Cizin glanced down at the targeting pipper, blooming bright on his chest, and he brushed at it dismissively, as if it were an insect crawling across his skin. He heeled away, presenting his back to Grant's gun bore. Instantly his warriors formed behind him and they marched out of the plaza.

Lowering his own weapon, Kane said curtly, "You should have given the word and saved yourself and your people more heartache."

Brigid grimaced at his morbid pun. "Ixchel, I know a bit about the Mayan culture, and how rulers were believed to be descendants of the gods and so their hearts made the ideal sacrifice, but even I have to confess I'm confused about what's going on here between you and Cizin."

Ixchel seemed lost in thought and did not reply for so long that Brigid almost repeated the question. Then the young woman swept the outlanders with a grim, determined gaze.

"Is it your intention to take the skulls to Xibalba and attempt to gain entrance?" she demanded.

Grant nodded brusquely. "We wouldn't be here otherwise."

Ixchel turned back toward the village. "I will guide you and I will ask only one thing in return."

"What's that?" Kane asked.

"I will tell you when—if—we make it inside the pyramid. We leave tomorrow at daybreak. Be ready."

Kane opened his mouth to ask another question, but Brigid said quietly, "That's probably about the best deal we'll get in this place."

"Do you really think we need her?" Grant rumbled distrustfully.

Brigid smiled wanly. "More than anything, I think we all need a good rest and some time to think."

Chapter 23

"It's too damn hot to think," Kane complained, wiping at the film of sweat on his face.

"And too damn noisy to rest," Grant said glumly.

The two men stood at the end of the wooden pier projecting into the brown waters of the Xingu River. The slanting sun cast heat that felt like acid on their exposed faces and drew sweat from their pores. It trickled down their necks and darkened the collars of their olive-green T-shirts.

Brigid Baptiste settled a long-visored cap on her head and showed discomfort only in a dewy film above her upper lip. Like her companions, she wore sunglasses, green camo pants, high-topped jump boots and a T-shirt.

They had removed the shadow suits the night before so they could bathe and forestall the inevitable rashes that came from wearing the one-piece garments for too many hours. Now all three people regretted divesting themselves of the climate-controlled suits, rashes notwithstanding. Even at half an hour past daybreak, the Amazonian air was oppressive with humidity.

A fifteen-foot-long dugout canoe bobbed gently on a tether in the river's current, bumping against a piling. They had stacked their ordnance cases, including the interphaser, neatly amidships and now they waited impatiently for the arrival of the rest of their party.

Consulting her wrist chron, Brigid frowned. "They're a little late."

Her hair hung down her back in a long braid, looking like a narrow flow of molten lava. "We're burning daylight."

"No," Kane retorted darkly. "Daylight is burning us."

He glanced behind him, first at the village barely visible through a grove of fruit trees and then to the rain forest. A dense screen of green decorated with looping, flowering lianas provided arboreal avenues for a screaming troop of howler monkeys.

"We can always get in the shade," Grant said, mopping sweat from his face and flicking it from his fingertips. "I feel like a nap."

Brigid arched an eyebrow above the right frame of her sunglasses. "In case you haven't noticed, it's barely dawn."

"I didn't sleep well," Grant admitted.

"Nightmare?" Kane inquired inanely.

"If you must know," Grant replied stiffly, "several of them."

"Yeah, me too," Kane said. "Ixchel's bedtime story didn't exactly soothe my nerves."

Brigid forced a smile to her face. "We've heard worse."

Neither man refuted her comment. In actuality, Ixchel
Fawcett's story was not as strange as many the three
Cerberus warriors had heard over the past few years.

The previous evening, after a ceremony honoring the
dead, Ixchel had related the background of her people's
society. Speaking in a calm, almost scholarly tone that
made the bizarre aspects sound almost deranged, Ixchel
told them how the little enclave of Mayan culture had
been nurtured and remolded by Fawcett and his fellow
Theosophists. They created a blending of ancient and
new, mundane and arcane wherein the pantheon of Old
Empire gods was reborn, both as personae to be worshiped and living examples to serve as inspirations.

People of Tulixin were selected, based on their birth
dates, genders and astrological houses, to bear the so-
called essences of the deities for a predetermined period
of time, usually no longer than five years. The Tulixinian citizenry chosen for these roles presided over all the
rituals and ceremonies associated with the individual
gods and goddesses whose names they bore.

During their period of service, they could consort
only with fellow members of the pantheon on the governing council. According to ancient Mayan lore, Ixchel, the goddess of fertility and childbirth, was the
wife of Cizin, one of the lords of death. The union symbolized the inextricable link between life and death.

Upon high holy days, Ixchel and Cizin would lead a
pilgrimage to Xibalba and engage in acts of ceremonial
procreation, to illustrate how life could spring from death.

When the term of Ixchel Fawcett's incarnation neared its end, she and her longtime lover, her high priest Ptalucan Whitley, made plans to marry. When Cizin was informed of this, he lodged many protests. Although he denied jealousy as a motive, Cizin still seemed unable to accept Ixchel's desire to be free of her role as goddess and live as a mortal.

Cizin undertook a lone pilgrimage to Xibalba, where he fasted and prayed for a fortnight at the foot of the pyramid. When he returned to Tulixin, he claimed the souls of their Mayan ancestors and English forefathers had bestowed upon him a vision of the future. He foresaw that their world would be destroyed if they did not revive the practice of human sacrifice, offering blood and hearts to their spirits.

However, he stated that the spirits would be satisfied with the heart of a goddess, that of Ixchel. But the spirits of Xibalba would accept her heart only while it still held the essence of divinity. Once she married, she would be mortal and her sacrifice would be spurned.

Ixchel instantly realized that Cizin was only cloaking his jealousy-fueled madness in the trappings of religious visions, setting up a situation where if he could not have her, no one could. While she still had the authority, she ordered him arrested, to be held until after her marriage was consummated.

Cizin, unfortunately, enjoyed the support of a number of like-minded members of the soldiery and priesthood. Swayed by his messianic proclamations of saving

Tulixin, a great many of them helped him to escape into the jungle, first looting the armory of weapons.

For weeks nothing was heard of Cizin or his followers. Then, during the wedding ceremony of Ixchel and Ptalucan, but before she would be ritualistically returned to mortal status upon the Altar of Tomorrow, Cizin's forces attacked, killing indiscriminately. Most of the Tuluxinians fled to their dry-well shelters in their homes, which led to escape tunnels beneath the village.

The Cerberus team arrived as Cizin's chief lieutenant, Cimil, was about to rape her, a symbolic act meant to defile her and brand her as the property of the lords of death.

Despite all of the complexities of religion and godly obligations, the foundation for the strife lay in nothing more than very mortal jealousy. Cizin wanted Ixchel. In their roles as god and goddess, she had played his wife during religious ceremonies, but Cizin had confused ritual with reality.

The story had disturbed the sleep of all three outlanders, filling them with fragments of dreams, some drawn from their imaginations, others springing from real experiences. Grant's slumber was so fitful, he was awakened by very faint chitterings that came from a corner of the hut. Lying in his hammock, he switched on his flashlight and saw four very black, very leathery bats hanging upside down from the wall. Under the light, they scuttled through an opening in the latticework and flapped out into the night.

Uncertain whether they were vampire bats or not, Grant decided it was futile to try to get back to sleep, particularly since it was nearly 4:00 A.M. He lay in his hammock for another fifteen minutes before rising to bathe and eat an unsatisfactory breakfast from their supply of MREs. As it was, as soon the first light of day peeped over the treeline, a chorus of hoots, chirps, clacks, howls and screams erupted from the forest.

He stood with Kane and Brigid upon the pier in the hot blast of early-morning sunlight and swallowed a yawn and a curse at the same time. Short-tempered by nature, Grant struggled to keep from plunging into a truly foul humor. He found himself half wishing Sindri would misbehave so he could take out his bad mood on him. At the moment, he wished he were anywhere else but where he was.

"Oh, you're here," a vibrant female voice said. "I feared you might oversleep, since I'd kept you up so late with my talking."

The outlanders turned to see a solemn-faced Ixchel approaching from the village, flanked by Sindri and Crawler. Upon glancing at the young woman, Kane felt his pulse speed up.

Ixchel Fawcett wore high-laced sandals and tight-fitting shorts that emphasized the ripe contours of her hips and rump. A blue cotton halter top held her firm breasts, and the gold chain danced between them. A red scarf bound her black hair. The golden bracelets were still upon her wrists, glinting in the sun. Every step she took bespoke a fatalistic resolve to complete an important objective.

Sindri wore a lightweight short-sleeved shirt and almost comically baggy khaki shorts, as well as hiking boots. The clothing apparently had been part of a child's wardrobe found in one of the Cerberus storage units, and not even Lakesh knew what it was doing there. He carried the containers holding the crystal skulls.

Crawler wore his abbreviated ensemble of leather harness and loincloth. Despite the heat, he seemed far more comfortable wearing it than the climate-controlled shadow suit.

As the three people joined the Cerberus warriors on the small dock, Kane observed, "There doesn't seem to be a bon-voyage committee."

"The less attention drawn to us the better," Ixchel said breezily. "As it is, if Cizin isn't aware of our expedition by now, he will be very soon."

"So you're sure he'll be coming after us?" Brigid inquired.

"Quite sure. To a dead, mortal certainty, I'm sure. An hour's head start is about the best we can hope for."

Sindri frowned, not caring for the implications. "So he'll be behind us all the way. Can you give us an idea of what's ahead of us?"

Ixchel smiled, but it didn't reach her eyes. "Jaguars and pumas, ocelots, tapirs, lizards, several venomous tropical snakes and piranha. Then there are the crocodiles."

"Caimans, you mean?" Brigid asked.

Ixchel shook her head and stepped lithely down into the canoe, ignoring Kane's proffered hand. "I mean crocodile and some of them are very, very large. But fortunately they're seldom seen."

"Sounds just like the kind of field trip we all enjoy," Grant grunted sourly. "The only thing that would improve on it would be some cannibals."

"Let's hope we don't run into the Yanomani, then," Ixchel said, settling herself astern.

"Why?" Crawler asked uneasily. "Will they eat us?"

"Probably not…but they'll most certainly take our heads."

Sindri reflexively hunched his shoulders, sinking his head between them. "Don't tell me…so they can shrink them?"

Kane snorted. "You could use a little head-reduction."

Sindri regarded him blankly. "Very glib, Mr. Kane."

"This sounds like another one-percent trip," Grant commented flatly.

Although Brigid and Kane smiled briefly in appreciation, Ixchel squinted up at them. "A what trip, Mr. Grant?"

He waved away her question, not wanting to explain the private piece of philosophy between him, Kane and Brigid that derived from the two men's long careers as Magistrates. Their half-serious belief was that ninety-nine percent of things that went awry could be predicted and compensated for in advance. But there was always a one-percent margin of error, and playing against that percentage could have lethal consequences.

"Well?" Ixchel challenged impatiently. "Are we going or not?"

Brigid eyed her closely. "Are you sure you're up to doing this, with what you just went through?"

Ixchel Fawcett met her steady gaze without blinking. Quietly, she answered, "Thank you for your concern, but I shall recover. A goddess always does."

Chapter 24

Sunlight filtered through the broad-leaved canopy, tinting everything with an emerald hue. Kane worked the paddle, grimacing at the way his sweat-soaked shirt pulled away from then re-adhered to his skin. He felt the physical weight not only of the heat and humidity but of the vast rain forest itself. The buttress roots of the giant hardwoods stretched out like gnarled tentacles to the river's edge. Because of their immense size, the trees were unable to send their roots very far into the ground and extended them outward instead.

Brigid maintained the canoe's position in the middle of the river with a long steering oar, trying to avoid low, overhanging tree branches. Ixchel had already warned them that venomous snakes, face-hugging spiders and even nasty-tempered, diseased monkeys had been known to drop down on unwary boaters.

The dugout wasn't an ungainly craft, despite its crude appearance, but even paddling downriver with the current was hard work. The moisture-saturated air was tainted with the muddy, tropical fecundity of the jungle that brooded on either side of the Xingu.

Within a couple of minutes of their leaving the pier, the river flowed in such twists and turns that the banks behind them seemed to merge together to form an impenetrable thicket of greenery, shutting off any sight of the village. With Grant in the bow, Kane and Brigid seated amidships, the canoe floated past overgrown islets and narrow-mouthed tributaries.

A black-scaled, yellow-striped caiman basked on the right-hand bank. Swiftly, it scuttled backward into the undergrowth when they paddled the dugout abreast of it. Its saurian eyes watched unblinkingly as the canoe went by.

"What do those things taste like?" Sindri asked.

"Like chicken," Ixchel answered blithely.

"What else?" Kane muttered under his breath.

A long-tailed red macaw flapped overhead, studying them with its wise, jade-ringed eyes. From its bright yellow beak issued a harsh, piercing cry, then it flapped away.

"What did that thing say?" Grant demanded, casting a glance over his shoulder at Brigid.

"How should I know?" she replied peevishly. "You think I speak parrotese?"

Kane refrained from commenting that if anyone aboard the boat did, it would be her. He kept his remarks to himself, deciding that a foul humor already predominated in the canoe.

His spirits lifted somewhat when the canoe pushed through a profusion of huge butterflies wheeling over the water. Their orange-and-yellow wings fluttered with an almost strobing effect as they darted and skittered through the alternating bands of shadow and shafts of greenish sunlight.

The river broadened to a hundred yards or more. After an hour of steady paddling and manuevering, they heard a faint ominous roar from around a bend. Ixchel announced, "Rough water ahead."

Within a minute, they entered a stretch of turbulent rapids, the dugout picking up speed as the prow clove through foaming white water. Brigid guided the canoe into the central cascade of the current while Kane and Grant, their biceps bulging, paddled and pushed the bow to port and starboard to avoid oncoming rocks. Spray drenched them, but since the river water was only slightly cooler than the air temperature, the relief was minimal.

The canoe lifted, fell and rose again, the jolts sending needles of pain lancing from the base of Kane's spine into the back of his neck. Sindri and Crawler clung to their equipment packs, keeping them from being bounced out into the river.

Once they were past the rapids, the muscle-weary Cerberus warriors turned over the piloting of the canoe to Sindri, Crawler and Ixchel. To Kane's surprise, none of the three protested, although Sindri, who took up the steering paddle, was very uncertain of what to do. Living most of his life on the arid plains of Mars had not made him much of an outdoorsman, but he gave a valiant effort. Ixchel offered instructions and words of encouragement.

The young woman's skill with the dugout was impressive but not really surprising. Even in America, outlanders, or anyone who chose to live outside baronial society or had that fate chosen for them, were a different sort from those bred within the walls of the nine villes.

Born into a raw, wild world, they were accustomed to living on the edge of death. Grim necessity had taught them the skills to survive, even thrive, in the postnuke environment. They may have been the great-great-great-grandchildren of civilized men and women, but they had no choice but to embrace lives of semibarbarism.

"How much farther?" Brigid asked Ixchel, taking off her cap and wiping at the layer of perspiration on the lining.

Arms working smoothly as she drove the paddle in and out of the water, the young woman answered, "We will not reach Xibalba today, but by late afternoon we should arrive at a permanent campsite established for people following the pilgrim path. We'll stay the night there and then finish the journey tomorrow morning."

Flexing his sore fingers, Kane cast her a glance, the surprise and suspicion he felt masked by his sunglasses. "Is that safe? Wouldn't that be the first place Cizin would think to look for us?"

"It's a holy site, a sacred spot," Ixchel replied. "To violate it would mean insulting the lords of Xibalba…the souls of those who do so will be banned from the afterlife for all eternity."

Sindri, his voice strained with exertion, half gasped, "That seems like a very risky proposition. If Cizin was really so concerned about observing holy rites and vows, he wouldn't have done what he did to you and your groom."

Ixchel nodded, her face expressionless. "Cizin thinks he is acting in accordance to a vision given to him by the lords of Xibalba."

"And who are they again?" Kane asked breezily. "Just in case we might run into them when we get to their crib."

Ixchel's strokes remained steady and a smile played over her lips. "The lords of Xibalba have their own separate dominions. There is Blood Gatherer, who draws blood from people. Pus Master and Jaundice Master cause people to swell, make pus seep from their legs, turn their faces yellow and cause jaundice.

"Then there is Bone Scepter and Skull Scepter who reduce people to bones and emaciate them to death. Trash Master and Stab Master, catch people who have trash on their door and stab them until they die. Wing and Packstrap cause people to die suddenly on the road. Last but of course not least are Bloody Teeth and Bloody Claws."

"Sounds like a nice bunch," Kane said dryly.

Ixchel lifted her brown shoulders in a resigned shrug. "Those are the lords of death, of Xibalba, whom Cizin believes have given him the vision."

"In which case," Grant pointed out, "he might think

he's been given a special dispensation to do whatever is necessary to fulfill the terms of the vision."

Ixchel blinked in surprise, the notion not having occurred to her before. She stopped paddling. After a thoughtful moment, she shook her head. "I don't think so. Cizin has lived for many years according to all the tenets and precepts of the lords of death. The laws of Xibalba have become as natural to him as breathing. He couldn't break his conditioning that easily."

"He already broke the taboo about human sacrifice," Brigid said tersely. "Violating a campground wouldn't be much of a step down."

Ixchel sighed. "Our religious rituals are elaborate— we have frequent festival occasions in honor of the gods of the winds, the rain, the cardinal points, the harvest, of birth, death and war. That's why the whole sphere of Mayan influence was dotted with temples, usually great stone pyramids, while certain sites, like the sacred city of Izamal and the pyramid of Xibalba, were places of pilgrimage."

"So?" Grant inquired impatiently.

"So, human sacrifice was forbidden by Kukulcan, and crept in only in later years. It was never a frequent or prominent feature of the Mayan culture except on occasion of some great national crisis."

Kane nodded in understanding. "And Cizin believes you're in the middle of great national crisis."

"Yes."

"Then you've just made our point," Sindri said, pausing in his paddling. Pushed by the current, the canoe began to slowly rotate in midriver. "None of the old rules apply."

"And even if they do," Kane declared, "all that means is Cizin and his boys will have to catch up to us before we reach the campsite."

Ixchel's eyes flickered with unease and she said quietly, "I've considered that, but I think that even if he learned of our journey and set off in pursuit, he wouldn't be able to overtake us before nightfall."

Crawler spoke for the first time, turning toward her, his sweat-pebbled brow furrowed. "I think you're very, very wrong."

Ixchel drew herself up haughtily. "And what is that judgment based on?"

With a solid thud, a crystal-tipped spear shaft miraculously appeared, quivering, in the thick hull of the canoe, barely six inches away from Sindri's right leg. He jerked convulsively to one side, a cry of shock bursting from his lips.

"On that," Crawler intoned calmly.

Chapter 25

The next twenty seconds were barely controlled chaos as Grant, Kane and Brigid snatched up guns, yelled orders and instructions.

"Somebody else take the paddle!" Sindri shouted.

"Stay where you are!" Grant bellowed, thumbing off the safety of his Copperhead.

"Everybody maintain your position and keep your head down," Kane said, putting his own subgun to his shoulder.

Ixchel's eyes flickered with fear, but she continued paddling frantically as did Crawler. Brigid worked the spear free, noting that the tip had sunk less than a quarter of an inch into the wood of the canoe, so the distance it traveled had been extreme.

"A lucky throw," she said, placing the projectile in the bottom of the boat and pulling her TP-9 autopistol free of its holster.

"Probably Cizin himself," Ixchel bit out. "He always had a magnificent eye."

Scanning the overgrown riverbanks behind them, Kane asked, "You sure it's him and his skull boys, not those Yanomani you mentioned?"

She ducked her head in a brusque nod. "Only the Tulixinians use crystal points."

Grant squinted, crouching near the stern. "I still don't see them."

"Good," Brigid said. "That means they can't see us."

"More rapids up ahead," Ixchel said. "Perhaps that will slow them down."

The Xingu widened and the current quickened as it rushed over half-submerged rocks, foamed brown and white and splashed over the canoe's prow. Brightly plumaged birds, disturbed in their perches among the great fronded trees overhanging the river, squawked angrily.

The paddles slashed in and out of the water in a frantic, fast rhythm.

Sindri gasped and strained over the long wooden handle. Strident yells wafted up the river from behind them. Jaw muscles bunched into knots, Ixchel grimly continued to work her paddle, sucking in great lungfuls of air, as she, Crawler and Sindri slid the flat wooden blades into the water, pulled and then mechanically repeated the motion.

The dugout entered a broad, straight span of open water, and harsh sunlight assaulted Kane's eyes as he stared behind them. Around the last bend came two canoes, both of them bearing six of Cizin's feather-bedecked warriors. Sunlight glinted from the tips of spears and swords. Kane estimated the boats were just a shade beyond the accurate range of the Copperheads.

Sindri's brow ran with sweat, and he squeezed his

eyes shut against the stinging stream. Hoarsely, he said, "I can't keep this up much longer!"

Kane gauged the distance once again and said, "Everybody take a breather."

He ignored the incredulous stares directed at him by his companions and snapped, "Do as I say. Stop paddling until I tell you to start again."

Sindri gusted out a sigh of relief and leaned on the wooden handle. Crawler and Ixchel withdrew their paddles from the water. Brigid cocked her head at him quizzically. "You've got some sort of plan, I take it?"

He showed her the edges of his teeth in a wolfish grin. "Some sort."

Kane's plan was a trifle ridiculous because it was such a long shot. It sprang full-blown into his mind in an instant. He decided to trust his instincts and seated the butt of the Copperhead against his shoulder, sighting down its short length.

The current carried their canoe a score of yards before the pursuers realized they were gaining on their quarry quickly. The warriors in the dugouts shouted in triumph and increased the speed and rhythm of their paddling.

As their two craft steadily closed the gap, one of the warriors stood up in the prow, cocking back his arm to cast a spear, tightly gripping the sleeve socket. His painted face split in a predatory grin.

Holding his breath, Kane squinted through the auto-targeter, centered the crosshairs on the man's forearm and squeezed the trigger. The report sounded like the breaking of a tree branch somewhere off in the jungle. The man clutched at his blood-spurting elbow joint, the spear and its socket sleeve spinning away into the brush along the riverbank. He tumbled headfirst over the side, into the Xingu. Crying out in dismay, the wounded man's fellow warriors hauled him back aboard. Blood spread out like a crimson smudge over the surface of the water. The water frothed and boiled around it.

"Discourage 'em," Kane said flatly. "Try to shoot to wound but discourage 'em."

He, Brigid and Grant opened up with their weapons, squeezing off shot after shot. Miniature waterspouts spumed in front of the canoes. Over the staccato drumming of the subguns and the cracks of Brigid's autopistol, they heard Cizin's voice lifted in frantic commands.

None of the Cerberus warriors wanted to shoot the Tulixinians—Grant and Kane had killed enough indigenous peoples in their years as Magistrates and preferred now to find alternatives to lethal force if possible.

The warriors began a desperate backwater maneuver, paddling against the current to slow their forward momentum. Bullets gouged sprays of splinters from the rims of the canoes and punched holes through the hulls.

A man cried out, slapping at his upper left shoulder. Convulsing, he twisted overboard, submerging completely in the river. As ripples spread, the water bubbled furiously. The man rose to the surface, his arms threshing in crazed semaphore motions. Silver-scaled, flat-bodied fish glistened on his hands, face and neck. They clung to his flesh by double rows of serrated, razor-keen teeth.

Uttering a gargling scream, the man clawed wildly at the piranha fastened to his face, trying to pry them away. As he shrieked, one of the carnivorous fish leaped from the water and sank its teeth into his tongue, instantly muffling his cries. The warrior rolled over and over, a red stain spreading around him in a cloud.

The Cerberus warriors ceased firing. "That ought to discourage the wedding-crashing bastards," Grant grunted.

Ixchel gazed worriedly over her shoulder. "Perhaps…or attract something far worse than a school of piranha."

Crawler glowered in her direction. "Which would be what again?"

Before she could form a reply, the river between the bodies swirled with sudden movement, wavelets forming and cresting. The Tulixinian warriors shouted in wordless terror, sliding their paddles in and out of the Xingu, attempting to turn their canoes around and row against the current.

Despite the heat, the back of Kane's neck flushed cold as a great sheet of water flew upward, crowned with foam. The body of the man beset by piranha abruptly vanished, snatched beneath the surface.

A heartbeat later, he reappeared, clutched at the hips between a pair of giant, fang-filled jaws. The creature only vaguely resembled the caiman they had glimpsed earlier. Dimly seen amid the churning waves created by its gargantuan body, the crocodile looked to measure at least forty feet from narrow snout to the tip of its lashing tail.

Its jaws were gigantic, nearly six feet long, with thick masses of scale-coated muscle swelling at the sides of its triangular head. Its armor-plated hide was of a repellant brown-black hue. The creature lifted the bloody, writhing warrior high above the surface of the river.

His legs kicked in a futile spasm as its jaws closed, the huge fangs shearing through flesh, crunching through bones. The upper half of the man's body splashed down into the Xingu. The lower half slid down the crocodile's gullet, swallowed in two snapping gulps.

A few warriors hurled spears at the monstrous, barrel-shaped body. All but one bounced off. The sharp point penetrated the scales shallowly and then fell away when the reptile turned its attention to the canoes.

Plunging his paddle into the water, Sindri said briskly, "I think we've rested for long enough."

No one laughed, but Ichel and Crawler followed his example, resuming their paddling with renewed vigor and determination. Gripped by a horrid fascination, Kane kept his eyes on the crocodile and the two canoes.

The creature dived under one of them and came up beneath it, pushing with its armored back. The craft tipped but did not capsize, although the men aboard it howled in terror and grasped the sides. Then their dugout rounded a small overgrown promontory and Kane saw no more of the struggle, but he heard panicky screams for another minute or so.

Repressing a shudder, Kane took the paddle from Ixchel. "I thought you said those crocs were seldom seen."

She nodded, relieved to hand the paddle to him. "Just because they're not seen often doesn't mean they're not around. If you had informed me of your plan, I would've mentioned that blood in the water was likely to attract any that might be in the vicinity."

Kane did not reply. He thrust the paddle into the river, very aware of Brigid's and Grant's eyes upon him. He had always prided himself on being free of phobias, but with a surge of shame he realized he had developed a fear of reptiles over the past few years. It wasn't an irrational fear, but derived from unpleasant experience.

Grant took Crawler's paddle. "Think Cizin and his men ended up as a croc buffet?"

Brigid shooed Sindri away from the stern and sat in his place, holding the long steering oar. "Even as big as that thing is, I doubt it could kill and eat them all."

"It certainly seemed big enough to do it," Sindri said contemplatively, rolling his shoulders. "Do you think it's a mutie?"

Brigid considered the question for a few seconds, then shook her head. "I don't know. The South American crocodile is definitely the largest species of crocodile, even bigger than the ones in the Nile River Valley. But as far as I know, their maximum length is twenty-three feet. This one was about twice that, so it could be a mutie strain."

Ixchel frowned. "What's a mutie?"

Crawler turned toward her, tapping his chest. "Me."

Ixchel's expression showed even more confusion, and Brigid said, "He means mutant, which is a term for life-forms whose DNA was rearranged."

"Like a form of evolution?"

"In a way," Brigid conceded, although she knew that negative mutations of the sort spawned by the nuclear holocaust played no part in evolution. Few of them lived long enough to reproduce.

However, one breed of human mutant that had increased since skydark was the so-called psi-mutie—people born with augmented extrasensory and precognitive mind powers. As Lakesh had said, those abilities weren't restricted to muties, since a few norms possessed them, as well, but generally speaking, nonmutated humans with advanced psionic powers were in the minority.

Because of Crawler's longevity, Brigid guessed his psi abilities derived from some form of mutation in his genetic material.

Lifting her gaze away from the dark surface of the river, she saw a broken line of distant mountains looming above the treeline. Over their peaks massed black thunderheads, and she glimpsed a flash of lightning within them.

Glancing over at Ixchel she asked, "Is that the Serra de Huanchaca?"

"Yes," the young woman replied. "The land of mists and mirage. We are making good time, but I think we should stop soon to rest and eat. There is a safe place not far from here."

Brigid didn't argue. The paddling had become so automatic she was barely conscious of the motions of her arms and shoulders anymore. But her muscles ached with a fiery insistence that grew worse with every passing second. The pain crept down her arms and settled into her wrists and metacarpal bones.

Their canoe rounded a hairpin turn, startling a lean jaguar that had come to the river's edge to drink. Snarling, the big spotted cat leaped through the brush and Brigid's eyes followed its fear-stricken flight automatically. She saw a small crescent of sand between the high grasses.

Ixchel pointed to it, announcing, "There."

They grounded the canoe, ignoring the parrots squawking and scolding them from the trees. Sitting in the shade provided by the overarching boughs, they ate from the MRE packs, drank sparingly from the bottled water and rested. Kane kept alert for any sight or sound of Cizin along the river, but after half an hour, he decided that the crocodile might have done more than just discourage the pursuit. Grant managed to nap, following the old Magistrate mandate of catching sleep whenever possible, so as to build up a backlog.

An hour later, shortly after high noon, they pushed off again. The Xingu grew progressively narrower and foam-

ing ripples scudded over its normally smooth surface. A
dull, endless roar came from around a bend upstream.

"More rapids?" Kane asked.

Ixchel shook her head. "No…falls."

Chapter 26

Grant fixed her with an angry, accusing stare. "You didn't say anything about a waterfall!"

"You didn't ask me," Ixchel replied tartly. "Don't worry—we'll be able to navigate around it."

The Xingu River continued to narrow steadily and as it did so, the swiftness of the current increased. The canoe bounced on the increasingly rough water as it entered a bottleneck, and spray spumed over the sides. Whitecapped rapids splashed violently around rocks thrusting up from the river bottom.

The dugout pitched to and fro and as it swept around a bend, they saw the cataract of water cascading over a ledge, a fine mist hanging over the drop-off like pale smoke. The way to the right-hand bank was blocked by driftwood torn and dislodged upstream, forming a logjam against a bastion of boulders.

A small channel cut between two of the rocks, but it was very close to the main spillway. Shouting in order to be heard over the roar, Ixchel said, "The water is shallow here! We can push ourselves clear!"

Grant and Kane climbed overboard into armpit-deep

water. The ferocious current and uneven footing of the riverbed nearly swept both of them away. They clutched at the stern of the canoe, their boot soles skidding on slippery stones.

Laboriously, they wrestled the dugout across the main rush of the cataract, waves slapping them in the face and forcing water up their noses and occluding their vision. Muscles straining, they directed the canoe toward the narrow channel between the upthrusts of rock while Brigid used the long steering paddle to keep the craft straight.

With the powerful drag of the river swirling around their bodies, Grant and Kane shoved the canoe by inches toward the opening. Both men realized that by fighting against the current, the only outcome would be to hold their own for a little while. Inevitably they would tire and even if their companions managed to make it to the riverbank, the canoe with all of their equipment, including the interphaser, would be carried over the falls and lost.

"We need somebody to pull while we push!" Grant shouted.

He had to repeat himself, yelling himself hoarse. Brigid nodded and handed the paddle to Crawler. But, to everyone's surprise Ixchel slid over the side. Gripping the prow, her head barely above the roiling surface, she motioned for Kane and Grant to start pushing again.

They did, digging their toes into the riverbed. The bow of the dugout eased between the two boulders and lodged there. Ixchel moved to the left so she wouldn't be trapped between the stone and the wooden hull.

Holding on to the side, she chinned herself up, opening her mouth to say something to Brigid. Then she disappeared, falling beneath the Xingu. Her body, swung by the current, plunged under the boat and slammed into Kane's legs. Both of them went down, hurtling toward the drop-off.

Kane surfaced, gasping. He glimpsed Ixchel's red scarf spinning past, caught in an eddy. The woman flailed the churning water, and Kane managed to clasp Ixchel's right wrist. With his free hand, he clawed out for purchase on the smooth rocks that had been worn glass-slick by centuries of rolling water.

Kane and Ixchel bobbed up and down in the foaming river, the current carrying them to the line of jutting boulders at the edge of the drop-off. Ixchel went under again, but Kane pulled her head up and she gasped in great shuddering mouthfuls of air. She wrapped both arms around his chest, linking her hands between his shoulder blades.

As she did so, Kane thrust out his arms and slapped his hands against two boulders, digging in his fingers. He braced himself between them, standing spread-eagled with his feet planted as securely as he could. Less than ten feet separated him and the woman from the precipice. Water flooded around them, buffeting them, pummeling them, pouring into a pool far below.

Although he could barely see, he glimpsed Brigid

Baptiste clambering atop one of the boulders that the canoe was jammed between. In her hands she held a coil of nylon rope. He gazed at her, noting aloofly that time had slowed. Every one of her movements took centuries to complete.

Suddenly a burst of static filled his head, followed by Brigid's crisp, matter-of-fact voice. "Kane, can you see me?"

He managed to cough out, "Yes."

"I'm going to throw you a line. I've already looped it, so put it over you and Ixchel both. Got it?"

"Got it—" He would have said more, but his throat was constricted due to the water he had swallowed.

Whirling the rope over her head, holding the slack loosely in her left hand, Brigid cast the lasso and missed. The rope splashed into the water several feet to Kane's left.

Ixchel gasped into his ear, "Can't hang on much longer—"

"Yes, you can." His voice was a raspy croak. "You're still a goddess and so you'll hang on."

Brigid made another cast and this time the lasso draped itself half over Kane's head and right shoulder. Ixchel carefully disengaged one hand to tug it down and the cinch the loop tightly around their waists.

"All right," Brigid stated over the Commtact. "We've got you. Let go and move in the direction we're pulling."

Bodies pressed together, their faces only inches apart, Ixchel impulsively kissed Kane's lips. Then he slowly relaxed his cramping muscles and lowered his arms. Instantly, his legs were scooped out from under him. He and Ixchel fell beneath the Xingu.

Feeling the steady pressure of the rope around their bodies, Kane kicked furiously, digging his toes into the river bottom. With a back-wrenching effort, he raised both himself and Ixchel clear of the torrent. Blinking the water from his eyes, he saw Brigid, anchored by Grant, hauling at the rope hand over hand.

Foot by foot, they were slowly pulled through the roaring, raging current toward the bank. Kane cradled Ixchel in his arms like a child, feeling her heart pounding hard against his chest. With her face buried in his shoulder, she murmured prayers to various gods and goddesses.

Finally, they reached a point where the current wasn't so powerful that they needed the rope to guide them through. Kane waded through the shallows to a strip of rocky bank and collapsed, sneezing water from his sinus passages.

Ixchel, bedraggled and taking in great gulps of air, squirmed away so she wasn't facing him. Then she vomited, a thin stream of brown river water spilling from her mouth.

Kane disentangled them from the rope and forced himself into a sitting position, breathing hard, wincing at the knives of pain stabbing into his shoulder muscles and forearms. Glancing toward Brigid and Grant, he snapped off a salute with the index finger of his right hand against his nose. "One percent," he rasped.

"Half that, I'd judge," Grant replied over the Commtact. "You want us to come and get you?"

He shook his head, running his fingers through his soggy hair. "Give us a minute and we'll come to you."

Brigid reeled in the rope. "Are you sure Ixchel is all right?"

"I think so, just a little sick." He glanced down at the young woman, impressed by her composure and how she had not panicked. "How are you feeling, Ixchel?"

Slowly, she sat up, fingering tangled strands of black hair away from her eyes. Hoarsely, she answered, "I believe I can walk."

"Good."

Carefully, Kane rose to his feet, grimacing at the various flares of pain igniting all over his body. He extended a hand to Ixchel. She took it, allowing him to pull her up. Her firm breasts strained against the thin, wet fabric of her halter. Not releasing his hand, she stared intently into his face with luminious, frank brown eyes.

Softly, she said, "You saved my life. Thank you."

Kane smiled crookedly. "Forget it."

She shook her head, still holding his hand. "I do not forget such things. You are a good and brave man, and I apologize for thinking you were anything else. I will make it up to you."

Kane did not respond to an unmistakable hint of promise in either her voice or eyes. He smiled what he knew had to have looked like an idiot's smile and gently pulled his hand away, moving across the bank. They picked their way over the wet rocks and around a fringe of jungle.

The dugout had been safely grounded and Sindri was passing their packs and equipment cases to Crawler, who then handed them to Grant. When the small man caught sight of Ixchel and Kane, he flashed them a toothy grin. "I'm overjoyed you survived your ordeal, Miss Fawcett, Mr. Kane."

"Spare us," Kane retorted coldly. "If it had just been me, you'd be overjoyed that I went over the falls."

Sindri shook his head in what seemed like mock pity. "You're such a cynical, unforgiving man, Mr. Kane."

Kane clenched his fists and teeth, his eyes glittering dangerously. Brigid stepped between the two men to stave off a verbal battle that quickly could become a physical one. Gesturing toward the stream branching away from the river, she asked, "Do we follow that, Ixchel?"

The young woman nodded, fingering the gold chain still around her neck. "For a few miles, yes."

"Then what?" Crawler demanded.

"Then we will reach the campsite I mentioned."

Grant took a pack from the crippled man. "For a mind mutie, you sure ask a lot of questions that you already ought to know the answer to."

Slipping his arms through the straps, Grant grunted at the weight. He carried the heaviest load, including the interphaser case. "Let's get going if everybody feels up to it."

Kane glanced questioningly at Ixchel. "How about you?"

Rubbing a dark bruise on her right thigh, she said bleakly, "I suppose I'll just have to be up to it, won't I?"

They began walking southwest. There were no trails in the endless blue-green forest that Kane could see, but Ixchel led them forward without hesitation. The ground was marshy underfoot so close to the river, and several times they had to wade through knee-deep bogs and over swamp islets. Without a word, Grant picked up Crawler and carried him over the deepest and swampiest sections. The crippled man did not acknowledge the help, nor did Grant expect him to.

Kane preferred Sindri to fend for himself, but to his annoyance, Brigid gave him a hand struggling through the soup of muck and sludge. She used the crystal-pointed lance to probe the ground ahead.

Within half an hour, a rain began to fall, a warm, wet drizzle that compounded their misery. Insects buzzed in clouds all around them, biting and flying, seemingly dedicated to achieving the single goal of crawling into mouths and eyes.

When they reached the higher ground, the terrain became less swampy, but the travel was still wearying as the six people wended their way among the endless columns of immense buttressed morabukea and greenheart trees. As they struggled over fallen limbs, Ixchel cautioned them to be alert for tarantulas, scorpions, anacondas and a countless variety of life-forms, both predatory and poisonous.

Purple orchids hung from tree branches and now and then ill-tempered monkeys screamed at them from above, pelting them with fruit rinds and nut shells. Brigid stumbled on a root and, overbalanced by her back pack, nearly fell, but Kane managed to catch her and set her upright again. The warm rain, mixed with perspiration, streamed down her face, plastered her thick red-gold hair to her head and made her clothing cling to every curve of her body. Ixchel trudged past without glancing at them.

"Much obliged," she said breathlessly. "Guess I'm a little out of shape."

"You could have fooled me," he replied, settling his own pack more firmly on his shoulders.

She directed a challenging stare at him. "Is that supposed to be a compliment or what?"

Kane only raised a sardonic eyebrow and Brigid responded in kind. Neither person said anything. They turned and started walking again and Kane repressed a smile. Even after five years together, he couldn't help but reflect that Brigid Baptiste was quite possibly the toughest woman—and one of the toughest people, for that matter—he had ever met.

During their three-hour-long march, the rain slackened, but still the water seeped everywhere. Wet heat rose from the ground, giving the jungle the atmosphere of a greenhouse in high summer. They walked out from beneath the canopy of the rain forest, and Kane was surprised by open sunlight. Tumbles of gray-green boulders led up to a high ridgeline. The slope was intergrown with vines, ferns and vermillion heloconia blossoms.

Favoring her bruised leg, eyes clouded with exhaustion, Ixchel could only point to a pair of rectangular huts on the ridgeline, in the shadow of a house-sized boulder. Their thatched roofs sloped to the ground on all sides.

"The campsite?" Sindri wheezed.

Ixchel nodded. After a few moments' pause to gather strength, the six people began to climb, scrambling for handholds on the face of the slope. As they struggled upward, Kane sensed they were being watched. He glimpsed no eyes in the shadows between the trees, no abrupt movement of brush to betray a presence, but he felt hidden watchers.

They scrambled up the incline, scratched by thorny vines and bitten by ants. Ixchel grimaced every time she moved her right leg. After nearly ten minutes and with groans of relief, the six people climbed to the crest of ridge, reaching it by squeezing between vine-clad boulders. Panting, Ixchel pointed into the valley on the other side.

Struck speechless by the sight, no one spoke.

Chapter 27

The grassy valley sloped gently downward, ending less than a mile away against an irregular gray rock wall that shot up vertically five hundred feet or more. The jagged, pinnacled ramparts were wreathed in tendrils of mist. Ravines and crevices slashed through the base of the stone palisades. Beyond them, rising in a series of staggered hills and ledges, loomed the face of a mountain. The summit looked like a dome of dark, buttressed rock on which little grew but patches of yellow grass.

"The foothills of the Serra de Huanchaca?" Brigid inquired, shading her eyes.

Ixchel nodded. "Beyond that wall lies Xibalba."

Sindri took a tentative step forward. "Then what are we waiting for?"

Ixchel declared curtly, "For me, you are waiting for me. I cannot walk any farther today, and you need me to show you the way or you'll be lost forever in the maze."

Gingerly she rubbed the blue-black bruise on her thigh. "I'm sorry, but I just can't do it. Besides, it would be long after dark before we found our way through the pass."

Slipping out of the straps of his pack, Grant rumbled, "In that case, I'm more than willing to spend the night here."

With a wan smile, Ixchel said, "We may, if the caretakers give us their permission."

Kane eyed her questioningly. "What caretakers?"

At the rustling sound from the hut nearest to them, they turned to see a man and woman emerge from a thatched door. Gun barrels snapped up, but the two people seemed oblivious to them. Heavyset in build and only a little more than five feet tall, their black hair was bowl-cut across their foreheads and napes. They wore apronlike garments made of tanned deerskin.

The woman's lower lip bore a puncture through which a thin sliver of bone had been inserted. Blue spiral tattoos adorned the man's cheeks and bare pectorals.

"Yanomani," Ixchel said, ducking her head toward the couple.

The man and woman responded in kind, faces expressionless. Sindri unobtrusively moved behind Grant, sinking his head between upraised shoulders. The jet-black eyes of the Amazonion Indians studied the newcomers intently but without any particular emotion. Two toddlers peered around their legs, their shoe-button eyes wide.

"Do you speak their lingo?" Crawler asked Ixchel sotto voce.

"Not very well," the male Yanomani said. "That's why we learned to speak yours, long, long ago. My name is Jarro. This is my wife, Vannu, and my children, Jarvinu and Kapola."

Jarro bowed formally before Ixchel. "It is good to see you again, Goddess, but we did not expect you."

Ixchel nodded in return. "Unusual circumstances in Tulixin necessitated this visit. These are my friends."

As Ixchel introduced the outlanders one by one, Jarro took their right hands, pressed it between both of his callused palms and gazed earnestly into their eyes for a long moment, as if seeking something lost but familiar there.

Sindri refused to allow Jarro to touch him, although Crawler permitted it and showed no emotion at all. When the Yanomani took Brigid's hand, his face creased in a broad smile. "I am honored to have such a wise woman of your years here. You and your friends are welcome."

Brigid's spine stiffened as she pulled her hand away. "My years? How old do you think I am?"

Jarro murmured deferentially, "You are very, very old on the inside." He glanced at Kane, adding, "As are you, but not as old as she."

"Thanks ever so much," Brigid declared with glacial sarcasm and turned away. As she did so, she glimpsed Ixchel unsuccessful trying to hide a smile beneath a hand.

Kane couldn't help but smile himself, but he understood the implications of Jarro's words. Normally he shied away from examining the bond he shared with Brigid. On the surface, there was no bond, but they seemed linked to each other and the same destiny. He recalled another name he had for Brigid Baptiste: *anamchara*. In the ancient Gaelic tongue it meant "soul friend."

From the very first time he met her he was affected by the energy she radiated, an intangible force that triggered a melancholy longing in his soul. That strange, sad longing only deepened after a bout of jump sickness both of them suffered during a mat-trans jump to Russia several years before. The main symptoms of jump sickness were vivid, almost-real hallucinations.

He and Brigid had shared the same hallucination, but both knew on a visceral, primal level it hadn't been gateway-transit-triggered delirium, but a revelation that they were joined by chains of fate, their destinies linked.

Kane shook his head to drive out the recollections of the past so he could focus on the present. The group unpacked its gear in a small walled compound between the two huts. Jarro and Vannu brought out armfuls of wood and tinder. Ixchel built a small fire and balanced cooking pots atop the logs. Tidbits from the MRE packages were mixed with bottled water to make a tasteless but nutritious stew. For flavoring, Jarro added a few chunks of fatty tissue he claimed was tapir meat.

By the time the sun had disappeared behind the mountain range, the meal was ready to be eaten out of clay bowls and mess tins. Jarro and Yannu supervised the distribution of the food, serving Brigid first.

"Age hath its privileges," Kane murmured.

Brigid's only response was to pretend he hadn't spoken or that he even sat anywhere near her.

The two Yanomani children hungrily swallowed the stew from the bowls, licked them clean, then asked for second helpings. Grant served them this time, saying as he ladled the broth into their bowls, "Must be tough finding enough food in this place to feed your family regularly."

Jarro nodded. "It can be, but as always, the lords of Xibalba provide. They always have."

"Yes," Ixchel said, showing surprisingly dainty table manners. She ate with a spoon, her pinky finger extended away from the handle. "Even my great-great-great-grandfather saw to that."

Jarro said gravely, "Yes, the legendary Colonel Fawcett. He was the first white man to come here."

"When was this?" Sindri asked.

Jarro shrugged. "A long time ago."

"I gathered that much," Sindri said impatiently. "I'd like an idea of the year."

Jarro regarded the little man with blank, grave eyes and did not reply.

"The Yanomani do not measure time the way we do," Ixchel interposed. "Just accept the fact Colonel Fawcett came here long before the memory of anyone living."

Brigid examined the crystalline tip of the spear she had brought with them. The firelight danced in shifting rainbow-hued patterns along its surface. "I can accept that fact, but I'm very curious as to how these weapons were fashioned. The Yanomani didn't have anything to do with it, I'm sure."

An uncomfortable silence settled around the cook-fire. Sindri said quietly, but with an unmistakable snide snicker lurking at the back of his throat, "How very ethnically insensitive of you, Miss Brigid. And all this time I thought you had one of the most enlightened minds on the planet."

Brigid shot him a green glare of irritation. "You know what I meant, Sindri."

Addressing Jarro and Vannu, Brigid said, "This spearhead, like the knives and swords we saw in Tulixin, have been manufactured, probably using the same process that made the crystal skulls. The technology is not only above that of the Yanomani but ours, as well. I'd like to know where it came from."

"And I'd like to tell you," Jarro replied, "but I don't know. Except for a few arrowheads, my people never used such implements."

"Their use has been restricted to Tulixin," Ixchel offered. "According to the chronicles of Xibalba, crystal tools and weapons were already in use when Colonel Fawcett and his people arrived. The wooden shafts and metal parts wear out, of course, but the crystals themselves never do and are always refitted."

Kane nodded in understanding. "That's really not too much different than some kinds of firearms in our own land. Moving parts will wear out and need to be replaced, but the framework, the operating platform of the weapon itself, remains the same."

Sindri tugged his backpack toward him and unzipped the rear pouch. "Let's do a little comparative analysis."

As he brought out the quartz skull, both Jarro and

Vannu uttered cries of shock and leaped to their feet, very nearly performing backward broad jumps so as to put as much distance between them and the skull as possible. Clutching at each other, the two Yanomani yammered fearfully in their own language. The children ran wailing into the hut.

Sindri chuckled, extending the skull toward them with both hands. Reflected firelight blazed with pulsating, prismatic shimmers in the eye sockets. "Don't be afraid…Old Mr. Grins here is harmless. All right, Mr. Grins?"

He moved the crystal jawbone up and down, miming human speech and said in a basso profundo voice, " 'Sall right, Sindri."

The Yanomani didn't seem convinced by Sindri's or Mr. Grins's words of assurance. They whispered to one another in urgent, almost frantic tones.

"What are they saying?" Grant demanded.

A line of consternation appeared on Ixchel's smooth brow. "I speak only a little of their tongue, but I've heard the words 'spirits' and 'punishment' a couple of times already."

Sindri moved the skull back and forth, uttering an eerie whistling sound. The wide eyes of Jarro and Vannu followed its motions like the fear-hypnotized prey of a cobra. In a melodramatic falsetto, Sindri declared, "Ooo-ee, I command the spirits of the skulls to mete out punishment to whosoever offers me insults and spoiled tapir meat, ooo-ee."

Noting the genuine fright in the expressions and postures of the Yanomani, Brigid said sternly, "Knock it off, Sindri. Put the skull away."

Sindri's grin broadened. "I'm not through playing with it."

Kane snapped, "The hell you're not. Do as she says, Sindri, or I'll take it away from you."

Sindri cut his eyes toward Kane, realized by the set of the bigger man's jaw and the angry glitter in his pale eyes that he had no intention of debating the issue, and returned the skull to the backpack.

"Wise decision," Grant rumbled.

Sindri smiled disarmingly. "All my decisions are wise ones, Mr. Grant. You, Mr. Kane and Miss Brigid should know that by now. What you so often interpret as caprice on my part has actually been thought out well in advance."

Sindri's silky lilting tone held an undercurrent of menace.

Jarro swallowed hard and said in a quavering voice, "The skull belongs in a sacred place. Spirits live there and mortals who trespass are punished...and all those who consort with the trespassers."

Kane and Grant exchanged uneasy glances, both men suddenly envisioning their heads being bashed in by clubs or shot by poisoned darts while they slept.

Ixchel said encouragingly, "Don't worry, Jarro. We go to the sacred place to return the skull to the spirits...only good will come of it."

The hard masks of naked fear on the faces of the Yanomani softened, but they didn't appear to be entirely comforted.

Ixchel stood up, automatically brushing off the seat of her shorts. "I suggest we all turn in. We should get as early a start as possible tomorrow."

The interiors of the two huts were surprisingly spacious, divided by flimsy partitions made of reeds and woven grasses. From the ceiling beams dangled dried herbs, desiccated birds, mummified reptiles and shriveled fist-sized objects that put the outlanders in mind of shrunken heads. No one asked Jarro for identification as he led them to various sleeping quarters within the two huts.

Kane chose a hammock strung between two posts in a small alcove. Stripping off his shirt and taking off his wet boots, he drew mosquito netting from his pack and draped it over his body. With the holstered Sin Eater in one hand, he managed to stretch out in the hammock without being dumped unceremoniously on his face.

The hammock was surprisingly soft and comfortable. Sleep tugged insistently at all his senses, lulled by the mournful calls of night birds floating in through the single small window. As he hovered on the brink of slumber, he suddenly felt a presence at the head of the hammock. Slitting his eyes open, he did not otherwise move, lying completely still, his nerves tingling, his muscles tensing. A shadow shifted over him and he set himself to spring up, but the touch of a warm, soft hand on his chest kept him from striking.

"Kane?"

Ixchel Fawcett uttered the breathy whisper, and Kane hitched around so he could dimly see her in the feeble light from the window. He saw she had tied up her long hair in a knot at her nape to relieve herself from the heat. Except for the golden chain around her neck, she was naked.

He sat up, suddenly, almost painfully conscious of her nude body with proud, full breasts and flaring hips. "What is it?"

Ixchel smiled almost sadly. "Do you have to ask?"

She leaned into him, arms around his neck, her breasts pushing his chest. Her nipples were hard and eager. Her ripe mouth sought his, making words with her lips against his in her panting passion.

"Twice you have saved me, and now I believe you were indeed sent by Itzaman. He could not save Ptalucan, but he sent you—therefore I am blessed. I make an offering to you."

It required all of Kane's self-control to keep from accepting what Ixchel offered. Gently, he pulled her arms away, saying softly, "Ixchel, this isn't right."

She clung tightly to him, whispering, "It is."

"No, you're in mourning…you're grieving."

Ixchel drew her face away from his, eyes glimmering with tears and an emotion he couldn't quite identify. "You don't want me?"

Sweat formed at his hairline, and he felt the physical stirring her naked proximity invoked in him. "It's not that, Ixchel…." He trailed off, groping for the proper response. "This just isn't the time, I'm sorry. I'd feel like I'm taking advantage of you while you're vulnerable. It's not that I don't want you."

"Cizin wants me," she murmured. "He wants me so badly he would rather take my heart so it could never belong to another."

"Would he really kill you?"

"Yes, he would do anything. He is so hungry for power, he would kill anyone who he perceived as an impediment." She stared at him levelly. "If I must die, let me make a sacrifice to you first."

Kane felt his body responding to her, to the musky scent and heat radiating from her. The image of the Devi Juballah who had trusted him and died ghosted across the forefront of his mind.

The moon came out briefly and he glimpsed her luminous brown eyes, her face close to his. Tremulously, she whispered, "I don't know what to do, what will happen. I'm very much afraid of the future."

Kane gripped the young woman by her upper arms, and said, packing his whisper with conviction, "Whatever the future brings, you're not going to die by Cizin's hand, I promise you that. You're just stressed out and exhausted. You need to get some sleep."

Ixchel sighed and leaned into Kane. "May I stay with you for a little while, please?"

Kane contemplated her question for a silent moment, then drew her by the hand to his side. The hammock was very comfortable for the two of them.

Chapter 28

Grant awoke before dawn with pains in his lower back, shoulders and rump. Although he had slept in a hammock like the others and had done so before, he had never cared for such a contrivance. He would have preferred to bed down on the floor of the hut, but the thought of insects crawling over his face made him opt to swing suspended between two posts. The hammock itself had sagged alarmingly beneath his weight, his backside barely an inch above the hard-packed earth.

As usual when he awakened from a night sleeping in his clothes, he felt rusty and mean. He swallowed a mouthful of water from his canteen, then went outside to relieve himself. On the way he passed the two Yano-mani children, snuggled together in a hammock, their faces in the repose of slumber looking innocent and cherubic. He tiptoed past, not wanting to awaken them.

The sun was just beginning to inch above the horizon, throwing a flood of orange light over the treeline. He watched it rise, thinking about parenthood and its awesome responsibilities. In the baronies, children were a necessity for the continuation of ville society, but only those passing stringent tests were allowed to bear them.

Genetics, moral values and social standing were the most important criteria. Generally, a man and a woman were bound together for a term of time stipulated in a contract. Once a child was produced, the contract was voided.

A number of years before, Grant and a woman named Olivia had submitted a formal mating application. Both of them had entertained high hopes of the application being approved, and they managed to convince themselves that it would be. After all, babies still needed to be born, but only the right kind of babies. A faceless council determined that he and Olivia could not produce the type of offspring that made desirable ville citizens.

Once their application was rejected, he and Olivia had drawn attention to themselves. Their relationship became officially unsanctioned and could not continue lawfully. In the years since Olivia, Grant had never given much thought to fathering children. But since pledging himself to Shizuka, he'd started thinking about it a bit more seriously. He wondered if creating a new life might not be a way to balance out the ones he had taken over the years.

Certainly Lakesh had tried his hand at bringing new lives into the world as a way cleanse his soul of his guilt over his involvement in the Totality Concept conspiracies. Kane and Brigid might not have even existed if not for his efforts to clean his conscience by manipulating the in vitro human genetic samples in storage.

With a degree of irony not lost on Grant, the current truce between Cerberus and Overlord Enlil was due to the fact that Balam held an infant as a hostage. The baby, carried to term by the hybrid female Quavell, had been bred to carry the memories and personality of Enlil's mate, Ninlil.

In actuality, Quavell had given birth to a blank slate, a tabula rasa, an empty vessel waiting to be filled. Although the child carried the Annunaki genetic profile, she was born in an intermediate state of development. Certain segments of her DNA, strands of her genetic material, were inactive and needed to be encoded aboard *Tiamat.*

Once there, through a biotechnological interface, she would receive the full mental and biological imprint of Ninlil.

Then the Supreme Council would be as complete as it had been thousands of years before, and *Tiamat* could set into the motion the rebirth of the entire Annunaki pantheon. Enlil would not be pleased with any overlord who put Ninlil and thus the long-range plan to remake Earth at risk. If not for Balam acting as mediator, a state of open war would have existed between the reborn Annunaki and Cerberus.

By the time Grant finished brushing his teeth, spitting into the ashes of the previous night's cookfire, he heard stirring from within the huts. As he returned, he glimpsed a blur of naked cinnamon-hued skin leaving the little alcove Kane had chosen as sleeping quarters.

He glanced in and saw the man sitting in the hammock, struggling to tug on his boots. He didn't look at all relaxed or rested. In fact, his expression was tight.

"Good morning," Grant ventured cautiously.

Kane shot him a glare. "What's good about—oh, never mind."

As he stood up, Grant asked, "You didn't sleep well?"

Kane ignored the query. "Let's get on the move early."

"What's the hurry?"

"I want to get this over with," Kane answered testily. "Is that all right with you?"

Grant shrugged. "Fine by me. Is Ixchel in as much of a hurry as you?"

Kane turned to face him, eyes glittering coldly. "As a point of fact, she is. She just told me."

"Does she usually discuss travel arrangements in the nude?"

"If Cizin is going to arrive," Kane said in a steely tone, "my gut tells me it'll be soon, thinking he'll catch everybody still asleep or just waking up. I promised Ixchel we'd protect her from the son of a bitch, and I think we'll do a better job of it away from here."

Grant nodded as if he understood completely. "You don't want to grab a bite of breakfast first?"

"We'll eat on the way." He reached into his pack and pulled out his rolled-up shadow suit. "It'll be a good idea to suit up, too. Then let's roust everybody and get moving."

Grant returned to his sleeping quarters, stripped out of his clothes and began pulling on the shadow suit by opening a magnetic seal on its right side. The garment had no zippers or buttons, and he put it on in one continuous piece, from the hard-soled boots to the gloves.

The fabric molded itself to his body, adhering like another layer of epidermis. He smoothed out the wrinkles and folds by running his hands over his arms and legs.

Carrying his pack, he entered the adjoining hut and found Brigid already awake and suited up. Sindri and Crawler had to be roused, first by calling to them, then finally by turning their hammocks upside down and dropping them face-first on the floor. Sindri objected vociferously to such mistreatment at so early an hour, but he sullenly complied with Grant's command to "get it together or be left behind."

By the time the outlanders assembled outside the huts, full dawn light spread across the sky. With the light came the screams of macaws and the rustling, cheeping, chattering of the jungle coming to wakefulness.

Ixchel bade Jarro, Vannu and the two children goodbye, telling them she hoped to see them again on their return trip. Judging by the tone of her voice and her haunted, haggard expression, she didn't find a reunion very likely.

She led the party of travelers down the face of the slope toward the mountain wall a little under a mile away. Early-morning fog swirled thickly on the pinnacled ramparts. The six people tramped through waist-high brown grass, nibbling at the contents of the MREs and washing them down with swallows of bottled water. Grant and Kane had strapped their Sin Eaters to their forearms and carried the Copperhead subguns in their arms.

Brigid noted that Ixchel looked wan and weary, as if she struggled to keep from succumbing to emotional exhaustion. The young woman tried to present a brave, stoic front, but the turmoil and loss of the past couple of days had taken a toll on her resolve.

She also noted how Kane kept casting apprehensive glances behind him at the huts of the Yanomani perched on the ridgeline. His watchful attitude filled her with a mounting unease.

Dropping back to walk beside him, she demanded, "What's bothering you?"

His initial response was a scowl, then he replaced it with a rueful smile. Jerking a thumb over his shoulder, he said, "I started feeling pretty damn claustrophobic back there. It would've been a good place for Cizin to trap us. I hoped I'd feel better out in the open, but I don't."

Brigid nodded. "I prefer to assume that Cizin decided against putting himself to any further risk. His pursuit yesterday didn't exactly reap any rewards."

"Ixchel told me that she's sure if Cizin is still alive he won't give up until he rips out her heart and kills us all."

Brigid started to reply, then a thought occurred to her. "Told you this when?"

"Last night," Kane answered dismissively.

Her eyebrows drew down at the bridge of her nose. "I saw the way she looked at you most of the day yesterday, but since she's scarcely more than a child, I'm surprised that you would—"

"Give me some credit, Baptiste," Kane broke in harshly. "She's scared to death and her heart is broken. I'm amazed she's made it this far without a breakdown. Other than that—"

He trailed off, biting off the rest of his words, jaw muscles knotted.

"Other than what?" Brigid pressed.

Kane gusted out a profanity-seasoned sigh. "Other than that, I promised Juballah we'd protect her from Nergal if she helped us. Look how that turned out."

Brigid ran her fingers through her tangled mane of hair and matched Kane's sigh with a frustrated one of her own. "You shouldn't hold yourself responsible for that."

"I don't," he retorted in a sharp, clipped tone. "I hold you and Grant as responsible as myself. But most of all, I hold Enlil, Nergal and the rest of the Supreme Council culpable."

"We didn't lie to Juballah, Kane," Brigid argued grimly.

"Maybe not, but like you said, it wasn't exactly our finest diplomatic moment, either. I'm not going to let something like it happen a second time."

Brigid bristled at the recrimination in Kane's voice, but she knew she had no real defense. "Assuming both you and Ixchel are right and Cizin is still active, his attacking the Yanomani outpost isn't a sound tactic."

"No?"

"No." She gestured to the field of grass all around them. "Getting ahead of us and laying a trap makes more sense."

Kane considered her words for a moment, scanning the terrain ahead. "Could be that's the strategy he has in mind, but there's no way to test the theory except to stroll right into a snare."

"There's one way," Brigid announced, turning around. "Crawler, may I speak with you for a moment?"

The crippled man scuttled forward, parting the grasses like a snake wriggling through a meadow. "Yes?"

"Can you give us a read on Cizin, on what he might be up to?" She asked.

Crawler blinked in consternation. "My abilities usually only work when the subject is right before me. I receive only impressions of emotions and intentions. I see colors, which denote feelings."

Sindri looked around nervously. "You saw Cizin, right? You know what he looks like, so you have a focus at least."

Crawler nodded uncertainly. "All I can do is try."

"Please do," Brigid said.

Ixchel and Grant joined Kane, Brigid and Sindri around Crawler as he began breathing deeply. His eyes widened, his lips peeling back from discolored teeth. He shivered, moaned softly, clutched at his brow.

Kane, Grant and Brigid had witnessed the mutie's performance before, as if invisible antennae sprouted from his psyche and quested for answers to Brigid's question. At one time the Cerberus warriors would have thought it was a sham, a very good piece of improvised theater on the part of the doom-sniffer.

Blinking his eyes rapidly, Crawler stared around as if he expected to see someplace other than the field of waist-high grass.

In a flat, uninflected tone he said, "I see red for pain of the heart, green for jealousy, black, black for hatred. Yellow for flames, orange for fire, white for heat, bright red for the fires of rage and vengeance."

He lowered his head, panting as if he had just propelled himself several miles by his elbows.

"Well, ladies, that tells us absolutely nothing," Grant said in disgust.

As soon as the last word passed his lips, they heard a faint pop and a tinkle of glass to their left. It was followed almost immediately by the same sound. The dry grass on both sides of them suddenly bloomed with hell-flowers of roaring flame.

"Son of a *bitch!*" Kane skipped around, heart racing and glimpsed coppery bodies rising from the sea of grass. Whirling the leather slings over their heads and letting fly with the incendiary globes, the warriors swiftly formed a tightening circle around the outlanders, making them the hub of a wheel of fire.

Chapter 29

Within moments, the entire valley seemed to be blanketed by billows of smoke laced with livid, bloodred flame. After each jangle of breaking glass, the ground erupted with mushrooms of flame.

The Sin Eaters in Grant's and Kane's hands quested back and forth but couldn't fix on targets. The death's-head warriors of Cizin revealed themselves just long enough to hurl a fire globe, then they dropped out of sight. Their strategy, as simple as it was, seemed to be working with a chilling effectiveness—surrounding their quarry in a ring of fire. The dry grasses blazed up like kerosene-treated tinder.

Glimpsing an opening in the closing circle of flame, Brigid raced toward it, crying out, "Over this way, hurry!"

Grant yanked Crawler off the ground, heaved him over a shoulder and followed her. Kane picked up Ixchel and bounded over the knee-high border of fire and put her down on the other side of it. "Now where?" he demanded.

Ixchel kicked herself into a sprint. "Follow me."

The party of outlanders ran frantically toward the mountain wall as the chemical fires ate through the grasses and weeds, scorching their way toward the palisades. Smoke rolled thickly, blotting out the sky.

As they raced toward the rock tumbles at the base of the mountain wall, the skin between Kane's shoulder blades itched in anticipation of a spear driving through the shadow suit and burying itself in his spine. He hazarded a swift backward glance but saw nothing but a haze of smoke.

Ixchel, in the lead, suddenly altered direction, heading for a scattering of tall flint outcroppings. Everyone followed her. Kane heard Sindri gasping, wheezing and cursing as he tried to maintain his footing on the uneven ground. Hurled spears clattered noisily against the stones.

They dodged among the larger boulders, banging knees and bashing elbows. The pain of a stitch stabbed along Grant's left side, the muscles of his legs feeling as if they were caught in a vise and his vision was shot through with gray specks. Nevertheless he kept running with Crawler over his shoulder, stumbling and lurching.

Ixchel picked a path between a heap of stones and emerged into a narrow pass, the sides of a fluted ravine rising sheer on either side. She gestured for her companions to follow, then plunged into the opening.

The cleft became a tunnel, a winding, widening passage and after a few yards, Ixchel motioned for everyone to stop running. Panting, she said, "Not even Cizin will order a head-on charge against your guns. That would be suicide."

Grant let Crawler slip to the ground and looked back toward the opening. "He's not so crazy after all, then."

They started walking and the smoke-occluded daylight quickly dwindled. Using their Nighthawk microlights for illumination, the outlanders saw a variety of mineral deposits embedded in the walls—glistening veins of yellow pyrites, silvery-speckled mica and geodes of quartz.

Overhead dangled slender, glittering stalactites. Several shards lay on the ground beneath them and Kane picked up one, turning it over in his hands to examine it. Its composition reminded him of razor-edged volcanic glass, but surprisingly lightweight. "This must be the raw materials for the Tulixinian weapons."

Brigid gestured to the gleaming clumps of quartz in the walls. "Not to mention the crystal skulls."

The tunnel turned, narrowed, but up ahead glimmered a tiny oval of daylight. Within moments a pale line of blue sky appeared at its top. Enough light filtered through the opening so they could see their way, so Kane turned off his Nighthawk.

The passageway ended at a semicircle of steps chiseled out of the bare rock. On either side of it stood eleven massive, squat statues with skeletal features.

"The lords of Xibalba," Ixchel murmured,

Head bowed reverently, fingers steepled beneath her

chin, Ixchel walked to the head of the stairs, then beckoned for her companions to follow. When they reached the topmost tier, they halted, blinking at the bright morning sunshine. No one spoke for a long moment, all of them studying the pyramid in silence.

The pyramid wasn't quite as impressive as they had assumed from the holographic image. In fact, the megalith bore only a superficial resemblance to what they had seen. They glanced around at the ruins surrounding the area, then at a colonnade of square stone blocks, and finally craned their necks to look up at the skull-roofed temple rising from the pyramid's summit.

Made of green-stained white stone, two of the megalith's walls were completely covered by flowering vines. Kane estimated the base extended well over three hundred feet from corner to corner. The topmost temple constructed atop the elevated superstructure measured a minimum of a hundred feet from the valley floor.

The structure was big, but barely a sand castle in comparison to a mile-high, five-sided pyramid-mountain he and his friends had visited on Mars. The risers of the long central stairway were hidden beneath snarled tendrils of greenery.

Crumbling walls surrounded the base of the structure. Blocks of smoothly hewn stone lay scattered about as if the valley had been the playground of gargantuan children, and they had left the place as it was after particularly protracted temper tantrums. Beyond them stood roofless buildings and eroded walls containing nothing but jungle foliage.

Stone stelae, covered with hieroglyphs and leering faces, rose from the undergrowth or leaned outward at sharp angles. Many broken statues lay on the ground, their features screened by the interminable sproutings of the rain forest.

Judging by the series of paving slabs leading to it, the pyramid had apparently been the focal point of the small city. Many of the slabs were cracked or upended, pushed from below by gnarled roots.

"Fawcett's lost city of Z," Brigid said softly. "Xibalba. It must have been very frustrating for him when he couldn't find his way inside."

Kane looked around the tangles of undergrowth with penetrating eyes, then stepped out of the mouth of cave. "Let's hope we don't have the same experience."

Brigid followed him quickly. "First thing on the agenda is to locate the threshold."

From his pack, Grant removed an apple-sized V-40 grenade, inserting a finger through the safety ring. "And the second is to make sure Cizin can't follow us."

Ixchel, in the process of leaving the tunnel, spun around, eyes widening with alarm. "What do you plan to do?"

Grant frowned at her. "Start a cave-in to block their way, what else?"

Shaking her head in furious negation, Ixchel exclaimed, "You can't!"

"There's got to be other ways out of here," Sindri argued. "This one tunnel can't be the only way in and out."

"You don't understand," Ixchel declared. "This is a holy site, this is *Xibalba!* You can't defile it without bringing down horrible punishment on my people!"

"I thought you were too intelligent to be ruled by superstition, young lady," Sindri said, sneering.

Ixchel ignored him, reaching out for the grenade in Grant's hands. "I can't allow it."

Grant evaded her hand, his eyes flicked questioningly from Ixchel to Kane and Brigid. They shrugged in response. Blowing out a sigh of irritation, the big man withdrew his finger from the ring of the grenade. "Have it your way, Goddess. But if Cizin gets a grip on your heart, don't blame me."

Ixchel's body relaxed in relief. "Thank you, Mr. Grant."

Grant had never been an avid subscriber to the benefits of sensitivity training, especially when it dealt with other cultures, but he realized the extent of the influence Xibalba exerted on Ixchel and her Mayan people. Her elemental belief in it bordered on the obsessive.

The outlanders moved through the overgrowth, stepping over fallen statues and stelae. The Xibalba site sprawled in all directions, and Brigid could easily visualize the city when it was in its glory, blazing splendidly with light and color and life. She pictured the jaguar-pelted Mayan nobles and the priesthood in elaborate headdresses of quetzal plumes, trudging up the long steps to pray to the lords of death who oversaw the afterlife.

The path they followed crossed a vast plaza filled with the wreck and ruin of Xibalba's once great buildings. Great blocks of basalt and granite had fallen from the pyramid, crushing statues beneath them. Others lay half sunken into the ground, their features eroded by the scourging hand of time.

Ixchel Fawcett touched the blocks of stone hesitantly, gingerly, as if she expected them to collapse beneath the pressure of her hand. In a small, hushed voice, she said, "I've been here several times, but I'm still awed by it."

"You should be," Brigid said. "While Europe languished in the Dark Ages, your people built architectural masterpieces like this."

Voice tight with impatience, Sindri snapped, "Can we find this damn threshold? Ixchel, you claimed you'd seen it before."

The young woman's eyes flashed with annoyance. "Yes, but I paid little attention to it. It's over this way, I think."

Ixchel followed the base of the pyramid, moving at an oblique angle toward its eastern face. Grant kept a watchful eye on their backtrack, but he discerned no movement from the mouth of the tunnel. Kane took the point position, hacking a trail through the thicket with his fourteen-inch combat knife.

"I rarely came to this side," Ixchel explained almost apologetically.

"Can't say as I blame you," Kane replied.

"Most of the religious ceremonies were held in the

plaza, although Cizin often climbed to the temple of Ah Puch to pray and purify himself."

"Sounds like if anybody needs it," Brigid observed dryly, "he does."

Their progress through the brush was slow. The air tasted faintly fetid and the interlocked barrier of ferns, branches and vines seemed almost impenetrable at times. They slogged on for nearly ten minutes, working their way among saplings and vines that sometimes almost obliterated where buildings had once stood. Hostility became evident in the faces of Sindri and Crawler, but Ixchel displayed an admirable impassivity toward their hardships.

Suddenly, Ixchel's hand closed around Kane's forearm. "There! I think...yes, that's it!"

Carefully, Kane, Brigid and Grant edged their way toward the free-standing archway sprouting from the jungle floor. Creepers wrapped it, crisscrossing between the support stanchions so thickly, the substance of which it was made was almost impossible to identify. However, they could tell it was not stone.

"It follows the general shape of the thresholds we've seen," Brigid said doubtfully. "The only way to make sure is find out if we have a key."

She extended a hand toward Sindri. "Give me one of the skulls, please."

The small man hesitated, then shrugged out of his pack and unzipped the rear pouch. "Which one?"

"It doesn't matter."

He handed Brigid the amethyst skull and she stepped close to the archway, moving the sculpted piece of crystal up and down, following the lines of the framework, duplicating the process she had seen Overlords Enlil and Utu perform. When nothing happened, Sindri uttered a wordless snarl of frustrated anger.

Expression composed, Brigid handed the violet-hued skull back to him and took the one made of translucent quartz. She turned back to the archway, repeating the motions. From within the skull pulsed a flicker of light.

It traced a glittering half circle of white fire along the contours of the arch. They heard a low, thrumming sound like a plucked harp string. Tiny strokes of lightning played along the edges, burning through the intertwined plant growth. The vines vanished in a brief flare of flame and a puff of smoke.

Within the frame of the threshold, hues of color shifted and wavered. An image strobed, rippled, then coalesced. Beyond the portal lay the vista of a dark passageway as seen through several feet of cloudy, disturbed water.

"I guess it's a threshold, all right," Grant commented unnecessarily.

Everyone stared, but other than an uncomfortable shifting of feet, no one moved.

Finally Kane asked, "Who wants to be first?"

At his words, Ixchel shrank from them, eyes wide with sudden terror. "This is blasphemy! This is the entrance to Xibalba where the lords of death sit in judgment of all those who come before them! The living cannot enter! We dare not!"

Sindri chuckled, his characteristic sinister rattle-snake laugh that always stood the short hairs on Kane's neck at attention. "Why, Goddess, are you *daring* me?"

Brigid glared down at the small man, snapping sarcastically, "Yes, Sindri, everything we've gone through to get here has led up to a double-dog-dare that you won't be the first to go through."

Kane turned to face Ixchel, forcing an encouraging smile to his lips. A shift of color, of movement in the undergrowth behind and to the young woman's right caught his attention. Without thinking, he lunged forward and swept up the young woman in his arms, pivoting at the waist to push her toward Grant.

A jarring impact on his left shoulder blade slammed him forward, his feet tangling in a cats' cradle of vines. He fell to his hands and knees, noting absently that although he felt no immediate pain, he was aware of a hot wetness seeping over the skin of his back.

Handing Ixchel off to Brigid, Grant opened up with his Sin Eater, firing a full-auto fusillade. The bullfiddle roar sounded obscenely loud. The stream of bullets raked the foliage, shredding leaves and shearing through wood amid sprays of splinters of pulped vegetable matter.

Glancing down, Kane saw a short-hafted spear on the ground near him, the crystalline tip gleaming with liquid crimson. More spears came whipping through the underbrush, invoking bleats of fear from both Sindri and Crawler as they ducked and dodged.

"Where the hell are they?" Grant snarled.

"We've got no more time for double-dog-dares!" Sindri cried out and bounded through the arch, carrying the amethyst skull tucked under an arm. Crawler followed him a half heartbeat later, vaulting forward by the strength of his arms.

Brigid and Ixchel pulled Kane to his feet. His shoulder muscle suddenly began to ache fiercely, and his skin burned where the spear point had penetrated his shadow suit and the flesh beneath.

Ixchel turned her face to his, her eyes wet but no longer wide and wild with terror. "You saved me again."

Between clenched teeth, he replied, "Told you I would. But you have to listen to us, and that means going through the threshold."

Grant swiftly examined the tear in the fabric and grunted. "You were lucky. The suit deflected most of the impact. You have a puncture wound in the muscle, but it's not very deep. Bet it hurts like hell, though."

Kane glared at him in angry incredulity. "You think?"

Brigid said worriedly, "We need to treat it as soon as possible. Even nicks can become septic very quickly in a place like this."

Kane turned toward the archway. "If we don't get out of the way of those spears, then all of us might find out how quickly nicks become septic."

Ixchel shook her head. "I can't do it—"

"Then I'll do it." Kane reached out, grabbed Ixchel tightly by the wrist and stepped through the threshold, pulling her with him.

Chapter 30

The undergrowth vanished. Vertigo assailed Kane's senses, as if he were a spoke in a giant wheel spinning so fast his mind did not have time to record or even register a sensation of movement. His stomach turned over twice, his ears popped and his vision smeared.

He was conscious of a split second of terrific, roaring speed, then he was on solid footing again. There was no shock of impact or a sense of a wild plummet coming to a stop, merely a strange, cushioning sensation, as if he had jumped into a wall of compressed air.

He stood with Ixchel in semidarkness. Releasing his grip on her wrist, she dragged in a lungful of air, then clapped a hand over her mouth to bottle up the scream working its way up her throat.

Sindri and Crawler stood nearby, looking around their dimly lit surroundings with surprisingly composed expressions. Turning to look behind him, Kane saw a duplicate of the threshold only a few feet away. The watery field within the archway rippled and disgorged Brigid and Grant. The linteled frame flashed, then showed nothing between the curves but darkness.

The six people stood in a small stone-walled chamber like an entrance foyer. The source of the pellucid light was a small square panel of a glassy substance inset in the ceiling. Grant, Kane and Brigid had seen the luminous panels before.

A short flight of stairs stretched upward at the far end. Sindri indicated them by inclining his head. "That looks to be the only way out."

Kane glanced over at Ixchel. "How are you feeling?"

She lowered her hands and nodded in response, not speaking.

"I'll assume you mean grand," Kane said, stepping forward. "I'll take point."

The stairs led to a dimly lit passageway, looking as if it had been hacked out of stone and reinforced with braces of thick, bevel-edged beams of wood. The Cerberus warriors paused long enough to put on dark-lensed glasses. The electrochemical polymer of the lenses gathered all available light and made the most of it to give them a limited form of night vision.

The group moved swiftly and fairly silently, the boots of their shadow suits making only faint rasping sounds. They stepped over irregularities in the floor and passed a number of the light panels set into the walls. They moved steadily ahead, none of them caring for the odd, faint sounds that came from the darkness ahead of them.

As they strode forward, Kane's imagination could not help but weave frightful visions from the whispers and echoes. Now and then he heard an eerie mechanical clanking and at other times he thought he sensed presences in the shadows. His mind toyed with skull-faced images of the lords of Xibalba, of Skull Scepter and Stab Master lurking the gloom, sharpening their bone knives, ready to chop his soul into easily digestible pieces.

The skin on the back of Kane's neck tightened and prickled as he became conscious of a distant, dull reverberation. The throbbing drone grew louder the farther they walked, like the murmur of a far-off crowd.

The composition of the tunnel walls and floor suddenly changed with a clear demarcation point. Abruptly both walls and the stone floor became softly gleaming metal alloy, much like the vanadium in the Cerberus redoubt. Neon strips on the ceiling replaced the light panels.

Running a hand over the wall, Sindri commented wryly, "This is a little different than the usual Mayan construction materials."

Ixchel eyed the passageway with confusion, then consternation. In a faltering tone, she said, "I don't understand."

"Don't worry about it," Brigid said. "There's probably been some remodeling over the last thousand years."

Their voices sounded hollow and muffled and echoed distractingly against the low roof. They continued walking as the tunnel passed through a square doorway that led into a vastly wider space.

The six people came to a broad shelf of alloy, thrusting out over a cavernous gallery nearly twenty feet below. They stood at a metal handrail and gazed down and saw the fusion generator. Twelve feet tall, it resembled two solid black cubes, a slightly smaller one placed atop the larger. The top cube rotated slowly, producing the drone. The odor of ozone was very pronounced.

"Now we know who really built this place," Brigid remarked quietly.

Neither Grant nor Kane bothered with a response. The sight of the strangely shaped generator was no surprise. They had seen identical machines in several places across the world over the past five years. The two-tiered generators derived from the same source as the light panels—the Annunaki.

Long ago Lakesh had put forth the initial speculation they were fusion reactors, the energy output held in a delicately balanced magnetic matrix within the cubes. When the matrix was breached, an explosion of apocalyptic proportions resulted, which was what caused the destruction of the Archuleta Mesa installation.

In a voice so faint and aspirated it sounded as if she were struggling to tamp down a scream, Ixchel said, "This can't be Xibalba."

"It's not," Brigid told her gently. "At least not the Xibalba of your religious beliefs. All of this is artificial."

"Man-made?"

Brigid smiled, but there was no humor in it. "I'm not sure about that, but gods didn't build it, either. You're not committing blasphemy by being here. This is technology, not magic."

Kane led them down a circular flight of stairs, passed through another arched portal and entered into a vault-walled chamber of huge proportions, made more so by the lack of any ornamentation or furniture. They felt like they were standing at the bottom of a stupendously huge dry well.

Ixchel gaped around in goggle-eyed surprise. Three circular tiers rose from the center of the chamber, surrounding a dais raised several feet from the floor. A short series of steps rose to the foot of a massive, high-backed chair. They could only see its back, but the surface bore ornate carvings and glittered with a variety of gems arranged in the squared-off geometric spirals favored by the Mesoamerican Indians.

Placed atop slender columns balanced on the rims of the three tiers were eleven crystal skulls. Their surfaces did not gleam—the sculpted features were dull, cloudy and opaque.

For a long moment, no one moved or spoke. Then Grant, unconsciously lowering his lionlike growl of a voice to a whisper, asked, "Now what are we supposed to do?"

"*Die,* if it were up to me."

The cold, grating voice spoke from the center of the chamber. The Cerberus warriors had heard the voice before. Hearts trip-hammering within their chests, they made reflexive motions to bring their weapons to bear.

With a swift scutter of metal-shod feet, shapes seemed to materialize out of the shadows. A dozen miniature snakeheads reared back, open jaws crackling and emitting tiny sparks. The armor-sheathed arms of three Nephilim were attached to them. They stood in a semicircle around Kane, Brigid and Grant, arms extended, faces impassive, white eyes unblinking.

"Oh, wait," the voice said. "It *is*."

The throne revolved on hidden pivots, revealing Nergal sprawled on the cushions like a basking lizard. His cold eyes glinted with mockery and a thin, triumphant smile creased his delicately scaled face.

"Kane...*buddy!*" Stretching out a red-gauntleted hand, he said, "I expected you here over an hour ago."

Sindri stepped forward and placed the quartz skull in Nergal's palm. "We were forced to deal with an unexpected distraction...milord."

Chapter 31

Kane felt a leaden weight gather in his guts. Suddenly he felt very tired and very foolish. He didn't move as the Nephilim disarmed him and his friends, pulling off their backpacks and dropping them carelessly to the floor.

Nergal briefly but critically eyed the skull, then flicked his gaze toward Crawler. "And where is the one I lent you?"

Crawler scuttled forward, removing the amethyst skull from Sindri's pack. "Right here."

His tone of address was considerably less formal than Sindri's, with a slight undercurrent of resentment. Kane wondered if he was the only one who noticed the absence of a "milord."

Surrounded by the contingent of armored Nephilim, a sparking viper's head barely an inch from her own, Ixchel started to whimper, then sank her teeth into her underlip.

As usual Brigid regained her composure and emotional equilibrium first. In a strong, clear voice she declared, "Nergal, I can't say I'm all that surprised to find you at the bottom of this, but how did you get in here?

The threshold looked like it hadn't been activated in centuries."

Hefting the crystal skulls in both of his hands as if he were comparing their weights, Nergal showed his teeth in a grin. "Very perceptive, Miss Baptiste. You're quite right….the threshold hasn't been used in many hundreds of years. But there's another way into this transmission control center if you know where to look. It's located in the temple atop the pyramid. Stairs and ladders, of course…rather a more prosaic means of getting around than the thresholds, but just as effective in the long run."

Sindri threw them a rather abashed grin over his shoulder. "Don't feel too badly. Even I have to admit this was my finest performance. I almost fooled myself."

"As when you saved my life?" Brigid countered.

Sindri's grin faltered and he laid a hand on his chest. "That act was truly from the heart, believe it or not."

"Not," she responded sharply.

Ixchel drew close to Kane, her eyes fixed on Nergal in fearful fascination. She murmured, "I don't understand any of this…is he one of the lords of Xibalba?"

Nergal rose from the throne, skulls still in his hands, assuming a haughty pose. "I am indeed."

Kane uttered a scoffing laugh of contempt. "You're one of the lords of bullshit, Nergal, like the rest of the frauds you call a family."

"Frauds?" Ixchel echoed faintly.

"Frauds?" Nergal repeated, rolling the word around on

his tongue as if testing the taste and texture of it. "In our former forms, as barons, we were frauds. But now—"

"Now," interrupted Grant, "you're just bigger and more overdressed frauds."

Nergal nodded toward Grant and the nearest Nephilim smashed an armored forearm into his belly. Breath gusted explosively from his lungs, and he folded in the middle, falling forward to his knees, clutching at his stomach.

Kane snarled and took a lunging step forward. "You lousy mother—"

Nergal nodded again, and a Nephilim clutched Ixchel tightly by the back of the neck, drawing a short, quickly stifled cry of pain from her lips. He pressed one of the ASP emitters against the side of her head.

"Leave her alone," Brigid snapped. "She's not part of this."

"I'll make that determination." Nergal's gaze fixed on Ixchel. "Who are you?"

The young woman met his gaze and bit out with a passable imitation of defiance, "My name is Ixchel Fawcett."

"Named after the Mayan fertility goddess." Nergal looked her up and down appreciatively. "You certainly seem to have all the necessary equipment to fill that role."

Kneading his midsection, Grant staggered to his feet. "Isn't it about time to tell us what this whole scam is about? Just to capture *Tiamat?*"

Nergal smiled a cold, enigmatic smile of malice. "Not to capture, Grant…but to convince her to combine resources with me. Accomplishing that one goal that you speak of so glibly will forevermore alter the history of Earth."

"From here?" Brigid demanded doubtfully. "With a baker's dozen of crystal skulls?"

Rather than respond verbally, Nergal slammed the skulls in his hands hard against the arms of the chair. They remained in place and almost immediately began pulsing with light. The skulls on the pedestals emitted a resonating whine, humming like harp music heard only faintly when carried by the wind.

The warbling climbed in pitch and swelled in volume. Whorls and waves of color passed through the skulls, swirling the most intensely within the pair attached to the arms of the throne.

A protracted, crunching grate of stone against stone echoed throughout the chamber. Slabs of stone on the walls shifted, long sections rotating on concealed pivots. On the obverse side of the panels, lights flashed and glowed from within glass-enclosed readout screens.

Ribbons of multicolored light shot across consoles, and instrument boards on all the walls flashed to life. A glass-walled box slid out like a drawer. It contained crystal shards sculpted like cylinders and pyramidal prisms. A series of monitor screens flickered simultaneously, images wavering across them. Within seconds they sharpened to display aerial views of Earth, the blue-green oceans and ochre deserts, as well as wide span of starfields.

Ixchel's head jerked to and fro, following each new movement, each new flare of light, her eyes wide and unblinking in combination of terror and wonder. Kane slid a comforting arm around her shoulders, but she didn't seem to be aware of his touch.

Sindri reached toward a skull on a pedestal, fingering the smooth cranial dome. "Despite their appearance, the crystals are superminiaturized subprocessing modules. The data storage capacity of each module is…well, let's just say it's immense, far more than anything in use during the twentieth century."

"What function do they serve?" Brigid asked, sounding enthralled in spite of herself.

Nergal gestured to the skulls, to the instrument panels. "They were crafted using natural materials in the area and they act as an Earth-based monitoring station of *Tiamat*."

A line of concentration furrowed Brigid's forehead. "You're talking about RMI, right?"

Sindri nodded in smug satisfaction. "Exactly, but this process is far, far more advanced and precise."

"What the hell is RMI?" Grant demanded.

"Remote Method Invocation," Brigid answered. "It's a way that twentieth-century computer programmers could interact and rewrite operational procedures through a distributed network from a remote location."

Nergal said, "The systems here, built by Annunaki techsmiths millennia ago, initially served as an adjunct to *Tiamat*'s navigational computers and were designed as redundancies, to act as a robot pilot in case her neuronic network ever suffered a catastrophic failure."

"That's all very interesting," Kane said diffidently, "but the last time I heard, *Tiamat*'s systems *hadn't* failed, catastrophically or otherwise."

Nergal chuckled with a sound like dry bones clattering in a metal washtub. "Very true…nor do I want them to. However, I intend to trick *Tiamat* into thinking she's suffering a major dysfunction and therefore permit ground-based telemetric signals to supplement her subroutines. Once that's accomplished, we can further insinuate a new program."

"For what?" Brigid demanded. "Surely *Tiamat* has the equivalent of firewalls and security restrictions in her central processing units to prevent an outside agency from succeeding at what you're attempting."

"Yes, you're quite right," Sindri said with a fatuous smile. "Security shields guard against technological forms of incursion, like memory core overwrites or uploading database infections."

He cut his blue eyes toward Crawler. "But of course, a psionic upload is not the same as technological, is it?"

Crawler's facial muscles twitched. In response to a beckoning forefinger from Nergal, he climbed up the dais and settled himself into the throne. The overlord smiled down at him fondly, patting his shaved pate. "Isn't it good to be together again, old friend?"

Crawler did not reply. He placed his hands on the pair of skulls on the armrests, tentatively at first, then his fingers stretched out over the craniums. The light swirling within them increased in intensity, and the monitor screens on the wall flickered and wavered.

"What we have here," Sindri said, as if he were lecturing students, "is the power of direct mind-to-mind communication augmented by an electronic propagation medium."

"They're two separate disciplines and biologies," Brigid snapped. "It's like trying to use a dolphin's sonar signals to interface with the navigational computer aboard a submarine. Just because they both swim in the ocean doesn't make them kindred organisms."

"Actually," Nergal replied, "Crawler's psionic abilities are governed by nerve centers, and a synaptic structure that isn't very different from electronic circuit analogues. Since much of *Tiamat*'s neural network is a blending of organic and inorganic synapses, Crawler will meld with her subroutines and telepathically convince her she is malfunctioning and allow us to rewrite her security codes."

Kane eyed Sindri suspiciously. "Do we need to ask who came up with this idea?"

Grant uttered a short, derisive laugh. "It's got egomaniacal pissant written all over it. I just wonder how you conned Crawler into going along with it."

Crawler declared, "I volunteered. Sindri and I work very well as a team."

Spots of angry color appeared on Sindri's cheeks. "What Crawler and I told you about running Sharpeville on our own was true. We did a good job of it, too…but no one can be content to control one small piece of acreage when the opportunity to expand your scope is offered."

Nergal said, "I had been searching for one of the memory modules for quite some time. When I returned to Sharpeville to reclaim the one already archived, I was impressed by the degree of order my two former subordinates had imposed upon the chaos left in the wake of my absence. I confided to them my plans to take control of *Tiamat.*

"So after you thwarted my attempts to regain the skull in Harappa, Sindri made a few suggestions about how the entire process could be streamlined, combining recovery of the thirteenth skull with interacting with *Tiamat.*"

Kane's stomach turned a cold flip-flop. "Do you really believe you can gain control of *Tiamat?*"

Sindri hesitated a moment before answering. "Not exactly…at this stage, we're only looking for the way to her core memory matrix instead of being redirected to a holding buffer. Once we reach the core, we can begin the judicious rewriting of code."

"And then what?" Grant snarled. "Send her out on seek-and-destroy missions against the other members of the Supreme Council?"

Brigid's face locked in a tight, pale mask. "That's a lot less important to Sindri than finally having what he's always lusted after."

Sindri grinned crookedly. "Other than you, Miss Brigid? I won't deny that I will have the power I've always sought, but it's a power I'll wield to reshape this sorry, violent world into one devoted to peaceful pursuits."

"Pursuits like bending knee and 'yes milording'?" Kane demanded, voice frosty with disgust. He gestured toward Nergal. "That's the kind of world he and his kind want, Sindri. And if you don't realize that, then you're a bigger fool—"

Kane stopped speaking, paused and stated with an icy calm, "No, you're not a fool, Sindri. You want exactly the same kind of world as the overlords. All you require is that you're in charge of some part of it."

Sindri's blue eyes narrowed. "Who wouldn't want to be on the top rung instead of the bottom? Once I establish the society that is in humanity's long-term best interests, I'll be relinquishing control."

Brigid's lips worked as if she intended to spit. "Bullshit."

"Anyone would make the same choice as me!" Sindri half shouted defensively.

"The eternal cry of the sociopath," Brigid retorted contemptuously. "Some of us aren't so consumed and crazed with hate we'd sell out every human being currently alive and those yet to be born into slavery. Didn't you lead a revolt of slaves on Cydonia?"

Sindri's shoulders jerked in reaction to her question. "That was a completely different set of circumstances."

"The circumstances are *exactly* the same," Grant rumbled. "Except now the stakes are higher."

"And the personal payoff is greater," Kane grated. "That is if your pal Nergal doesn't order one his white-eyed zombies to flash-fry you after you've outlived your usefulness."

He made an exaggerated show of consulting his wrist chron. "Which I calculate will be any time now."

Sindri turned around to face Nergal, who affected not to notice his stare.

"Enough of this," Nergal announced, fixing his attention on Crawler. "If you would begin initialization—"

The crippled doomseer nodded and squeezed his eyes shut. A deep humming note arose from the instrument panels, and the two skulls beneath Crawler's hands glowed and pulsed in a throbbing rhythm.

The monitor screens fluttered, flickered, then blurred pixels formed into the image of a sleek, dark shape sailing majestically through the sepia sea of space. The bow resembled a gargantuan horned head crafted from alloy, and the back-swept pylons supporting twin engine nacelles put him in mind of the wings of a raptorial bird.

Weapons emplacements looked like stylized foreclaws. The tapered configuration of amidships and stern suggested the tail of a huge sea creature—or a dragon.

Like the first time Kane had seen *Tiamat*, he experienced a surge of blind xenophobic terror as of a cold fist knotting in the pit of his stomach. When he gazed at the dark dragon sailing over the face of the world, he knew that under the armor that plated the enormous sweep of its metal hull, the ship was a living, thinking entity and was aware of its own power, its own invincibility.

The concept that Nergal, Sindri and Crawler believed they could take control of her, force her to do their bidding seemed more than arrogant—it seemed suicidally insane.

Kane sensed rather than saw Ixchel tensing up beside him, but he heard her hoarse, frightened whisper of "Oh, my *God.*"

"Goddess, actually," he corrected softly.

Nergal strode over to the transparent box containing the crystal points. His long fingers manipulated tiny colored tiles over a flat surface. As he slid the tiles from one section of the board to the other, he studied the sequence and the color of lights shimmering within the crystalline shards. They emitted semimusical notes. After a moment, he announced, "Upload achieved."

Sindri's face stretched into a grin, but it looked forced. "We won't have to wait much longer now."

Chapter 32

The pulsing blue halation spread from the skulls and crept over Crawler's tensed arms, sheathing them with light. He compressed his lips as if trying to tamp down a cry of pain, then they peeled back over his teeth in a rictus of silent agony. His entire body shuddered with a violent spasm.

Sindri leaned away from the chair, looking toward the monitor screens. "What's happening?"

"Exactly what I hoped would happen," Nergal responded, unruffled.

Crawler shook with another tremor, and he bit down on his lower lip to choke back a scream as the blue light blazed brightly from the skulls beneath his hands. Veins swelled in his temples, his hairless scalp throbbing as if tiny worms wriggled and squirmed just beneath the surface. Scarlet oozed from his nostrils, then droplets formed at the corners of his eyes as if he were weeping blood.

"Nergal—!" Sindri's voice hit a high note of alarm.

"It's nothing," Nergal declared indifferently. "As his mind fully interfaces with *Tiamat*'s neural net, there's bound to be a physical reaction. It's transitory."

Sindri glanced uncertainly from Crawler to the monitor screens. "When will it pass?"

Nergal lifted an epauletted shoulder in a shrug. "I couldn't say. Perhaps when his metabolic functions cease."

Sindri's eyes widened in consternation. "You mean when he *dies?*"

"Of course," Nergal snapped impatiently. "Now stop distracting me."

Brigid uttered a taunting laugh and when Sindri turned his gaze to her, she said, "So it's not just us you lured into a trap, but poor Crawler, as well. You betrayed and abandoned him just like you betrayed and abandoned your own people, the transadapts."

Faintly Sindri said, "I didn't know this would happen."

"Didn't know and wouldn't care if you had," Grant interjected coldly.

Sindri's face turned the color of old ashes. He balled his fists, the knuckles straining at the skin like ivory knobs. His small body trembled with the intensity of his emotions.

He whirled toward Nergal. "Stop this now. Let Crawler go."

Nergal spared him a scornful glance over his shoulder. "I couldn't even if I wanted to. His mind energy has been uploaded and is enmeshed with *Tiamat*'s neural pathways."

"You didn't say anything about sacrificing Crawler!" Sindri shouted. "He was your friend, too! For many years!"

"He was Baron Sharpe's councilor," Nergal retorted. "To me, to Lord Nergal, he was nothing but a commodity. As are you."

He half turned away from the consoles. "A commodity that has, as Kane observed, outlived its usefulness."

He nodded toward the Nephilim standing beside Ixchel. The armored man instantly extended his ASP emitter toward Sindri, the viper mouths flaring brightly. Sindri took a staggering half step backward, face slack with astonishment and fear.

Suddenly, there came a flashing gleam of light, a clatter of sound and the meaty thud of an impact. The Nephilim stumbled backward, hands reaching for the shaft of the spear protruding at a grotesque angle from his throat. His knees buckled and he collapsed to the floor.

Dark shapes plummeted from the darkness of the ceiling amid a glitter of spear points and wild screams, only somewhat muffled by their death's-head helmets. The warriors bounded into the chamber with the swiftness of a tropical storm.

"Cizin!" Ixchel screamed.

Kane immediately realized that Cizin was probably more familiar with the layout of the pyramid than Nergal himself. He and his warriors had entered by the same way as the overlord and his Nephilim.

Whirling from the console, eyes wide with astonishment and fury, Nergal bellowed a word in liquid Nibiruan. The Nephilim standing on Grant's right fired a bolt of coruscating plasma at one of the keening helmeted warriors.

The wafers of crystal protecting his chest instantly turned to black slag, and the force bowled him off his feet, spark-shot smoke pluming from the point of impact. The stench of cooked flesh filled the chamber with a throat-closing reek. Sindri crouched on the dais, at the foot of the skull throne, shouting in wordless fear.

With the ASP emitter trained on a target other than his head, Grant shouldered the Nephilim aside, at the same time bending and snatching up his Copperhead.

Brigid shoulder-rolled over their piles of equipment, grabbing her TP-9 autopistol. She raised it hastily, framed the white-eyed face in the sights and squeezed the trigger. The round smashed into the Nephilim's forehead. His eyes rolled as if to look at the small round hole just above the bridge of his nose. Without a sound, he fell forward on his face.

At the same time, Kane wheeled on the remaining Nephilim, barely managing to shunt aside the ASP emitter with his right forearm. The ball of plasma went wild, scorching across the chamber at an upward angle and exploding against the opposite wall with a blizzard of sparks and rock chips.

Kane threw himself to one side, clawing for his own weapons on the floor. He only dimly heard the faint tinkle of breaking glass, but then the Nephilim's body was draped in a cocoon of fire. Flames licked over his armor as the man tried to slap them out, turning in blind circles like a dog trying to bite it's own tail.

Kane slammed a heel into the back of his right knee,

and the Nephilim tottered at the mouth of the stairwell, arms windmilling. Then he fell, crashing loudly against the risers, trailing a tail of flame like a meteorite following a crazed trajectory.

Not sure if he had been the true target of the fire globe, Kane shot out an arm for his Sin Eater, but a sandaled foot came down hard on his hand. Biting back a cry of pain, he looked up into the scarred, sweat-slick face of Cizin.

A spear flew toward Grant and he fell flat, banging his elbows painfully. He heard the crystalline point clanking against the wall behind him. He glimpsed a skull-helmeted man sliding another lance into the socket sleeve in his right hand.

Grant lined up the Copperhead's muzzle and squeezed off six shots in a long, rattling burst. The stream of 4.85 mm rounds caught the man in the center of his stomach and rapidly tracked upward, cracking his body armor, punching him backward, then pounding his brass visor out of shape.

Raising her TP-9, Brigid squeezed off three rounds just as several warriors circled the throne. The warriors flattened against the wall as bullets tore white gouges in the stonework above their heads.

Grant got to one knee, the Copperhead in his hands blazing on full-auto, playing the subgun back and forth. Ricochets whined and buzzed all around.

A hoarse cry of shock bursting from his lips, Nergal stumbled back from the console as the crystals dissolved in a spray of glittering fragments. A tide of dazzling lightning flashed along the skulls atop the pedestals, arcing from one to another in a blinding display.

A tendril of energy touched a warrior's helmet and with a sharp, eardrum-compressing report, his head was instantly enveloped in a fireball, turning most of it molten. Flying droplets of superheated bronze struck his companions and they began a screaming, stumbling retreat.

With a muscle-wrenching effort, Kane jerked his hand from beneath Cizin's sandaled foot and rolled frantically to the left. He came swiftly to his feet as Cizin attacked.

Cizin missed his first slash with the saw-toothed sword blade, and his second fanned the air scarcely a centimeter from Kane's groin. Cizin's mouth was bared in a grimace, saliva slicking his lips. He was a madman, infuriated beyond any hope of reason.

On Cizin's backswing, Kane seized the sword arm and locked it at the elbow under his own. The man's left hand closed over his face, hooked fingers seeking his eyes. Although Kane's knowledge and skill in an eclectic mixture of martial arts was deep, he didn't bring any of them into play. Instead, he opened his mouth and bit Cizin on the wrist, sinking his teeth deep and drawing blood.

Cizin screamed and tried to drive a knee into Kane's groin. He twisted so the blow landed on his hip, but still it hurt. His mouth opened reflexively and Cizin tore his wrist free. Kane clutched his breastplate of crystal wafers, using it to muscle him toward the stairwell.

Cizin struggled and hacked at his head with the sword, face contorted in maniacal fury. Kane kicked himself backward, and with a popping of leather thongs, he wrenched the man's armor away from his torso. As he backpedaled, he tripped on a backpack and fell heavily. Desperately, he flung the vest at the man advancing on him.

Cizin didn't seem to notice, lifting his sword in a double-handed grip, bracing himself to deliver a chopping stroke that would cleave Kane's cranium like a melon. Then a spear pierced his unprotected left breast, flying as unerringly as if it had rails to guide it.

A shocked gasp tore from Cizin's lips, followed by a gurgling sound. He glanced down at the slim column of wood projecting from just beneath his pectoral. His uncomprehending eyes darted back and forth and settled on Ixchel Fawcett standing over the body of the Nephilim from whose throat she had ripped the spear. She stared at him expressionlessly.

He lurched back a pace, the sword falling from nerveless fingers. He gazed at Ixchel imploringly, lips writhing, as if he were trying to speak, to ask her a question.

Ixchel said unemotionally, "The lords of Xibalba have claimed your heart…and now you have fulfilled all your duties as Cizin and Ah Puch will welcome you."

The glint of madness faded from Cizin's eyes. He nodded as if he agreed with her and opened his mouth. A flood of scarlet spilled over his lips and chest, and he carefully sat down on the floor, then fell over onto his back, hands clutching the haft of the spear.

Ixchel did not move. She stood, hugging herself, gazing at Cizin without expression.

Kane rose to his feet and said, "I said you wouldn't die by his hand."

Before Ixchel could answer, he whirled at the concussion of a brutal thunderclap. From the consoles erupted crackling fingers of energy. Gauges on the panels burst in sprays of glass shards.

Nergal staggered back, arms crossed over his eyes. When he lowered them, blood oozed from a laceration on his chin. His face was distorted into a mask of utter fury, and he swept the Cerberus warriors with a glare of unregenerate hatred, roaring, "I couldn't complete the interface initialization and *Tiamat* became aware of what we were doing! She's feeding back the impulses as pure energy, overloading the power generators to burn everything out so it can't be done again!"

Sindri reached for Crawler, shouting, "Then help me get him out of this damn chair!"

When Sindri touched Crawler's arm, fire flashed and he jerked backward with a howl of agony, clutching at his burned and blackened hand.

The skulls on the pedestals exploded in showers of glittering glass. Crawler's body seemed to ignite from within, tiny pinpoints of blue flame flaring up from the pores of his skin, covering him in a sheath of sizzling plasma. His hands fell away from the skulls on the armrests.

The flesh on his scalp stretched and split amid spurting scarlet geyers. His brow bulged and with a sound like a wet paper bag bursting, his cranium cracked open, splattering the back of the throne with a slurry of blood, cerberal fluid, brain matter and bone fragments.

Sindri's howl of pain changed to one of horror, and he scrambled away from the dais. At the same time, Brigid bounded atop it. She avoided looking at Crawler, contorted within the throne. She closed a hand around the quartz skull attached to the armrest, setting her teeth, expecting to feel a sear of heat even through her glove. Instead, she felt only a mild warmth and a pins-and-needles tingling sensation.

The skull came away easily. Pivoting on a heel, she shouted to Kane, Ixchel and Grant, "Grab our stuff and go! Get to the threshold before the main generator goes!"

Lightning flashed through the chamber, and Nergal and Sindri cried out in fear. Ixchel and the Cerberus warriors ignored them, snatching up their backpacks, rushing down the stairwell, jumping over the burning body of the Nephilim.

The skull in Brigid's hand activated the threshold, and the four people plunged headlong through the archway and into the jungle. They sprinted away from the pyramid, tearing through the underbrush.

"Why are we running?" Ixchel panted.

Grant husked out, "That big generator in there—if it goes, it could destroy this whole area. Seen it happen before."

Ixchel asked no further questions; she only forced more speed into her pumping legs. Breath burned in all of their straining lungs. As they ran deeper into the wilderness, the structure shrank behind them. At the outermost ring of ruins, they paused to catch their breath, turning to look back.

Tongues of white flame shot from the pinnacle of the pyramid, arcing straight up into the sky. Then, with a grating of stone against stone, the megalith began to come apart. Black cracks zigzagged through the stairway, fragments of facing crumbled and fell away, crashing against the ground. A network of cracks and splits shot through the base, and the entire structure trembled.

Kane, Brigid, Grant and Ixchel stood rooted with awe and terror, remembering the apocalyptic effects of fusion generators that went critical in the past. Fortunately the pyramid broke apart but didn't explode. Slabs of stone thundered down to shatter into heaps of rubble.

With almost majestic lethargy, the mass of rock collapsed inward and seething dust clouds whirled up through which the lurid flicker of plasma energy blazed.

Finally, the cataclysmic crashes and cracks faded, replaced by the crunch of settling stone. Planes of dust and smoke rose toward the sky.

Ixchel passed a hand over her forehead. It did not tremble and in a surprisingly steady voice, she asked, "Do you think either one of them survived?"

Kane did not want to commit to an answer. If there

was a way to escape death, the more certain the better, he knew Sindri would find it. He wasn't so sure about Overlord Nergal, but he found himself caring less about the possibility of his survival than Sindri's.

"Let's just say it's over," Grant said flatly.

"Is it?" Ixchel looked up toward the column of smoke rising into the sky and her gaze climbed higher. "That thing, *Tiamat*, is still up there, somewhere over our heads. She will always be there from now on, like the conscience of humanity."

"Or an avenging goddess," Kane stated quietly. "You ought to be able to relate to that."

Ixchel's dark eyes questioned him. Then she nodded. "I think I do. Perhaps before you depart, I will teach you how to relate to a goddess, as well."

She turned and walked toward the tunnel in the mountain wall. Kane gazed after her for a silent, thoughtful moment, then slid into his backpack. Grant and Brigid Baptiste gazed at him with expectant expressions on their faces.

"What?" he asked impatiently.

"Ixchel is really smitten with you," Brigid said. "I don't know if you've noticed."

"I'm not blind, Baptiste," Kane replied, pitching his voice low so the young woman couldn't overhear. "But I make it a policy to never get involved with women more divine than I am."

Brigid arched a challenging eyebrow. "That must limit your opportunities pretty severely."

Kane met her penetrating gaze and smiled wistfully. "You have no idea."

He extended his hand. After a moment's hesitation, Brigid Baptiste took it, her fingers locking in his. They walked together, with no more questions asked.

JAKE STRAIT

DAY OF JUDGMENT

BY FRANK RICH

INNER-CITY HELL JUST FOUND A NEW SAVIOR— THE BOGEYMAN

The damned, the dirty and the depraved all call the confines of inner-city hell home. And that's exactly where Jake Strait finds himself when a gorgeous blond angel hires him to infiltrate a religious sect to find her sister. But what he discovers instead is a wild-eyed prophet on the make, putting everyone at risk.

Available July 2007, wherever you buy books.

GOLD EAGLE®

GJS3

TAKE 'EM FREE
2 action-packed novels plus a mystery bonus
NO RISK
NO OBLIGATION TO BUY

SPECIAL LIMITED-TIME OFFER

Mail to: Gold Eagle Reader Service™

IN U.S.A.: P.O. Box 1867, Buffalo, NY 14240-1867
IN CANADA: P.O. Box 609, Fort Erie, Ontario L2A 5X3

YEAH! Rush me 2 FREE Gold Eagle® novels and my FREE mystery bonus. If I don't cancel, I will receive 6 hot-off-the-press novels every other month. Bill me at the low price of just $29.94* for each shipment. That's a savings of over 10% off the combined cover prices and there is NO extra charge for shipping and handling! There is no minimum number of books I must buy. I can always cancel at any time simply by returning a shipment at your cost or by returning any shipping statement marked "cancel." Even if I never buy another book from Gold Eagle, the 2 free books and mystery bonus are mine to keep forever.

166 ADN EF29   366 ADN EF3A

Name	(PLEASE PRINT)	
Address		Apt. No.
City	State/Prov.	Zip/Postal Code

Signature (if under 18, parent or guardian must sign)

Not valid to current Gold Eagle® subscribers.
Want to try two free books from another series? Call 1-800-873-8635.

* Terms and prices subject to change without notice. N.Y. residents add applicable sales tax. Canadian residents will be charged applicable provincial taxes and GST. This offer is limited to one order per household. All orders subject to approval. Credit or debit balances in a customer's account(s) may be offset by any other outstanding balance owed by or to the customer. Please allow 4 to 6 weeks for delivery.

Your Privacy: Worldwide Library is committed to protecting your privacy. Our Privacy Policy is available online at www.eHarlequin.com or upon request from the Reader Service. From time to time we make our lists of customers available to reputable firms who may have a product or service of interest to you. If you would prefer we not share your name and address, please check here. ☐

GE07

AleX Archer
THE LOST SCROLLS

In the right hands, ancient knowledge
can save a struggling planet...

Ancient scrolls recovered among the charred ruins of
the Library of Alexandria reveal astonishing knowledge
that could shatter the blueprint of world energy—and
archaeologist Annja Creed
finds herself an unwilling
conspirator in a bid for the
control of power.

**Available May 2007
wherever you buy books.**

GRA6